Winner of the 2017 Scotiabank Giller Prize

#1 National Bestseller

A *Globe and Mail* Best Book of 2017

A *National Post* Best Book of 2017

A CBC Best Book of 2017

A Kobo Best Book of 2017

A *NOW* Magazine Best Book of 2017

'To borrow a line from Michael Redhill's beautiful *Bellevue Square*, "I do subtlety in other areas of my life." So let's look past the complex literary wonders of this book, the doppelgangers and bifurcated brains and alternate selves, the explorations of family, community, mental health and literary life. Let's stay straightforward and tell you that beyond the mysterious elements, this novel is warm, and funny, and smart. Let's celebrate that it is, simply, a pleasure to read'
**– The 2017 Scotiabank Giller Prize Jury**

'The opening chapters of this new opus, *Bellevue Square*, stick closely to the grip-lit script: simple, compelling prose, sudden plot twists, looming violence and a female narrator who swiftly proves unreliable. But as the reader becomes more and more absorbed in the story, the book quietly becomes something else. Something mystifying and haunting and entirely its own... reading *Bellevue Square* is as captivating as it is unsettling... This modern ghost story... will not soon be forgotten'
**– *Toronto Star***

# ALSO BY MICHAEL REDHILL

# BELLEVUE SQUARE

## MICHAEL REDHILL

**NO EXIT PRESS**

First published in the UK in 2018 by No Exit Press,
an imprint of Oldcastle Books Ltd, P O Box 394,
Harpenden, AL5 1XJ, UK
noexit.co.uk

ISBN
978-0-85730-267-0 (paperback)
978-0-85730-268-7 (epub)
978-0-85730-269-4 (kindle)

2 4 6 8 10 9 7 5 3

Typeset in 10.75pt Sabon
by Avocet Typeset, Somerton, Somerset, TA11 6RT
Printed in Great Britain by Clays Ltd, Elcograf S.p.A.

*For Elizabeth Marmur and Ruth Marshall*

'I and this mystery here we stand.'

WALT WHITMAN
'Song of Myself'

MY DOPPELGANGER PROBLEMS BEGAN ONE afternoon in early April.

I was alone in the store, shelving books and humming along to Radio 2. Mr Ronan, one of my regulars, came in. I watched him from my perspective in Fiction as he chose an aisle and went down it.

I have a bookshop called Bookshop. I do subtlety in other areas of my life. I've been here for two years now, but it's sped by. I have about twenty regulars, and I'm on a first-name basis with them, but Mr Ronan insists on calling me Mrs Mason. His credit card discloses only his first initial, G. I have a running joke: every time I see the initial I take a stab at what it stands for. I run his card and take one guess. We both think it's funny, but he's also shy and I think it embarrasses him, which is one of the reasons I do it. I'm trying to bring him out of himself.

He's promised to tell me if I get it right one day. So far he hasn't been Gordon or any of its short forms, soubriquets, or cognomens. Not Gary, Gabriel, Glenn, or Gene and neither Gerald nor Graham, my first two guesses, based on my feeling that he looked pretty Geraldish at times but also very Grahamish, too. He's a late-middle-aged ex-academic or ex-accountant or someone who spent his life at a desk, who once might have been a real fireplug, like Mickey Rooney, but who, at sixty-plus years, looks like a hound in a sweater. There is no woman in his life, to judge by the fine blond and red hairs that creep up the sides of his ears.

I know he likes first editions and broadsides, as well as books about architecture and miniatures. I keep my eye out for him. And he's a gazpacho enthusiast. You get all kinds. I always discover something new when Mr Ronan comes in. For instance, you can make soup from watermelons. I did not know that.

He came around a corner and stopped when he saw me. He was out of breath. 'There you are,' he said. 'When did you get here?'

'To the Fiction section?'

'You're dressed differently now,' he said. 'And your hair was shorter.'

'*My* hair? What are you talking about?'

'You were in the market. Fifteen minutes ago. I saw you.'

'No. That wasn't me. I wasn't in any market.'

'Huh,' he said. He had a disagreeable expression on his face, a look halfway between fear and anger. He smiled with his teeth. 'You were wearing grey slacks and a black top with little gold lines on it. I said hello. *You* said hello. Your hair was up to here!' He chopped at the base of his skull. 'So you have a twin, then.'

'I have a sister, but she's older than me and we look nothing alike.' I don't mention that Paula is certain that G. Ronan's name is Gavin. 'And I've been here all morning.'

'Nuh-uh,' he said. 'No, I'm sure we...' He left the aisle. My back tingled and I had the instinct to move to a more open area of the store, where I could watch him. I went behind my cash desk and started to pencil prices into a stack of green-covered Penguin crime. I flipped up their covers and wrote 5.99 in each one, keeping my eye on my strangely nervous customer. Finally, he came out of the racks with *The Conquest of Gaul* and put it down on my desk.

'Oh... Mr Ronan? I wanted to tell you I found a pretty first edition of *Miniature Rooms* by Mrs Thorne. Original blue boards, flat, clean inside. Do you want to see it?'

'Yes,' he said, like it hurt to speak. I brought it out from the rare and first editions case. 'It's just uncanny, it really is,' he said.

'This woman.'

'Yes! She said hello back like she knew me. I swear to god she called me by name!'

'But I don't know your name. Right? Mr G Ronan? I think you dreamt this.'

'But it just happened,' he said, like that explained something to him. 'And you knew my name.'

'Mr Ronan,' I said, 'I am one hundred per cent –'

I didn't like the look in his eye. He began edging around the side of the desk, coming closer, and I backed away, but he lunged at me with a cry and grabbed me by the shoulders. Despite his size, I couldn't hold him off and he backed me up, hard, against the first editions case. I heard the books behind me thud and tumble. 'Take it off!' he shouted in my face. With one hand, he tried to yank my hair from my head. 'Take off the wig!'

'Get back!' I shrieked. I pushed against his forehead with my palm. 'Get off me!'

'Goddamn you, Mrs Mason!' When a fistful of my hair wouldn't tear off, he leapt up and stumbled backwards, his eyes locked on mine, but washed of rage. The blood had drained from his face. 'Christ, that's real!'

'Yes! It's real! See? Real hair attached to my own, personal *head*.'

'Oh god.'

'What is *wrong* with you?'

He grovelled to the other side of the desk. 'Oh my god. I'm so sorry. I must be having another attack.'

'Another attack! Of what? Do you want me to call an ambulance?'

'I'll be okay. I'm really sorry. I don't know what came over me, Jean. Forgive me.'

That was the first time he had ever used my name. 'You scared me. And you hurt me, you know?' I began to feel the pain seep through the shock of being battered. 'Are you sure I can't call a friend or someone?'

'No. I'll go home and lie down. I'm just so sorry.' He took his wallet out and put his trembling credit card down on the cash desk.

I tapped it for him. We stood together in a dreadful silence until I said, 'Gilbert.'

'No,' he replied.

I LIKE SYSTEMS. ORDER IS good. I can pass a whole day in front of bookshelves alphabetizing, categorizing, subcategorizing. I look forward to shelving. I have the image, in my mind, of a beam of used books shining in through the door and through a prism in the middle of the shop. The beam splits and the books leap into their sections alphabetically.

I am the prism.

But alphabetical is not the only order. I'm not a library, so I don't have to go full-Dewey. A bookstore is a collection. It reflects someone's taste. In the same way that curators decide what order you see the art in, I'm allowed to meddle with the browser's logic, or even to please myself. Mix it up, see what happens. If you don't like it, don't shop here. January to June I alphabetize biographies by author. July to December: by subject.

There are moral issues involved, too. Should parenting books be displayed chronologically by year of publication? I don't want to screw someone's kid up by suggesting outdated parenting advice is on par with the new thinking. Aesthetic issues: should I arrange art books by height to avoid cover bleaching? Ethical: do dieting books belong near books about anorexia? And should I move books about confidence into the business section? And what is Self-Help? Is it anything like Self Storage? (Which is only for *things*, it turns out.) In Self-Help, I have found it is helpful not to read the books at all.

And what about the borderline garbage that people like to buy – tales of clairvoyance, conspiracy books, fake science? I'm duty-bound to stock some of this stuff, but I like to put it on a higher shelf and force the customer to find the kick-stool. Take a moment to rethink your life choices.

I called Mr Ronan a few days later. I didn't want to be nosy, but he'd left the store in such distress. I got his voicemail twice and left a message the second time. 'Mr Ronan,' I said, 'it's Jean Mason from Bookshop. I just wanted to ask you if you were feeling any better. I'm sorry for whatever fright you had, but I hope you've worked it out. Well. I guess I'll see you next time. Bye.'

I put the phone away and at that exact moment a woman I would later be accused of murdering walked into my shop. She wore a green dress embroidered with tiny mirrors and had warm, buttery skin.

She browsed with her neck bent and looked sideways at me a couple of times through a drape of hair. She wasn't really looking at the books. She was acting suspicious, like she was going to steal something. You can always tell the shoplifters. They act nervous until you make eye contact with them and then they act über cool, like they're obviously the last person who would ever steal from a bookstore. 'Can I help you?' I asked her.

'Maybe. Maybe not.' She had a Spanishy accent. 'Tell me, do you know who I am?'

*Shit*, I thought, *another author*. 'Should I?'

'I work in the Kensington Market. My name is Katerina.'

'I'm Jean. I own this bookstore.'

She stood in front of the cash desk with her hands clasped in front of her. Her dress winked at me. The mirrors stitched onto it were the wings of butterflies. She folded her hands in front of her pelvis and took a deep, stagey breath. 'If I call you out,' she said gravely, 'you must to come out.'

'I'm sorry?'

'If I call you out, you *must* to come out!'

16

In downtown Toronto, you have to be prepared at all times to intersect with people living in other realities because they pop out at you when you least expect it. In the liquor store, in the lineup at Harvey's, shouting about today's god or just asking you *whassup*. 'I'm sorry,' I said, 'I really don't know what you're talking about.'

'I followed a rumour that there was a Llorona about. The Llorona of Ingrid. And if you are Ingrid's Llorona, and I call you to come out, you *must* to come out!'

'What the hell is a yorona?'

'The Llorona cries for a lost child, and tries to steal one from its mother.'

Now she was beginning to scare me. 'Are you serious? Are you accusing me of something? What do you think you know about me? We haven't met before.'

'I know.'

'So?'

She kept her dark eyes locked to mine for a three-count. Then she relented. 'Okay, Jean. So maybe you're not Ingrid's Llorona. You could be Sayona, but I don't think so. You live near Kensington Market, Jean?'

The way Mr Ronan had acted seemed to be of a piece with this woman's behaviour. I felt a need to see where she was leading. It was none of her business, so I lied. 'I live around the corner from here, up a side street. Concord Avenue.' I changed the name of the street, but I was honest about the neighbourhood. I also left out the words *ramshackle* and *hut*. It's not like we couldn't do better, but Ian says he's not moving again for ten years. 'If "near" is five kilometres, then I guess I'm near. But I never go to Kensington Market.'

'Why?'

'I don't know. I have my local shops. I don't have to go.'

'You mean you don't *like* to go, right? You think it smells bad?' She leered at me. 'Maybe *you* have a Llorona following *you* around.'

'I want you to go now.'

'Do you have children?'

'I don't,' I lied.

'Do you have a twin?'

Goddammit, what the hell was this? 'No. I have a sister, but she's older than me, and we look nothing alike. This Ingrid you're talking about...?'

'Yes,' she said. 'She is *absolute* your twin. Only her hair is shorter.'

'Who told you you could find me here? You know Mr Ronan, don't you?'

She gave me another galactic stare, her mouth clenched. She was very pretty, well dressed, smelling of some floral balm. 'Who is Ronan?'

'You might meet him in a waiting room one day. Anyway, if this is a joke, it isn't funny. I know people will do anything to go viral these days, but I'm not falling for it.'

'Is not a joke! You *might* have been an evil spirit. I called both Sayona and Llorona out of Ingrid and they did not come out. So now I know: I am witness a miracle.' Her eyes welled up. 'God bless the baby Jesus.'

'Stop it. I'm sure she looks more like herself than she looks like me.'

'No, no. You must come see now. She buys my pupusas!'

'Your what?'

'My pupusas!'

'Katerina –'

'Jean?'

'The human face has millions of combinations. I mean, there's Catherine Deneuve but there's also Andre the Giant, right? But still we see people who look like each other all the time. It's common.'

'Who is Catherine Deneuve?'

'A professional wrestler.'

She laughed. 'You will see. You have Spanish books, by the way?'

'I have some foreign-language back there,' I told her. If she wanted to browse instead of leave, that was fine. As long as the conversation was over. 'I have the *Don Quixote* Penguin in English.'

'*Don Quixote* does not exist in English,' she huffed, wagging her finger at me. She crouched in front of the poetry section. 'And Catherine Deneuve was a old movie star.'

'Humphrey *Bogart* was an old movie star. Deneuve is still alive.'

'He was very ugly.' She returned with a Celan. 'She has *exactly* your eyes.'

'Deneuve?'

'Ingrid.'

'Do you know her last name? Maybe I should look her up.'

'Fox. F-O-...' She had to draw the X in the air.

'Really. Ingrid Fox.'

'Maybe she will look *you* up.'

'I hope she does!' I said, with forced good nature. I spun her book around to face me and flicked the upper right-hand corner of the cover to see the price. 'You'll read German poetry in English, but not *Don Quixote*.'

'Don Quixote thinks in Spanish. Is impossible to be any other way.'

'Just take it,' I told her. 'A gift. It's been nice meeting you.'

'Really?'

'No, but I want to give Torontonians a good name.'

19

'This is a wonderful city, but it is *cold*. Weather *and* people.'

'We don't mean to be. We're just shy.'

'No, you're just boring. But *you* are very good and nice. Hey, I bet you don't think I can do Bogie.'

'It hasn't occurred to me to wonder.'

She tightened her jaw. 'I come to Casablanca for some water,' she said.

It wasn't bad.

IN THE SPRING OF 2014, I chose a location for Bookshop out on the revamped part of Dundas Street around the top of Trinity Bellwoods Park. I saw coffee shops springing up and decided to cast my lot. Now we have artisanal cheese shops, a pet store, and some good restaurants. And Ossington Avenue. Ten years ago the only nightlife on Ossington was drive-by shootings. Now you can get Italian shoes and chocolate for wine tastings.

We're only in Toronto by a lucky stroke. If not for Ian having had some good fortune playing marijuana stocks on the TSE (husband: '*Skill!*'), I'd still be working at the college in Port Dundas; he'd still be in the Ontario Police Services. We'd all be back in that quiet, safe little town. But as my ex-cop likes to say, 'I smelled the coffee on the wall.' The country was going to legalize pot. He'd busted some growers in Westmuir so many times he'd become friends with them, and some were liquidating in the lead-up to legalization to buy stocks instead of plants. Ian didn't warn me that he was retiring and putting all of our savings into stocks with names like Gemini Pharma and GreenCo. Luckily for him and us, it was a good bet, although I was furious not to be consulted.

Every place you live has its own rhythms, and it can take a while to get used to it or fit in. After two years, I was still decoding Toronto, and I certainly knew what Katerina was talking about – the friendly coldness of Torontonians – but many things about the city were becoming clearer. Torontonians wanted to get on with it, but they were generally courteous. If someone let you into a car lane, for instance,

21

you were expected to wave with casual gratitude, like you expected it, but thank you anyway. Toronto's panhandlers say thank you when you give money, and also when you say 'Sorry.' In fact 'Sorry, thank you,' may be the most common exchange between citizens. Toronto's reputation when I lived outside it was that it was a steely, arrogant place without a heart, but now I see it likes outsiders and it draws on a deep spring of weirdness. Maybe that's the source Katerina came from.

I dwelled for a while on these two encounters in my shop and then, to satisfy my curiosity (or to have my gullibility further tapped), one day mid-month I closed the store early and went down to the market. Apart from our move, nothing as interesting as Katerina and her Ingrid had happened to me in a long time. I planned to keep the whole thing to myself, because Ian is a worrier and this was only a lark. Who wouldn't want to know what was going on? And a part of me was thinking: what if this turns out to be a good story?

May was on its way, thank god. We were getting inoculations of sun. Winter here arrives, stays, persists, goes away a little, then comes back and people start leaping off the bridges. That's approximately March, when jumping is at its apogee, but even then, winter isn't over. What it likes to do is go away for a week in April and then return for three days and finish grandpa off.

Katerina hadn't said where she worked, but Augusta Avenue in Kensington Market was crowded with Mexican, Chilean, Middle Eastern, and Portuguese businesses. I looked for her in all of them. The last time I'd been in the market – years ago – its identity as a countercultural space had already been scrubbed clean. It was a hodgepodge now, but something was happening: it was young like it had once been, the coffee was excellent, and I saw a couple of restaurants I'd risk eating in. The smell of weed hung in the air, advertising the dozen or so medical marijuana dispensaries that had appeared since the Liberals were elected.

No matter your approach, once you crossed College Street or Spadina Avenue or Dundas, you were somewhere else when you entered Kensington Market. It's like if I cross the Canadian border in my car, I *know* I'm in the United States. Even before the signs for Cracker Barrel come up, I'm feeling hustled. Kensington Market's energy was hustle too, plus bustle, a lot of movement right in front of your eyes, and a shudder or rattle behind it. Countercultural, but bloody and raw. The organic butcher beside a row of dry-goods shops offered, in one window, white-and-red animal skulls with bulbous dead eyes, and in the other, closely trimmed racks of lamb and venison filets, displayed overlapping each other like roofing tiles. Then some stranger rustles past with blood on his cheeks.

There was no sight of Katerina on Baldwin Avenue, either. It had been about a week since she'd appeared in my store, and I wasn't entirely sure I remembered what she looked like. I've had this problem before. When I first meet someone, my mind must be busy noting other details, because I don't always register what they look like. Sometimes I even forget the faces of people I know. There have been times when I haven't been able to bring my own sister's face to mind. Not even if I look at one of the few pictures I have of her. I'll look away from her image and close my eyes, but she won't be there.

Katerina was not on the lower part of Augusta Avenue. I looped back and forth over the street, going into a fish and chips shop, a vegetarian wok spot, the coffee corner, and looking at the people behind the counters, sometimes searching their faces as if a person I spent ten minutes with not very long ago could change that much. On Augusta I crossed with throngs of every station back and forth and back over the street.

I found her at last, working a flattop in a Latin American food court. The only sign over the entrance said CHURROS CHURROS CHURROS. Seven or eight food stalls went back inside the narrow space. In the front window, an elderly man squirted batter into a decapitated three-gallon jerry can of boiling oil. Brand name Cajun Injector.

'How are you!' Katerina came around her counter to hug me. I stiffened in her embrace. 'Are you okay? I worried about you, you know.'

'About me?'

'Of course! Come in the back, I make a coffee.' She ushered me toward the rear of the food mall more quickly than necessary, I thought. I smelled coconut and coriander as we went past the stalls. 'Miguel won't be happy to see you after what you did.'

'What *I* did?'

'Yeah! Did you go to the doctor?'

She walked into my back.

'Katerina,' I said, 'I'm Jean. Who do you think I am?'

'Jean!' she said. 'So stupid of me. You are the other one!' She admired me. 'Incredible.'

'I'm the other one now?'

'I thought you didn't believe.'

'I don't know what I'm not believing in. What did Ingrid do? Why did she have to see a doctor?'

Katerina showed me to the patio. 'We talk out here. Are you hungry? I have to look busy a couple minutes.'

'I'm not hungry. Just hurry.'

'Go sit.'

24

I hesitated, or resisted, but then I obeyed. At the back of the building, a red rusted VW Bug stood on blocks, and behind it, in a garage partially closed off by tarps, I heard voices and smelled weed again.

In one of the chairs, my legs sprawled out in front of me, I laid my head back and closed my eyes. Now I felt stupid. I was almost certain that Katerina wasn't a threat, but between her and Mr Ronan – who had not returned to the shop – I probably should have started to get a little suspicious. Something was definitely wrong, but what? When I opened my eyes, the clouds had amphibious underbellies and were ringed in a menacing shade of grey. I leaned forward and looked into the food mall, but it was too bright to see in.

I got up and left the patio. This was foolish. I walked partway back to Augusta Avenue along the alley and stopped. I stood with my back against the wall. I imagined I could feel the graffiti skirling out in twisted bands behind my shirt like tentacles of smoke.

'You want to eat in the alley?' Katerina said. She stood at the edge of the patio with a styrofoam plate of food in her hands. I returned to the table. I didn't know it yet, but by returning to the patio instead of walking away, I had sealed Katerina's fate.

She put the plate down in front of me with an orange Jarritos. There was an albino hamburger on the plate that smelled the way my grandmother's kitchen sometimes smelled: of comfort. 'This is called the pupusa,' she told me. 'You eat it with your hands. Like a sandwich. Go on,' she said, 'eat it.' I tried to figure out how to pick it up. 'And because you weren't listening the first time, I will tell you *again* about the Llorona and the Sayona.'

'It's not necessary,' I told her, but the moment I'd taken a bite of her pupusa, I didn't care anymore. Its scent was how it tasted. The shell contained a mixture of avocado, white cheese, corn, and a greeny-brown salsa that tasted like roasted tomatoes and garlic. The shell was made of white cornflour; the hot and crispy-hard surface perfectly burnt in a few places, and it was warm and bready on the inside. Katerina grinned at my pleasure, and I concluded that, at the very worst, she was only a nuisance.

'So,' she said. 'My mother has told me I was visited by a Llorona myself. When I was a baby. An old woman was coming to the house one night to ask for a cigarette. My mother gave her one. The old woman comes back two more times, and she doesn't want to be rude, my mother, so she brings her into our house. She makes her tea and the old woman tells she has a daughter my mother's age and my mother feels warm toward her. After that, she comes and visit from time to time, always after I go to sleep, and my mother was smoking with her and making her hot tea and sometimes a tortilla with a egg inside it.

'One night, the old woman wants to use the *anexo*. To make her water. My mother show her out back. She tells me that the old woman went away for too long and she felt something was going on. So she goes to my room, and my door is open. She goes in and she sees a woman who look exactly like her! Standing beside my crib! And I am inside the crib, standing, reaching to her, who I think is my mother. My real mother, she shouts and stamps her feet and the spirit goes out through the curtains! Straight out the wall. My mother picks me out of my crib and holds me the rest of the night.'

'How do you know she was your real mother?' I asked, trying to make her smile. 'Maybe it was a bait-and-switch-and-bait.'

'She was never visit by the old lady again. Later, *her*

mother, my grandmother, tells her who it was. The Llorona! Sometimes she comes to visit crying with a baby in her arms, sometime to see if a baby is in the house. If she come in three times, then she will try to take!'

I chewed calmly. 'This is delicious, by the way.'

'Now you see what we are dealing with, you and Ingrid.'

'I thought you concluded neither of us were Guatemalan spirits.'

'There are more than two spirits,' she said. 'I have not ruled out for Ingrid that she is La Siguanaba.'

'Speaking of Ingrid, why did she go to the doctor? Did she try to walk through a wall or something?'

'You are joking.'

'A little.'

'I can make you believe,' she said, and her tone of voice made me want to jump up and run. She leaned over the table and tucked her hair behind her left ear, revealing three blue dots tattooed on her temple. A triangle of pinpricks still red and raw around the edges. 'Look at this. She give these to me.' The dots gleamed like spider eyes.

'What is it?'

'A trick with a sewing needle!' Katerina laughed and fell back into her chair. 'I invite her over one night! We have some drinks. She's a good talker. She was drunk. She tells me...' She lapsed into silence and a trickle of blood came out of her hairline. 'She said she was sick. Here.' She tapped her head, right on the tattoo, and noticed the blood on her fingertip.

'I think you scraped it with your nail.' I passed her a napkin. 'Why did you let her do that to you?' I asked. 'What does it mean?'

'We get drunk and she give me a tattoo. Big whoop.'

'Jabbed you in the temple three times for the hell of it.'

'It means therefore, she says.' She looked at the blood on the napkin.

'Therefore.'

'She says it is my own personal therefore. I think she fell in love with me.'

'Wow. Do you usually drink so much?'

'Yes.'

'And that night?'

'Of course. What do you think? I do anything for company here. I think maybe Toronto is a fuckless city. It was nice that she come over. But you have to be careful, if you ever meet her, don't believe *everything* she say.'

'Like what?'

'She thinks she has a doppelganger!' She laughed and I suddenly felt really scared. My heart hiccupped behind my ribs.

'This was great, Katerina. How much do I owe you?'

'You should go to the park,' she said. 'That is where she will come. One day again soon.'

I struggled for a moment over whether I really wanted to know. 'Which park?'

'Her again?' said a man in the doorway. He wore a white apron stained with chocolate sauce.

'No. Another one! See?'

'Hello,' he said to me. 'You pay on the way out.'

'It's on me,' Katerina said.

He switched to Spanish and harangued her. It was obvious they were, or had once been, lovers. But he was also the boss.

'I'm allowed to do nice things for people,' she said in English. 'Miguel was a mathematician in Chile,' Katerina explained to me. 'But here he is only Churros Churros Churros.'

For that, he came out and grabbed her by the arm. I was on my feet before I knew it. 'Let her go! Let go of her right now! We don't grab people!'

'She owes me four hundred dollars.'

'I'll give you the money,' I said. 'Let her go.'

Katerina came and stood beside me. She rubbed her upper arm. 'You don't have to do that. I don't owe him anything. *Ingrid* owes him.'

Miguel said: 'She dented the flattop with a cast-iron pan!'

'Ingrid?' I asked. 'You've seen her, too?'

'*Who?* This one!' he said, pointing at Katerina. 'Miss Hot-and-Cold!'

'And he makes fun of my English!' she said, and started to cry. 'Shithead. I break up with him because he is so mean. And a *sucio cerdo*, a pig, a dirty pig!'

'You go,' he said to me.

Katerina tapped her tattooed temple. 'Don't worry. I don't belong to him. I am with you and Ingrid, miracle women, and you protect me.'

'I'm a witness,' I warned him, sliding past. 'Don't touch her again!' To Katerina, I said: 'I'll come back soon. I wrote my phone number on the napkin.'

THE PARK KATERINA MEANT IS called Bellevue Square. I saw what she was talking about right away: you could see anyone or anything in that park. I sat on one of its benches after leaving the food mall and watched people coming and going for two whole hours. I had to remind myself to keep looking for my twin, but the passing parade was so gripping that from time to time I forgot my stakeout. The park was a clearing house for humanity. I saw no sign of my lookalike.

The following week I went back, and the week after, too, a couple more times. I walked through the square, or sat for an hour, sometimes two. For cover, I had one of those puzzle magazines full of sudokus and crosswords, and I occupied myself with filling them in when I wasn't doing my regular sweep of the park. I figured out which restaurants would let me use the washroom, which store sold the cheapest water. As my main lookout point, I settled on the low wall that half encircles the playground on the north side of the square. It gave me a vantage to the south as well as both sides of the park, and I could easily scan the path that cut it in half diagonally, southwest to northeast.

I found reasons throughout the second half of April to drift toward the park, or pass the park, or sit in the park. There were times when I was at home or in the store when I felt a need to go there. And other times, I sat on the low wall overcome with a feeling of *wrong*, as if I were forgetting something important, or being watched myself. It wasn't anxiety. It was something that was present everywhere all at once: a climate. Something I was in.

At the very beginning of May, I started buying my

groceries in the market, too. That gave me extra days to have a reason to go. The temperature shot up into the twenties, and the park swelled with people and animals and garbage. I began to count the number of people who weren't Ingrid, and I kept track of them on my phone, giving every person an identifying name so I wouldn't count them twice, like Earlobe Mole and Triple Sweater Man and Bendy, who was a woman whose head sat askew on her neck and who walked serpentine.

The puzzle book did its task so well that in those early weeks no one so much as acknowledged my existence. Then, almost exactly a month after Mr Ronan had first warned me of Ingrid's existence, a woman walked clear across the park toward me like she recognized me, and I thought, *Ah, this woman knows Ingrid*. She wore two pieces of clothing: a tight white halter top with white spaghetti straps cutting into her burnt shoulders and a pair of white Lycra shorts. White sunglasses, a layer of lipstick red as a car crash. Also, I had to presume, no underwear: the front of her shorts looked like someone had painted over a tarantula. She kept coming, even though I'd put my head down to write feverishly in the margin of my magazine. I saw her light blue toenails and silver sandal straps come to a stop inches from my feet. She said, 'Do you have what time is it?'

I told her it was almost four o'clock and she sat down on the wall beside me, as if giving her the time had been an invitation. She took a bottle of beer out of her purse, twisted off the cap, and began drinking. It was twenty-six degrees and the cold green glass was sweating. I noticed a child on the wall of the sandbox looking at the bottle. Spandex had hiccups and burps, which made her sound like she was beat-boxing. She must have come from one of the rooming houses down Denison Avenue. Got a beer out of her minifridge and came to sit in the park. She drained her beer and put the empty into her purse. It clinked. If you can get two in, that's what you want. Two was always enough to renew the drunk for my father. Her second beer was sweatier than the first.

On some days, I ate pupusas and continued my little friendship with Katerina. I kept her off the topic of my 'miracle' sister, and eventually she told me more about herself, about her home and where she grew up in Guatemala. By coincidence, she'd come to Toronto when Ian and I came with the kids, within days of each other, we discovered. 'Now we're like twins, too,' she told me. 'We become Torontoners almost on the same day!'

Miguel had stopped harassing her. But when I went to sit at the back of the shop, I would face the front so I could tell her if her sometimes-lover came in. In none of my brief visits to Katerina, however, did Ingrid ever come in.

And she seemed to be staying out of Bellevue Square, too. Or maybe she was avoiding it. It certainly felt that, if she existed, she wasn't all that interested in meeting me. But now that we knew about each other, there was no reason not to put the mystery of our lookalikery to rest.

Within this time, I'd worked out a general taxonomy for the park. Many homogenous groups had formed. I identified, in discrete subsets: obsessives, paranoiacs, zombies, professional clowns, hair eaters, weepers, chatters, schizos, aliens, psychotics, dipshits, ferret keepers, goths, takeout eaters (a hugely varied group in and of itself), tourists, police, masturbators, shouters, air-guitarists, CD sellers, city workers emerging from the ground, and cat walkers, to name a fraction.

The volume of a person's voice appeared to be a barometer of their sanity. The silent, dirty, downcast men holding furred paper cups, with sooty eyes and scars for mouths, were the ones who developed a sudden taste for murder once in a while. Even the ones who were usually alone joined up with others from time to time. On a typical afternoon, one of these broken types, say Jimmy, will be making some terrible noise, roaring so loudly you can hear his voice shred – but in rage or grief or desolation? He'll slump against a tree in his blue shirt not dark enough to hide the filth on it, his beard going down to his navel. I've seen or imagined little black mice scurrying around in that beard. It's impossible to know what the face under it looks like. The first time I saw Jimmy, he was reading *Us* magazine in the shade of one of the willows. I looked at the cover a moment too long – Tom Hardy was on it and I have a debilitating weakness for Tom Hardy – and Jimmy said, 'They're just like us!' I pretended not to hear him, but he called to me. 'Hey. Don't be scared. Celebrities are just like us, so it follows we're just like them. They live our secret lives out in the open and we hide their public lives in our thoughts.'

One afternoon, a young couple crossed the park to see him. The woman, a girl really, gave him a king can of Brava. She wore a polka-dotted skirt over black leggings. She told him how the cops knew it was him and he better get off the streets. They left and he walked back and forth over a worn patch of grass smoking a bent cigarette and sucking at the beer with flared lips. He finished it and pulled his shirt off. I saw the knobs of his vertebrae range up and connect to the base of his skull. He crossed the park and sat under another tree. Immediately, two dipshits came over and sat right in front of him and I braced myself for violence, although nothing happened.

(The dipshits are the ones with glue dripping from their

noses. I guess Jimmy knows they're worse off than he is. He's got a nice warm bed if he wants one, a five-minute walk from here, and he's not really an addict, he's sick. The addicts are sick too, but the glueheads, specifically, burn off their personalities, while there's still a Jimmy in Jimmy. Or so he's told me. The dipshits sleep in the park. From time to time there are fights at night, so you have to stay out when it's really dark, like after the bars have closed. Gluehead violence is common. Punks come and roll them where they're sleeping, but they don't wake up. Not because they're dead, but because getting mugged is not enough to wake them.)

Even with its menaces, the square's playground has kids in it. Kids in the wading pool, kids on blankets sitting in the grass. Lunatics are a hazard if you live downtown, but your kids still want to go to the pool, right?

I stayed a watcher for much of these weeks in Bellevue Square. I remained apart from the passersby and the regulars. I was different because I didn't belong; that's what I told myself. One afternoon I was sitting on the wall and struggling with a corned beef sandwich on a paper plate. I don't like to drip on myself or eat messily. If something I'm eating falls apart, say a taco or an ice cream cone, I get angry. I know (because I've had therapy) that I get angry at myself because I no longer have my father around to get angry at me. For being a slob or a clumsy moron.

It had turned windy, and the sandwich was coming apart in my hands. For a reason lost to time (I should ask Ian's mother), it's traditional to make a corned beef sandwich with two asymmetrically cut pieces of bread that had been nowhere near each other in the bag, arranged into two sandwich halves, and held together by flimsy toothpicks. I'd removed the tooth-picks and lathered mustard on the bread.

I sat with my knees pressed together, using the second half of the sandwich to weigh the plate down on my lap.

The first half was scrumptious, even though some of the meat squelched out and fell onto the plate. I started on the second half, and this time the two peninsulas of rye that were holding the meat in place were so insubstantial that much of the sandwich fell apart at the same moment as the wind blew my plate into the playground.

I looked down at the splat of pink meat and streaky mustard on my jeans and muttered: 'You idiot.' In my mind, I continued: 'You can't even eat a sandwich. Look at all this wasted food, you pig.'

My inner scold was interrupted by the appearance of two feet in dirty Adidas in my line of vision. I looked up into a pair of hands holding napkins, and above them, into the eyes of a man I had named Zippy because he had a small head and a protruding nose. He was dressed in what he always wore, a black quilted parka vest, with a camera around his neck. He said, 'I hate when that happens.' I accepted the napkins, and he sat beside me.

'Thank you.'

'I put the plate in the recycling because it was dirty and the pigeons will eat the bits of meat and I'm a photographer. My name is Ritt. I've seen you twelve times.'

'I'm Jean,' I said.

'Are you from the bin? The loony bin?'

'No,' I told him. 'Are you?'

'I'm a member of that establishment. I perform there often.'

'What do you perform, Ritt?'

'My photographs. I have more napkins and I also have photo albums and a two-terabyte SDXC card. Do you need more napkins?'

'I'm good now. Thanks for your help. That was good timing.'

'Can I show you something?' He had a photo wallet in his hand and he unsnapped its clasp. 'These are ginna blow your mind, I swear.' It was an album of flowers, snapshots in plastic sleeves. 'Ten point two pixels. Crystal clear, high fidelity.'

'Interesting,' I said, although it wasn't. He flipped slowly through, giving me enough time to take in his portraits of rhododendrons, tulips, and hyacinths. There were sprays and starbursts of white hydrangea. 'Do you take pictures of people?'

'People don't hold still. You get blur and you get double exposure and people aren't interesting! People are people, you know, like the song. Being good looking, an example of humanity, doohickeys with eyes in 'em? That doesn't mean you're a nice person! Look at hands and feet, if you want to know someone, hands and feet, and *corpuscles*. That'll tell you the truth, hands and feet.' He put a finger beside his nose. 'And corpuscles.'

'Did you take all of these in the market?'

'Most of them.'

'This one?' I asked. It was a picture of deep pink lotuses floating in a small pond. I could almost smell them. It was a low-angle shot taken in someone's garden and in the distance, people sat around a glass table, eating dinner. 'There are people in this one. And were you *at* this dinner? It almost looks like you're hiding in the grass.'

'A fence,' he said. 'I took it through a wooden fence.'

It was a good photo. It had an aura of memory to it, as if I'd been in that garden. Then something about it began to bother me.

He said, 'This is art, you know. If you see something

36

and take a picture or write it down, it's art because you're the one that did it, you know? Before I took pictures of these things, they were only things. Do you believe that art exists?'

'Oh. Sure,' I told him, and then I saw it. I recognized one of the people at the table: a woman with long hair who even through the photoblur I recognized, although it couldn't be. 'Oh god,' I said. I took the album out of his hands.

'Hey – !'

I breathed in through my nose and out through my mouth, the way my therapist had shown me. I looked more closely. It was me. I recognized the shirt, the earrings, even my posture. But I didn't know any of the people and I'd never been in that garden. I was sure of it. I didn't want to puke on Ritt's flower album so I flipped away from the lotuses and started counting my breaths. 'Sorry,' I said.

'They're for sale, you know. You can't just have them.'

'Oh yeah? Can I buy the lotus picture?'

'That one? I like my daisies better.'

'The lotus speaks to me. How much?'

'Two? Bucks?'

'I'll give you five.'

'Wow.' He got the picture out before I changed my mind. 'Have you heard a band called A Band Called?'

'What? No.'

'They're good, but you have to like caterwauling. Do you want any other pictures?'

'No. But if you see this lady again,' I said, showing him the woman who had to be Ingrid, 'I'll pay you five bucks per picture.'

'Right on,' he said. He leapt up to return to whatever he'd been doing before he rescued me from my sandwich and gave me my only solid lead.

Ritt erased the fourth wall between me and them. I began to notice parkies more; they were people who, in addition to being troubled, full-on mad, or lost, were also persons with beer preferences, party affiliations, kids, and manners, too. They were entire, and they were sick or addicted or in the thrall of an awakening or fervour. There were the drunks, of course, and they are ghastly and scrubbed-out people. But almost everyone I met or spoke to in Bellevue Square was a decent soul. As was my new friend, Katerina. It was as if the park and its environs had been, at least temporarily, made into a mysterious little paradise for me, with entertainment and pastimes and the promise of something marvellous, something absolutely marvellous coming, something that would bring with it the answer to the *wrong*.

Once I began to interact, I joined the ranks of regulars. It felt strange for only a very short time, being brought into their circle, but I realized I already had a place in its ecology. I was paying for sightings, real, false, and rumoured, as well as ones that were convincingly told, and I spread prosperity in a thin, useful layer. I became a resource, and in return, the people of the park and market opened up to me. Everyone had a role to play. Miriam, who owned the sidewalk space in front of the recessed fire hydrant beside the synagogue, put herself in charge of ensuring we all got milk. I took a carton of 2% every time I was there. Why not? I was paying for it.

Cullen became my most 'regular' informant. He's an old man with a fanlike grey-and-black beard. A custodial figure. He brushes off the seating areas with a copy of the day's *Metro*; keeps his eye on the wading pool. I heard he once rescued a child from it, but he was still taken away by the cops. Because a black man rescuing a white child and all that, he told me, like he accepted it. I couldn't see him harming anyone, but I don't really know what happened. He's peaceable enough. His uniform is faded jean overalls with a woollen shirt underneath to keep his rangy body warm, even in summer. His work entails going around the benches as well as sitting-stones and the wooden playground wall, in a kind of lazy surveillance. When he's idle, he stands on the Augusta side of the park, near the south corner, looking up the street expressionlessly. He's told me this is his 'no-mind' time. He thinks nothing, he sees nothing. 'It's my practice,' he's told me. He's the only one Miriam doesn't give milk to. He says it's because she's a racist bitch, but I think they were once an item, a long time ago. I have a feeling for these sorts of things.

Cullen is a social type and he likes to stick around after he gets paid and tell me disconnected stories from his life. He told me his mother always knew when a storm was coming because one of her dogs would wait at the basement door. The other was deaf and got struck by lightning. Also, he said he taught biochemistry at the University of Toronto, but quit to 'study chemicals in their natural habitat.' His sightings have been disconcertingly consistent. His Ingrid shops for fruit, weighing oranges in her hand and knocking melons, but never buying. I've asked him why she never buys and he says she might be allergic. He claims to have spoken to her only once, and just the first time, when he greeted her thinking she was me, and she asked him to move along. 'She has a hungry look,' he told me. 'I don't think she's really after fruit.'

'What do you think she's after? It can't be me. I've been coming here a month without a single sighting.'

'I'm not sure, but she may be after my great-great-great-great-great grandfather's magic horn.'

'Your what?'

'But she can't steal it because I don't have it yet! Charles is bringing it to me. One day! One day Charles will bring me Katterfelto's Horn!' His shiny eyes became distant, his mouth frozen in a half smile. It seemed to me he was in a place that was beyond madness. He was ecstatic.

ON MAY 15TH, I DID a tally of all the people I had individually witnessed in Bellevue Square, comers, goers, and stayers. Among my most interesting sightings was a drunken teenager making out with the Al Waxman statue, as well as a man sitting in the grass with a bottle of Vaseline and a single, disgusting Q-tip, which he inserted into his nostrils loaded with petroleum jelly. I also saw people getting each other off under blankets and a nudist who was ushered out of the park by police officers. But none of these people had been Ingrid. To be precise, by the middle of May, Ingrid Fox had not been 4,233 people.

WE ALL KNOW THAT BAD things are coming. Advice: don't get too comfortable. Read short books, don't see your doctor too often. Example of this: on one of my visits to my old GP, Gary Pass, I learned the name for the bony protrusions that had started to poke out of my skull. They were aneurysmal bone cysts, benign (1997). Then Pass pronounced I had polyps. They flourished in such places as my armpits (2001, 2006, 2010), my cervix (2007), and my rectum (2012). It's no small thing to have a half-dozen growths fried off your cervix, but I would take that over two in the fundament. Paula, my sister, called the second operation 'Fire Below.' She's been allowed, since 2007, to make fun of my aches and pains because she has a case of the brain tumours. Paula used to live in Phoenix with her husband, Chase, but now she and Chase are quits and she lives alone in Phoenix, convalescing or dying. Nine years after diagnosis, the tumour has doubled in size, but she lives on. It's inoperable. We keep our Skypes on and I have a huge data plan on my phone, which means I can talk to her while I walk down the street if I want. I'm all she has now. Our deadbeat father died last year, and our mother alternates between Toronto and Key West, where she cures herself to kid leather six months out of the year. Once in a while she'll go see Paula, but my mother *has a life*. She says you shouldn't have to take care of your kids past their eighteenth birthdays.

During times of peace, when people are surviving from one week to the next, a kind of holy feeling comes over me. I try to live by the belief that almost everyone who is likely to make it through the day does, and although this is an argument for some ordering presence, I'm sure it's not one we've thought of. You can't talk about God around Ian. He's a piercer of fictions. He knows too much, and he doesn't hide it from you. Men want to be right. Let them, I say. It drives him crazy when I won't take the other end of the rope. 'Okay, you're right' are three devastating words.

Mostly he is pleasant about issuing corrections. He is capable of a warm, giving smile. It can be dangerous to ask him for advice or even just his thoughts on something because he fancies himself an expert on just about everything. I guess he is. After my first few fruitless weeks in the park, I wanted to know how detectives found stuff out.

'You mean how they solve crimes?'

'Yeah.'

He closed the magazine he'd been looking at and put on his thinky face. 'Well, it's different depending on the type of crime, but the two most important things about a crime is the scene of the crime itself with its attendant evidence, and witnesses. Detectives and specialists collect evidence from the –'

'How do you find witnesses? Isn't it hard sometimes to find people who are willing to talk?'

'Often, yeah.' He paused. 'Why are you asking?'

'I was just wondering if the way they look for witnesses in movies and on TV is really how they do it in reality. Knockin' on doors, 'scuse me, ma'am...'

'There's lots of that. Anyone hanging around the crime scene is worth talking to. They might know whose house it is, whose car it was, what the victim's name was, and so on. You take notes, write down people's names. You have to keep your ear tuned for inconsistencies in people's stories. Are there hours missing from their day? And watch where their eyes go.'

'What do you mean, where their eyes go?'

'If they won't look at you, or, conversely, they won't *break* eye contact, something's wrong. People's faces twitch, too, when they're trying to control their responses.'

'And that means they're lying.'

'Not necessarily. But they might be hiding something. You have to reassure them they're doing the right thing cooperating with the police.'

'And then what?'

'You take pictures. You go away and think about it, you come up with a theory, and then you test that theory.'

'And then you solve the crime.'

'Eventually. You thinking of a career change?'

'Another one? No thank you.'

'Anything else, Miss Marple?'

'No. I'm going to go check on the boys.'

I look at Ian sometimes and wonder how we actually ended up together, given the odds as he's explained them to me:

*What was the likelihood that we'd ever meet? Never mind how right we are for each other. We have no idea what other lives we might have led.*

His philosophy is that as soon as something bad happens, it's already in the past, but good things reach into the future. So he ignores the bad things. I accuse him of toxic positive thinking; he says he's making his own reality to counteract the odds.

Ian: You are one person only, and only once, and so how is it you are born a woman in the twentieth century, at a time when life expectancy is double what it was even one century ago, and for the first time in recorded history you have rights, and you're a Canadian, and white, *and* you got to marry me and pass on my genes, which is awesome *for you*! Calculate the odds of that happening. Being happy is a choice!

Me: I am happy! Jesus!

My sister: The odds are *someone* is going to marry a decent man, and maybe you did.

My mother: If something is too good to be true, then it's probably not true.

Ian is scrupulous about his taxes, and not because of his background as a lawman but because his mother raised him right. In our old hometown, he'd had the reputation of a minor superhero, although equal numbers of people hated as loved him.

His mother: I raised him right. What are *you* doing with him?

To my case for a numinous order *maybe* existing in the universe, Exasperated Rationalist will ask me how do I think a woman living on a garbage tip in Calcutta would see my theory? What does it mean about *her* that there's supposedly some order in the universe? That you really have nothing to complain about makes you lucky, it doesn't mean you're good or that there's a god who loves you personally. Ian preaches randomness and claims he finds it as mesmerising as any other philosophy.

He says: You can stop taking everything personally. Nothing is meant to happen or not to happen. You're one of the fortunate ones. Don't be an idiot and not enjoy it!

Of course I know this is true. But really, how can you be this unromantic?

I MARKED THE END OF my sixth week in the park with no verifiable sightings, although I was now bringing an entire roll of loonies with me every day I went. Which was, more or less, every day. I'd hired a hand for the bookstore, a PhD candidate named Terrence whose specialty was female sci-fi writers like Ursula K. Le Guin and Nalo Hopkinson. His thesis was called 'Stellar Reproductive Technologies.'

I'd put on four pounds since the beginning of my vigil, many of which were the result of a superior ice cream store being within a hundred metres of the park. I was trying to cut down on their malted milk chocolate by switching to their hazelnut and fig, but I wasn't making much progress. Cullen came to sit beside me in my usual spot on the low wall surrounding the playground. I gave him half my ice cream and felt virtuous. He had a sighting he wanted to be paid for. No one saw Ingrid as often as Cullen did, but he was good company and he needed the money.

There'd been no persuading Miriam to take Cullen off her shit list. Most of the time she's sentinel at the front doors of the Kiever Synagogue, across from the square. The synagogue – which has a fascinating history, she'll tell you if you so much as glance at it – looks like a Communist wedding cake. It looms over the northwest corner of the park. Miriam collects tips by warning people when they've parked too close to the recessed fire hydrant beside the temple. It's countersunk into a fence, set back an extra three feet, and people always miss it. Even in broad daylight they miss it, although Miriam makes more money when it's dark. She darts over when she sees someone backing into one of the two trouble spots, the ones within three metres of the hydrant. She'll come calmly by and 'notice' that someone has just parked too close. Her patter goes: Oh excuse me, sir/ma'am, you might not want to park there. Yessir, that's a hundred and eighty-one dollars you won't be spending today. If the person is Jewish (and she is never wrong), she'll ask if they're coming to services. If they are, she adds: You don't want to take God's name in vain the second you come out of *shul*! No members ever park in front of the hydrant: they know it's there. But Miriam always has fresh meat. Out-of-towners, new members, people in for the high holidays, the only time they ever come.

She makes forty or fifty dollars a day. She distributes half of it to parkies, in the form of those half-pints of 2% milk, and she keeps the rest of it for herself. There are people of every colour in the park, and she gives to all of them. Except Cullen.

'What was Ingrid doing?' I put a loonie in his palm. 'How close were you?'

'She was sitting right here. Where we're sitting. I thought she was you.'

'How'd you figure out she wasn't?'

'She told me she wasn't. I said to myself, Cullen, this one really does have a twin, or she's goofy. She didn't know your name yet so I told her.'

I made a game-show buzz. 'Wrong. Katerina's already told her my name. Give me back my dollar.'

He tried to return it, but I pushed the coin away. 'She said she didn't know it. She gave me more money than you ever have.' He unsnapped a breast pocket and removed a ten-dollar bill. It was a bill that had been old when I was a kid, light purple with shadings of burnt orange, and a kaleidoscopic background of spirographic rosettes. It had a restrained psychedelic vibe. Behind Sir John A. Macdonald, the word *CANADA* was chiselfonted in a dark, authoritative violet. On the current bill, our first prime minister looks like he's recovering from a bender.

'Ingrid gave you this? Ten dollars from 1971?'

'I guess so.'

I gave him another loonie. 'Keep up the good work.' He went away without saying thank you and reappeared ten minutes later with a cigarette in his mouth and one over each ear. I could see the bill still crumpled up in his shirt pocket.

'I've had cancer twice,' he offered. 'Lung once. They told me I was terminal but I wasn't.' He drew on the cigarette like he was sipping champagne. 'Except in the usual way. What are you doing if you quit smoking when you get a diagnosis of terminal lung cancer? Presuming it doesn't hurt to smoke, why not keep on keepin' on? The conclusion is foregone and change is pointless. You feel gratitude and happiness in being alive.'

'While you kill yourself?'

He mimed sprinkling bread crumbs to invisible birds and a couple of real ones flew up and came near. Maybe I was as gullible as they were. 'I laugh in the face of people who recycle their fast-food wrappers and detergent bottles full of poison,' he said. 'Too little! Quitting smoking is like being environmentally conscious in 2016.'

'You don't care that we're killing the planet with our filthy habits?'

'The planet isn't dying because we're bad and we poisoned the oceans. It's dying because nature is death on the hoof.' (Puff puff.) 'The destruction of the planet and the extinction of all life is stamped upon it, my dear. Now take us: what a weapon.' (More puffing.) 'The adaptations of bipedalism, the opposable thumb, and face-to-face sexual congress sealed the planet's fate the moment all three were within the same animal.'

Once Cullen hits a vein, he can take off on amazing flights, and I listen with admiration for what the human mind can do with its talent for missed connections. First you had to figure out what the puzzle was, then you had to solve it. 'These three things,' Cullen continued, crushing the cigarette underfoot, 'guaranteed that the human species would have a large territory – in the end it is all of the habitable land on Earth, and much that isn't – that they could hold and finely manipulate objects and therefore invent tools, and that it would develop culture. My god, it's wonderful and sinister! Do you know, Jean, we're the only species that looks into its mate's eyes during intercourse? It developed our concept of the other, and therefore we also conceived of ourselves. *There is another*, said the monkey, *I am the same*. Face-to-face intercourse makes the passing on of genes a *personal* thing. Empires came of it. And empires and cities made overpopulation inevitable. Overpopulation was the mother of invention in the Industrial Age and the exploding costs of keeping billions of people alive led directly to going off the gold standard in the 1970s, when it was already too late to do anything about the inevitable outcome of all this success. When money becomes metaphorical, we go extinct.' He mimed taking a puff from an invisible cigarette and then he got up and walked away.

Of course, I didn't believe that Cullen had seen Ingrid. But still, I thought about her sitting there, imagining her body present within mine. I let her fill me, starting from my heart and spreading out to my trunk and my limbs. I even felt heavier.

My phone made its Paula Skypesound and I cleared my passages and squinted. In public, sometimes I talk to Paula as if I'm on a regular phone call, with my iPhone against my ear, but she complains she doesn't like staring into my head. Even in a world where people bark into Bluetooth mics while walking down a street, I'm not yet comfortable conducting video conversations in the wide open. This time, however, I needed the grounding of Paula's eyes and mouth and I lay the phone in my lap and looked down at her pixelated face. 'Hey.'

'You're in romantic silhouette,' she said. 'With the sun behind your head and all. What time is it there now?'

'I don't know, it's... just past four. You can't see the time on your phone?'

'I wanted to know what time it was where *you* are.' She had her phone mounted on a selfie stick, giving me a panoramic view of her lying-in on her sick-couch in the middle of her depressing condo. 'Is the background supposed to make you look holy?'

'No,' I said. 'I'm leaning over. I don't want to be too obvious, talking into my own lap.'

'Ashamed of me?'

'Uh, yeah.'

'Are you there right now? In the park?'

'Yes.'

'Do you see her?'

'I wouldn't be on the phone with you if I did.'

'Show me the park.'

I held the phone out and panned left to right while I narrated. 'Disgusting restrooms, drug dealers, wading pool with waders, pigeons and ducks, the street, the path, trees, Giorgio the stand-up comic, trees, pot smokers, pot dealers, Ritt the photographer, King of Kensington bench, nappers, the synagogue, cheap clothing, the playground, me.' I put the phone back in my lap.

'The park has its own comic?'

'He's a homeless guy who does a routine about poo. You have to pay him five bucks to hear the whole thing.'

'How are you?'

'Feeling insubstantial.'

'Suck it up, girlfriend.'

Her tumour is a vestibular schwannoma, which Paula says is German for getting fucked in the ear. It's a tumour that forms on the eighth cranial nerve, below the brain. When at last she'd been bullied into seeing a physician, the tumour was already too big to remove. She's left with a permanent ringing in one ear, wonky balance, and a paralyzed cheek. She looks drunk and leers a lot, not on purpose, and prefers to stay indoors. I send books to her Kindle to keep her busy. I also write her actual letters once in a while. For a shut-in person like my sister, getting mail is like having someone visit you.

Paula is the first person I confide in, which sometimes has unintended consequences. She takes the other person's point of view readily if she thinks it's correct. She says it means I can trust her. And I do, of course. Her own problems have made her no less practical than she was when we were younger and more carefree.

'Have you been outside in the fresh air recently?' I asked her.

'I went on the balcony. It was raining.' She raised the stick to show me the grey Phoenix skies. 'Who's cooking your children their suppers?'

'Ian is defrosting, reheating, or ordering in.'

'How long have you been there today?'

'Just a couple of hours.'

'Anything?'

'No.'

'What's her name again?'

'Ingrid.'

'And how do you know that?'

'Katerina – a lady from the market who knows her – she told me. She's seen us both.'

'And what does Katerina do? Sell drugs?'

'She works at a pupuseria.'

'A poo-poo what?'

'A pupuseria.'

'Does she talk like Salma Hayek?'

'Salma Hayek is from Mexico,' I said, hoping no one could hear either end of our exchange. 'Katerina is from Guatemala.'

In my lap, Paula dropped her jaw halfway down her neck. *'There is nathing fonny about my Eenglish.'*

'Katerina's accent is a little more subtle than that, superstar. *And* she does Bogart.'

'Where does she know Ingrid from?'

'From the *market*, Paula! Listen to what I'm saying.'

Suddenly she squeezed her eyes shut.

'What's wrong?'

'Pain,' she mouthed.

'Your head?'

'Your face.'

We waited it out. I wanted to ask her what to do, but there's never anything I can do.

'God,' she said, exhaling. 'It's like someone's stirring my brain with a chopstick. Hold on.'

The view of the room changed as she stood. It takes considerable effort for Paula to rise from a seated or a prone position. She gets 'overlaps,' where some part of the previously seen angle is still visible while she is in motion. It looks like a screen wipe from *Bonanza*, she says. The camera at the end of her stick pointed down at the floor and I watched her feet shuffle back and forth, first over the broadloom and then over the ticky-tack kitchen tiles, grey with fake marble streaks. She leaned the camera against the counter while she shook out her pills and I got a view of the interior of her sink. It looked like a badly loaded dishwasher, with plates and pans and utensils standing pressed against each other. She capped the pill bottle and ran the water. Her palm came into the frame shaking, containing five pills, a quintuple dose. My disembodied voice said, 'Whoa,' into the sink.

'Am I getting a lecture now?'

'*Five?*'

'Lowest effective dose.'

'Lowest effective overdose!' She returned to the couch, vorkapiching the view of the floor as she spun the selfie stick in her hand.

'I better take Gravol next time we talk. Why can't you just hold that thing still? Or call me back!'

'I want you to get a feel for my actual life.' The scene returned to Paula lying on the couch, the houseplants drooping behind her, and the wall adorned with her idea of fine art: calendar pages, old ads framed in cheap IKEA frames.

'I wish you'd let me come and see you,' I told her for the umpteenth time. Paula refuses visitors to her *tomb*, as she calls it. Even delivery boys are told to leave their pizzas on the hall carpet and go away.

'You know you can't see me, darling. I'm barely here. What could you do?'

'I could give you a hug.'

'Your arms would go right through me.' She pushed the pillows up behind herself and got settled again. 'How long has it been, anyway? I bet we don't even recognize each other in person.'

I'd tried to go down once or twice after her diagnosis, to see her, but there was always a reason I couldn't, or she stopped me from coming. Being apart this long makes me feel closer to her than maybe I would feel if we had regular visits.

'This vigil you keep, what's it really about? See a couple new wrinkles beside your eyes?'

'Mr Ronan saw her, too. It's more than just Katerina. And those two people I'm sure have never met.'

'Who's Ronan again?' she asked.

Cullen waved to me from the sidewalk. He had an aggravated expression on his face and I felt guilty of something. I waved back with two fingers and he got into a black Corolla that was parked at the curb. Passenger side. The car drove off.

'What are you looking at?' Paula asked.

'Mr Ronan is the gazpacho guy.'

'Oh, *Gavin*!'

'Him. He's seen Ingrid too.'

'Well, that's proof, then,' she mocked. 'How are my nephews?'

'Reid is still a space alien and Nick has grown two inches since last summer.'

'Any hair on his upper lip?'

'A small, blond caterpiller.'

'God, getting an adult in return for a child is a *bum* deal.'

'Agreed.'

'I would have loved your boys.'

'You mean having kids of your own?'

'Having a family would have been better than this. Anything would have been better than this, but I didn't think it through.'

She began to drift. She couldn't stay focused for very long. 'Should we say goodbye for now?'

'Goodbye for now,' Paula said, and she collapsed the selfie stick. Her face flew at me. 'In case you're interested in my opinion, I think you're bonkers.'

I HAD QUITE A SHOCK when I got off the phone: it was nearly nine at night. I'd lost all track of time. I'd also forgotten it was a Friday, and I had five texts from Ian. They were increasingly splenetic. The final one read: *I thought we had an agreement. If I don't hear from you by 8, I'm making a missing persons report.*

He picked up halfway through the first ring. 'Are you okay?'

'Yes! I'm sorry, I'm sorry! I was doing inventory and the system crashed and I had to call Terrence to come in... I just lost all track of the time. What a mess! Did you eat?'

'I was worried sick.'

'I hope you guys ate.'

'Of course we ate. It's *Shabbos*. We ate almost three hours ago. Which was two hours *after* you were supposed to be home.'

'Are the boys okay?'

'Are you kidding me? They barely registered that you weren't at the table.'

'Did they register that *you* were at the table?'

'No. Why are you laughing?'

'A missing person's report?'

'Are you coming home *now*, Jean?'

'Yes. Immediately.'

'How delightful. I'll be upstairs working when and if you do. Goodbye, Wife.'

'Goodbye, Husband,' I said, in my meekest voice. Forgiven through mockery.

When I got home, I found that Ian's mother was still at the house. She'd waited for me. So I wouldn't have to eat alone. 'We girls have to stick together,' she said.

Beatrice hadn't liked me when Ian brought me home fifteen years ago, and she didn't like me at the wedding, either. But as soon as I started popping out her grandkids, she turned sweet as pie, at least officially. We both understand she still doesn't like me, but we each come with the package now, so why not be nice? I've asked Ian how it is his eyelids don't close sideways, and he claims his father, who I never met, was only part-lizard. Beatrice's tongue is pinned to the floor of her mouth owing to some childhood incident involving a pencil, so you only ever see the pristine pink tip of it. This is only one of the things I'm not crazy about. She was also born smelling of bronzer.

I play a game where I am twice as polite as she is and see if I can make her burst into flame. 'That's so super of you, Bee, to wait,' I said. 'At least there's *one civilized person* under my roof.'

'I'm heating a microwave in the leg for you,' she said. 'We'll have a little picnic.'

I sat at the one place setting left at the table. It was a large white plate on a plastic placemat. When the microwave dinged, she removed a casserole with a steamed-up lid. My children, who had yet to say hello to me, were on the couch, engrossed in their phones. In Reid's lap, Lefty was curled up in his usual place. The only sound coming from the room was purring. 'Hell*oooo*?' I called.

Beatrice put a casserole on the table and removed the lid. Inside, resembling a crime photo, was a single chicken leg.

'Is there any salad left?'

'I'll look. You eat, you're hungry!' She rummaged in the fridge, her broad rear end blocking my view of the boys.

I heard Nick say: 'Do you know what rage means?'

'Angry,' Reid answered. 'A lot of angry.'

'I got salad,' said Beatrice, backing out of the fridge and standing with a showy groan. 'And I found something to nosh on with you. Gotta keep up my strength for these little gangsters.'

I was still half-listening to Nick.

'Do you know what inducing means?'

Reid's shoulders bounced up and down. He didn't know and he didn't care.

'It means make something happen,' Nick explained. 'Angry Birds is a rage-inducing game.'

Nick had lately been sprinkling his conversation with words that belonged to a more adult vocabulary, like *inducing*. I wanted to hear my children talk to each other more, but that was it for their conversation. They'd been drawn back into their several screens, and they sat together isolated, their phones in their hands with the television still on in front of them. I'm not certain either of them can function with fewer than two screens. Reid's eyes were dead – fixed and dilated.

'Why is that one so *schvartze*?' Beatrice asked me.

'Sorry?'

'Nicholas. You don't think he's darker than his brother?'

'I've never thought to compare them.'

She looked over her glasses at me. 'Have you always been so fair?'

'Yeah. My sister too.'

'Your *sister*? Well, maybe it skips a generation. Or maybe,' she said, winking, 'you got it on with the postman!'

Her mouth churned with white meat. Her 'nosh' was a whole chicken breast from the fridge. 'How's your chicken?' I asked her.

'I don't mind having cold. You eat.'

Ian's mother eats chicken like a Jewish Inuit. She eats the skin, then the meat, followed by the gristly, translucent grey knobs at the ends of the bones. These she breaks to suck out the marrow. I pray she doesn't have a chicken breast when she comes for Friday dinner, because she eats the ribs and makes barbaric smacking and crunching sounds.

'AAAAGH!' Nick shouted. 'This shithead game is glitched!'

'*Nick!*'

'Well, it is!'

'It doesn't require such colourful language.'

'Ech,' said Beatrice. 'Shithead isn't so bad. Do you remember when he was two and he'd ride around on that plastic tricycle and go *fuck fuck fuck* every time he bumped the stair?'

'Ha-ha-ha-*haaaaa*!' Reid shrieked.

'SHUT THE EFF UP, LIMPDICK!' Nick shouted.

The chaos ignited something in my duodenum. My stomach lurched and I felt the back of my throat being pulled downwards. Then something came out of me. No one could see it, but it was in the room with all of us. I felt it go through Nick and Reid and I heard Beatrice chewing bones and swallowing them.

She tapped the edge of my plate with a sternum. 'Stop dreaming, dear. It has the most bacteria when you eat it at room temperature.'

I tried to go back to my food, but the panic was rising. It wasn't panic, though – it was density and intensity, it was volume and pressure and brightness, like somebody had tightened the room tone. My ears tuned tinnitus and my eyes focused to five hundred dots per inch. Now I saw, impressed into the tip of Beatrice's index finger, the outline of her nail before she cut it. I saw the light in the kitchen behind her head grow a nimbus. A thought appeared in my mind and the thought was 'I'm inside of what I'm inside of,' but I don't have thoughts like that. Then the sound of Beatrice chomping the wishbone – a moist splintering – made me jump up and my chair hit the wall behind me.

'HO-lee!' she shouted.

I ran upstairs to the hall bathroom and locked the door behind me.

Ian stomped down from his office. 'Oh my god, Jean! What is going on!' He tried the handle. 'Hell-o? Are you okay?'

'The chair tipped over.'

'What happened to you today?'

'I just – I lost all track of the time.' I ran cold water over a facecloth, loud enough so I had cause not to hear what he was saying. 'Did everyone have a nice supper?' I called.

'Reid ate buns and dipped French fries into sauce. Nick ate half a chicken.'

'There were French fries?'

'You sound strange. Can you unlock the door? Can I talk to you?' He rattled the handle. When I didn't reply, he went away for a minute, but returned with something that clunked against the door. It sounded like a chair. I stepped backwards into the tub. 'Jean?'

'I'm okay,' I said. 'Just had a little tumble downstairs. Everything's fine.'

'All right, but where have you been all day? Before inventory, or whatever it was you were doing.'

'I went and sat in a park for a couple of hours, and I had a call.'

'With who?'

'Whom.'

'Don't do that.' He tried the handle again. 'Can you open the door?'

'I'm taking a shower,' I said, turning the water on. 'I'll be out in a sec.' He just sat there. I could sense his weight behind the door. 'Are you going to listen to me shower?'

'Turn the water off, okay? Enough.'

I did. I didn't need this to escalate.

'You promised to talk to me if you ever had another... attack. So talk to me.'

*Fuck*, I thought, *I did*. But did I mean *this*? Did I mean anything out of the ordinary, or did I mean only, and specifically, if I suffered postpartum depression again? 'Nothing like that is going on,' I said. 'There's nothing to tell you about. It was a beautiful day, I went to a park, I had an ice cream, and I lost track of the time. And then I had to go back to the bookstore because Terrence, and there was inventory...'

'The *bookstore*? Because you *what*? You're lying. You're lying to me, Jean, why?'

The anguish in his voice hurt to hear. I unlocked the door. He came in. I saw him look for anything I might have been planning to harm myself with.

'See? I'm fine.'

'So why lock yourself in the bathroom?'

'I wanted to be alone for a couple of minutes.'

'I heard you come up the stairs like there was something chasing you –'

'I know what you're thinking. But that was then and this is now. You don't have to worry about me.'

'I can't ever stop worrying. I saw what happened to you. You didn't see it. You didn't even know you were sick when you were sick.'

'I know,' I repeated. 'Okay. What happened tonight

wasn't exactly as I told you. But if I tell you, I just want you to listen. Okay?'

'Yes! Please!'

'I did have... a little attack,' I began, making it up as fast as I could. 'When I was out getting a coffee, my heart just started going bump bump bump, and I got *scared*. I had to walk it off. Like Dr Pass told me, you know? I walked and I... I don't know how long I walked, Ian. But my mind cleared –'

'You said you had a call. From who?'

'I talked to my mum, I talked to a friend... so I could ground myself. It was good to hear their voices.'

'Why didn't you call me?'

'Because I thought you would do this. Get worried or get angry. I took care of it,' I said. 'I'm sorry I gave you a scare.'

He went into himself for a minute, weighing. He took my chin in his palm and kissed me. 'Okay. I'm sorry that happened. I'm glad you're feeling better.'

'Carry on,' I said. 'I'll release your mother back to the wild and put the kids to bed.'

'Okay. Next time call me, though. I won't judge you. I want to help.'

'Sorry. Thank you.'

He started up the stairs.

'By the way, have you noticed your mum's been getting mixed up lately?'

'How do you mean?'

'She put a microwave in the leg for my dinner. That's how she said it.'

He continued to his office shaking his head slowly, Ianese for *if it's not one thing, it's another.*

THE FOLLOWING DAY, OVER A stewed chicken and avocado pupusa, Katerina told me she'd seen Ingrid the previous evening. She'd come in for churros, then popped back to say hello. She was feeling better, but the results from the doctor were worrisome. She was having seizures, and they'd started her on a drug.

Having recovered from the previous night's vapours, I had a new perspective on Katerina. It was good that Ian had questioned me so directly, because afterwards, I felt myself click back into place. Of course I wasn't getting sick. I knew what that felt like, and this wasn't that. But it only made me want to know so much more. And I wanted to show Katerina the picture.

'Has she said she wants to meet me?' I asked her. 'Why don't you just give her my number?'

'She says she can't be reached. Better to wait until she's feeling better.'

'She'll see *you*, why won't she see me?'

'She's not ready, Jean. She says she's not herself. And I think she is scared.'

'She must think you're full of it.'

'Do you know what she says? *Oh no, not again!*'

I showed her my forearms, bumpy with gooseflesh. 'You're actually freaking me out. Look.'

'Her husband is very handsome. Maybe *you* can have him after she's gone?'

'I have a husband. And what do you mean, after *she's* gone?'

'You call her doppelganger, I call her Llorona, someone

63

else calls her Ra, but she always bring death. I'm not sure, but I think it's *hers*. Her own death.'

'What does her husband look like?'

'I don't know. I never meet him.'

'And how sick *is* she?'

'She says it has happened one time, and after, she got better. But I'm not sure. I care about her a lot, but I don't trust her.'

'Do you trust me?'

'No.' She squared herself to me, to look me in the eye. 'Let me ask you something. Do you like Jimmy?'

'*Jimmy?* He's crazy, but I guess he's okay. Not for a date, though.'

'Oh we already have gone,' she said. We sat at a table at the back of the food mall, hidden among other customers. I had a sightline to the front, and if Miguel came in she was going to dart into the walk-in freezer, then come out with something.

'You've already gone on a date with Jimmy?'

'You have only been here one month. Jimmy is here for years. He's not always like that, he cleans up. Then he's only the same trouble as the rest.'

'What did you do?'

'There was a French chicken place. It comes to the table whole, and inside with olives and prunes, and they bring us a nice bread, you know, a baguette. We ate the whole thing with our hands.'

'Sounds like it went well.'

'My *chichis* smelled like chicken fat for three days!' She laughed a deep, lungy laugh and her eyes teared up. I passed her my water, but she waved it off.

'Why are you asking me about Jimmy?'

'I asked *if you* like him,' she said, blotting her eyes.

'Oh. No. Yes, but not like that. And anyway... I'm married!' Katerina crushed the napkin to her mouth to stifle more laughter. 'Okay, ha ha. Yuk it up.' I finished the last bite of my pupusa and let her collect herself. 'Can I show you something?'

'Of course!' she said. She cleared her throat.

'There's a guy in Bellevue Square named Ritt. He's there a lot, and he talked to me yesterday. He showed me a photo album, and in one of the pictures...' I looked in my bag and found the slot I'd stored the picture in. I hadn't looked at it again – I was too frightened to. 'Here,' I said. 'Tell me what you think.'

She studied it for a moment. 'They're beautiful. He took this?'

'Look closer.'

She had to bring it to her face. Finally, she asked, 'Do you know those people?'

'Do *you*? Do you recognize any of them?' The picture wasn't *that* blurry. 'That's me!' I said. 'Look!' I took it from her and held it beside my head for comparison. Her eyes went back and forth.

'Oh, wow,' she said, 'right! I guess... your head is a bit turned away, but now I see.'

'Those are my earrings. I'll wear them here next time. And that bracelet, that's mine. Ian had it made for me on our tenth anniversary. Four colours of gold wound together, a strand for each one of us. That's *my* bracelet.'

'Okay, so it's you.'

'Yes, except I don't remember this evening. I don't recognize anyone else in the picture. This man' – a warm-looking dad type with a soft belly and a grey-chinned beard – 'is completely in focus, and I am one hundred per cent certain I've never seen him in my life.'

She nodded along to my Sherlocking. 'So it *is* Ingrid. Somehow your friend takes a picture of Ingrid. It's for sure she lives near here.'

'I thought so too, but Ingrid has short hair.'

'Maybe this is a old picture?'

'How long has she been here, though? Why haven't I seen her yet? I've come here a lot. You see her, but I don't.'

'I see her at least five times before I meet you in your bookshop.'

One way or the other I wanted to erase all hint of doubt for myself. The picture was troubling, because either this woman truly existed or I had forgotten an entire evening and all the people in it. 'I'd like you to do something for me, Katerina. I want you to give Ingrid a letter from me.'

'You wrote her a letter?'

'Yes, and I want you to deliver it. Wherever she is, home, here, the hospital. Take it to her in the hospital if you want. I'll give you five hundred bucks, too.' I put the envelope on the table.

'I don't want money.'

'I spent a long time writing it, Katerina. It's important. I want to be sure she gets it.'

She snatched it up. 'I do this for free! Such a good idea!' She put the envelope into her pants pocket. 'Miguel will come back soon. Stay as long as you like. I have to peel corn.'

I TROLLED THROUGH KENSINGTON MARKET after my pupusa. If Ingrid had been there the previous night, she might have had cause to come back in the daytime, say to pick up a repaired item, or I might get lucky running into her as she returned to fetch a pair of sunglasses she left at the pupuseria. I went into some of the shops on Augusta and Baldwin, again. And again, no one greeted me as a woman named Ingrid, although I asked a couple of people if we'd met before. (We hadn't.) I made sure to check into the other Latin American and Mexican and Argentinian places. If she liked pupusas, Ingrid probably liked arepas and enchiladas and tamales, but not today, apparently. Katerina remained the only person who had seen her more than once. I'd wanted to speak to Mr Ronan again, and I called a few more times, but there was never an answer. It seemed wrong to leave him another message, but the third time I got his voicemail, I told him I'd located a first-edition Römertopf clay pot cookbook from 1969 and did he want me to set it aside? He didn't return my call.

I don't keep my customers' addresses, but I used Canada411 to look for other Ronans, and there were few enough that on the first phone call, I found myself speaking to an older woman who knew exactly which Mr G Ronan I was talking about. She told me they'd discovered Graham (for that was his name) hanging in his apartment at the beginning of April. I'd braced myself for bad news, but not death, not suicide. I couldn't hear anything else she told me at first because I was in that moment when he'd grabbed my hair at the bookstore. I saw his face, clear as day. His round Grahamish face and his hairy Geraldish ears. I had a pang of anger. I'd guessed his name, but he hadn't admitted it. He'd lied and broken a promise and I'd tried to be his friend.

I expressed my condolences and told the woman that I knew Graham for a while, that he'd been a regular customer of mine. He gave me a list of things to keep an eye out for, I told her, books he wanted, and she asked me to send the list to her. I later did. It was handwritten and signed G.

May 20, 2016

Dear Ms. Ingrid Fox,

Please forgive me in advance for what might seem an invasion of your privacy. I will only write to you this once.

Katerina is convinced you are my double. Except for our hair – you wear yours short, I wear mine long – we are supposed to be identical. She's told me that you've been unwell, and that you're seeing doctors for a neurological condition. However, I wonder sometimes if Katerina is the one who might be unwell and if she should tell a doctor about you. I know she has friends who would accompany her to appointments if she wanted. She also claims you gave her a tattoo that I think she gave herself. I'm a little worried because I really care about her.

I have kept a lookout for you for almost two months now, and if you are actually out there, I think the reason I haven't seen you is that we look nothing alike. However, Katerina is my friend, and she believes you to be her friend as well, so if you are really out there, I know you won't allow me to worry about her like this. I propose we simply meet and put any doubts to rest.

I will wait from dawn until dusk in Bellevue Square next Friday, May 27. You are welcome to come at any time. Katerina is also welcome.

Yours,
Jean Mason

BY MAY 27TH, APPROXIMATELY 7,500 people who had passed through the park were not Ingrid. This confirmed my two top hypotheses: that she didn't exist at all and Katerina needed a shrink, or she did exist but she looked nothing like me. The third possibility, that *I* was crazy, I deemed distant but possible. Ian has his reasons to be concerned, but if I've gone mad, then it's nothing like the last time, which was already twelve years ago. Of course I get low from time to time, most people do, and probably the majority of them would never call it depression, but that's what it is. I imagine depression as a concavity in the spirit. Something gets scooped out. The first time, the concavity was Nick. After he was born, I got sick and I had a hard time bonding. Accept the baby, they said. I love the baby, I said. It's hormones, they said. Take the medicine. I took the medicine, I did the yogic breathing, I loved the baby. It would be nice to spare the people you care about the most the experience of seeing you get sick in that way, but so many of us are only a few squares away from pure lunacy anyhow. That you so rarely get to the final square gives you and everyone around you the reassuring illusion of your solidity. For most of six months, I wouldn't eat because I worried that if I got food poisoning, it would make my milk toxic. I denied that I was worried someone was poisoning my food. I drank organic whole milk and I ate applesauce I made myself, and almonds. It happens to a lot of women. It's nothing to be ashamed of and I had the love and support I needed, which is all anyone ever needs. And time.

The fourth and final hypothesis, that Ingrid actually

existed and was my identical twin, I put at 'basically' impossible, which still allowed for the slimmest chance of possibility because impossible has stringent, but not unmeetable, requirements. Impossible is choosy. For instance, merely unlikely things are bound to happen to you and the people you know almost all of the time. Still, if you think about it, you know a person whose guitar teacher's best friend's son survived being shot six times. Or we settle Mars. Or Donald Trump becomes president.

I tried to rise above myself and see this all from a psychological point of view: maybe I was pre-grieving my sister's death (*eventual* death, I argued: unilateral vestibular schwannomas are rarely fatal, even among those who are only eligible for radiation); or maybe some part of me knew Ian was in money trouble or there was another woman and *this* fantastical goose chase was how I was dealing with it. Or maybe I, myself, had a brain tumour. But what was this tumour doing beyond making me more credulous than usual?

I knew I was close. Ian would have been horrified at the thoughts evolving in my mind as I sat in the square, waiting for Ingrid. I remained locked to my position, from dawn till dusk, with only three bottles of water and a bag of apples. Miriam brought me my carton of milk around three, but she didn't linger. I hadn't seen Cullen since he waved to me getting into that black Corolla.

Evidence was mounting that nothing beyond someone else's overactive imagination was at work here. I watched the sun sink in the western sky. Unless they were being as fashionably late as possible, neither Katerina nor Ingrid was showing. I even waited until it was dark. In the dark, nothing happened.

IAN JOKED ABOUT MY BEING good enough to join them for Friday dinner, but I was hardly late. It was only seven. Beatrice was making up a mess of *biximol*, which is a fry-up of beef cubes, red and green peppers, and mushrooms, with a dash of Worcestershire, that she claims to have learned from Ian's first nanny, a Swedish au pair. It's served normally with scrambled eggs, but tonight she'd made it to go in vol-au-vents. Both boys looked at the semi-burnt towers of puff pastry running over with glistening *biximol* and pulled their upper lips back in disgust. She brought one for Ian, and then one for herself, and sat down.

'Um, Ma?' Ian said. 'Is there one for Jean?'

'Oh god!' My mother-in-law jumped up to grab me a plate and the children said in unison: 'She can have mine!'

'So sorry, Jean!' Beatrice put a plate down in front of me. The pastry was cracked and dribbling its contents.

'It's okay, Beatrice,' I said under my breath. 'I only live here.'

Ian tilted his head at me.

'I'm just joking,' I added.

'Maybe I forget to serve you because your chair has been empty so many Shabbats. You don't like to eat dinner with your family?'

'No! I eat dinner with –'

'When Ian was a boy, Shabbos was *obligatory*!'

'You're only here one night a week, Bee. Don't make it sound like you keep the place running.'

'Jean,' Ian warned.

'It was a night for family,' Beatrice continued, as if I

72

hadn't said anything, 'not for work.'

'Did everyone get a plate to eat from for Shabbos or only the blood relations?'

Ian's fork hit his plate with a clank. 'For chrissake.' The boys stopped eating.

'Let her go,' Beatrice said as I got up from the table. 'It's better you don't fight in front of the children.'

He was still good and angry when he came into the bedroom an hour later. 'What the hell was that all about?'

'It's like I'm not even in the room, like I'm invisible to her. She doesn't talk *over* me, she talks *through* me!'

'Keep your voice down. If she didn't notice you, how would she know how often you've missed Shabbat dinner?'

'I'm sure she prefers it that way. Then it's the perfect family. No crazy mummy, the kids get fed –'

'Jean, come on. You're the mother of her grandchildren. She loves you.'

'She wouldn't mind if I got hit by lightning.'

'I don't know what's happening with you right now,' he said. 'Nick says you haven't been home after school for three weeks, and when you *are* here, it's like you're being broadcast from another planet. You tell me nothing's wrong, but given what I'm seeing, that answer is starting to be part of the problem.'

'So *I'm* the problem, eh? Have you had your mother's head checked for bugs? Did she heat anything up in the leg today?'

'Why are you acting like this? I don't believe your story from two Shabbats ago anymore. What's happening on Fridays that you can't make it home for dinner? Is there someone else?'

'Oh! No, god no.' I had to tell him *something* now. 'Look,

I wasn't sure what it was at first, so I didn't want to talk to you about it because I figured you'd worry.'

'It.'

'It... I ran into this woman in April,' I said, watching his face. 'Never met her before. New to Canada. Anyway, she works in Kensington Market. She introduced herself to me and we became friends.'

'Okay, so?'

'She told me she saw a woman in the market who was my exact twin. Said she even had my voice. Just listen before you say anything. She was going to introduce me to her. To Ingrid –'

'Ingrid,' he grunted.

'But she never did and I didn't – and I *don't* – believe her. But it was weird. I wanted to know more.'

'What could you have wanted to know? She's a scam artist. How much did you lose?'

'Don't be like that. Don't be so cynical. She didn't ask me for a thing. She told me Ingrid had been in and out of hospital with seizures and she didn't want to meet me until she felt better. Finally, I asked her right out, would she give Ingrid a letter from me. In the letter, I asked her to meet me in Kensington Market today. And I waited in the park all day for her, but she didn't come. And I *knew* she wouldn't. Because my friend is sick. I've had problems before, so I guess I recognized it and I wanted to help. Because we're friends.'

'How are you going to help your friend?'

'By letting her know I'm here for her.'

He was shaking his head, but I knew he was processing it. 'But are you sure you don't believe her? A little bit?'

'I don't. I tested it today, and this Ingrid didn't show.'

'Show me the letter,' he said. I shrugged and pulled it up

on my phone. He read it quickly, his eyes vibrating left and right. He passed the phone back to me. 'You wrote that?'

'Yes.'

'How much time have you been spending there? In the market?'

'An hour here and there. Looking around to see if *maybe* there was someone who looked a little like me. I wanted to judge for myself. Is there anything wrong with that?'

'Here and there? What's here and there? How long has this been going on?'

'About a month.'

He was becoming agitated again. 'What's "about a month"? Three weeks? Six?'

'About that.'

'Which is it?'

'Maybe five weeks.'

'So... that means two months, right?'

'I'd like you to stop this.'

'I'll stop. But you're going to take me there. Tomorrow. And show me what you're talking about.'

PEE, DOG TURDS, AND DECOMPOSING mice are only some of the fragrances of Bellevue Square in springtime. I'd long ago stopped noticing these undertones to the market's stinky chiaroscuro, but it can be a challenge for first-timers, and when we walked into the park, Ian pulled his head back, as if he could save his nose from going in. 'That's... fucking *foul*,' he said.

Miriam greeted us as we entered.

'Friend of yours?' Ian asked.

'A local,' I said.

'That makes you...?'

'I told you, I got to know a few people over the weeks –'

'*Months.*'

'– that I've been coming here.' I told him Miriam was a Turkish lady who'd worked her corner since 1995. I told him how she was the market wet nurse. Ritt wasn't around from what I could see, and now Cullen had been missing for the better part of a month. The last few things Cullen had talked about before he vanished had unsettled me. He claimed to have invented a drug that allowed him to upload his thoughts into a computer.

Ian and I sat on the top of the playground wall.

'This your post?'

'Yes.'

'Other people have seen this Ingrid, and they're sure.'

'Yes,' I lied, Graham Ronan being dead, and the local lunatics unreliable.

'But no one's actually seen you two together. In the same space.'

'If they did, they didn't tell me. What they *did* tell me was that she looks more than passingly like me. Apparently my hair is longer.'

He digested this. Someone called my name from some distance, and we both looked across the wading pool. It was Ritt, coming toward us with a photo wallet clutched in each hand. *Oh boy.* 'Hey Ritt,' I said, hailing him before Ian could wonder if this man with the strange-shaped head was a threat or not.

'Hello, Jean, and hello,' he said to Ian, and Ian sort of nodded. Ritt gave me one of the albums and handed Ian the other. 'You can look at gears while Jean checks out carved keystones.'

'What is this?' Ian asked me, but Ritt answered.

'These are snapshots I take with my DKS-09 and save to a deep memory card and at Shoppers Drug Mart there are more than drugs and I develop my pictures there.'

'Thanks for that,' Ian said.

Ritt reached into the inner pocket of his parka vest and removed a small sheaf of loose photos. 'I did what you asked,' he said to me. 'I got some more shots.'

There were eight different pictures, all of me sitting in the square, wearing eight different outfits, and eating in three of them. Over the eight pictures, the trees in the background grew leaves. 'Oh, these are great,' I told him, sweating.

Ian stuck his hand out. 'Let me see those.' He shuffled through them. 'Are you her personal paparazzi?'

'She asked me to take pictures of that lady and I did.'

'You know these are pictures of *her*,' he said, talking to him like he was an idiot.

'I don't know who she is, I'm only doing what Jean asked me to do.'

'It's okay,' I said, trying to take the photos back. 'Ritt and

77

I started talking about portrait photography one day –'

'Jean and I have never discussed portrait photography but I gave her napkins and that's how she saw the lady in one of my pictures. Jean?'

'Yes?'

'I've been thinking about whether you should pay me for all eight pictures or only for the ones you want to keep and I decided that you should keep all of them but that I would give you a discount and you could pay me four dollars each which is a total of thirty-two dollars.'

Ian shoved the photos back at him. 'She doesn't want these crappy pictures.'

'I only have a twenty,' I said, handing him the money. 'I'll give you the rest later.'

'Okay, Jean. Thanks, and thanks,' he said to Ian, 'for enjoying my images of bicycle gears and other types of gears as well.'

Ian, defeated, plopped the photo wallet back into Ritt's hand. Ritt headed off, to spend his earnings. Ian swung his head toward me. 'Speechless,' he said.

'He's harmless.'

'How much has he taken off you?'

'It doesn't matter. But I'm sure I've spent five hundred bucks here in handouts. What does it matter to you? It's my money. I earned it in the bookstore.'

'Oh, yeah, right. In your bookstore.' His phone rang. He showed me the screen: a beaming Beatrice. He'd asked her to take the kids. 'Hi, Ma. What's up? I'm busy.'

'Everything okay?' I asked him, but he got up to take the call in private and stood with an elbow balanced on a wrist, listening.

Ian's voice arrived at my ear as a murmur punctuated with stertorous *uh-huhs*. At the bottom of the park, I saw

Jimmy coming up Denison. He was doing what he called the long circuit, a walk that took you down Augusta to Queen, Queen to Denison Avenue, then north until you arrived back at the Kiever. I got up and walked over to him. His matted beard had potato chip crumbs in it. 'Ripples?' I asked him.

He swatted at his chin, and sparrows instantly gathered around his feet. 'That your boyfriend up there?' he asked me. 'I saw you sitting beside him.'

'He's not my boyfriend. Are you on day pass?'

'Yeah. Except it's from yesterday.'

'They'll take away your privileges, you know.'

'Fuggit,' he said. 'Privilege to hang around crazy people? No, I'm better like *this*. I'm more *me*.'

Ian put away his phone and came over. 'You guys know each other, too?'

'This guy's wearing a wedding ring,' Jimmy said. 'So if he's *not* your boyfriend he's cheating on his wife.'

'Jimmy, this is my husband of fifteen years, Ian Mason. Ian, this is Jimmy. Jimmy hangs out in the park sometimes.'

'Like her,' Jimmy said, offering his hand. 'Are you cheating on your wife?'

'*This* is my wife. We're looking for a woman who looks exactly like her. You ever seen her?'

'Your wife?' Jimmy slid me a swirly look. '*Very tricky opening*,' he said.

'He wants to know if you've seen Ingrid.'

'Oh. Yeah. A coupla times, but I'm never totally sure it's her because sometimes it's Jean. I mean most of the time it's Jean, or all of the time, but if I think back, in my own mind there were a coupla times I saw Jean before I met her, so that *must* have been Ingrid. It's just hard for me to sort out who told me what.'

'Who told you *what*?'

'Exactly.'

'Sorry,' Ian said, over-patiently, 'what did Ingrid tell you?'

'You'll have to ask her yourself,' Jimmy replied, nodding to me. 'She probably knows. I don't have time for this, though. I have to find Colleen.'

'Who's Colleen?'

'Who else would she be?' Jimmy replied, and walked away.

'Hey –'

'Leave him,' I said. 'He's a mental patient.' We watched him stalk over the new grass, his arms wide and his hands in fists at the end of his scrawny arms. When he reached the other side of the park, he went 'BEH-HEHHHEH!!' like an enraged goat, and crossed to the Kiever side, mad as hell.

I tugged on Ian's sleeve. 'Let's go get pupusas.'

'You want to go in the same direction he's going?'

'We're going this way,' I said. I led him up the path to Augusta.

'So this is how you've been spending your time? With these kinds of people?'

We got to the street, but the way north was blocked by a crush of people. It was springtime in the market on a Saturday morning. At the T-shaped intersection of Baldwin and Augusta, bodies jostled for space with cars and bicycles. As we got nearer, the back of the crowd ruptured and people surged toward us.

They were letting cops through from the north. They came down driving the wrong way and cars had to back up and drive on the sidewalks to let them pass. We stopped at the edge of the crowd. Ian looked over the heads in front of us. 'I don't know what this is,' he muttered.

'What did your mother want?'

'She said Nick was throwing up.'

'Oh no! Is he okay?'

'They had one of their all-nighters and ate gummy worms and Vachon cakes in front of her TV until four in the morning. She said they watched three movies in a row.'

'Great. Maybe they had some bridge mix for breakfast.'

'Hold on,' he said. 'They're going into an alleyway up there.'

I stood on my tiptoes to see which alley he meant, and when I saw, my heart sank into my stomach. I'd stood in that alleyway, thinking about walking back into the mass of humanity and leaving Katerina's story behind.

The front of the crowd pushed back as the ambulance parted it, throwing red and white light and making urgent whooping noises. Cars honked on Baldwin and the voices around us called *what happened*, but nobody knew.

Then someone shouted, 'That's her! That's her over there,' and I turned to look behind me, but the coatbacks were running away in every direction, down the street and into the park, like they were fleeing.

Ian pulled me onto the sidewalk. 'Are they pointing at you?'

'Are they? Hold on a second!' I got my phone out as if I had to answer a call. 'Hello?' I said into dead air.

'Where are you going?'

'Sorry! It's Nick! Hey, sweetheart! Daddy told me you weren't feeling well.' I put a finger into my other ear and walked away from the thronging, and when I looked back, a policewoman was approaching Ian. The moment she put her hand out to shake his, I made a sprint for the alley that leads to municipal Green P parking lot number 071 and I ran behind it and climbed the fence into the residential parking area. The ambulance was already around the back of the food mall and I crept closer, keeping to shadow and breathing one two three four. The attendants jacked a gurney down from inside the ambulance and rolled it toward the crumbling patio where Katerina had served me my first pupusa.

I took a few more steps, my dread thickening, until I came close enough to see that it *was* her. It was poor Katerina. She lay face down on the white paving stones in a pool of blood, her arms and legs twisted in different directions, her face turned toward me. One of her eyes was a red disc and the other stared out clouded. I must have made a sound, because one of the officers hurried over to me and asked if I knew the victim.

They needed someone to identify her. The officer, name Sanchez, had to pull me toward the body. My nostrils felt like they were the size of quarters, and oxygen swamped my head and made me dizzy. The words *Careful: she can still hear you* came into my mind and 'she' was Katerina, the woman, my friend, sprawled dead on the back patio of a makeshift food mall. I started to cry.

Sanchez led me over to her. There was a purple hole in the side of her head, right through her tattoo. 'Can you please cover her face!'

A pair of blue gloves pulled a sheet over her and a red ring soaked through. 'I know her first name,' I said. 'It's Katerina. She works here.'

'How well did you know the victim?'

'Victim!' I sputtered. 'Oh my god, I can't believe this. I met her in April.'

'Were you her friend?'

'Yes. We were friends.'

'Did she have a husband or a boyfriend, you know?'

'A guy named Miguel.' A man in a suit and tie was drawing

a chalk line around Katerina's body. I sobbed and Sanchez put his hand on my shoulder. 'Why did this happen?'

'Will you please wait here, for two minutes?' he asked. 'I want to get a statement from you, Miss...?'

'Fox,' I said. 'Ingrid Fox.'

SANCHEZ WENT OVER TO TALK to the suit and I slipped back to the streets through the parking lots and went into Bellevue Square. Crying endorphins made me feel calm again. I bought a four-dollar hat from Smart Wear, a floppy beige number that would come down over my eyes if I lowered my gaze. My jaw ached. I went and sat in my usual spot.

Did Katerina kill herself? I'd thought that maybe she wasn't well, but she wasn't depressed, she was *lively*! She was looking for love, she was making friends...

It could have been Miguel. I'd given his name, so no doubt Sanchez would find him and question him. I'd only seen them together once, and there had been a troubled connection between them, but I couldn't see him killing her. But if it was him, they'd know it.

Jimmy? Could Jimmy kill?

There were voices behind me. 'That's her! She's right there!' It was Ian. He came toward me with a female constable. 'Where did you go? Whose hat is that?'

'I've been here the whole time.'

He thanked the cop and she returned to the street. 'Come on, Jean. Someone was shot. They're taping off the whole street.' He offered his hand, but I didn't take it.

'She's coming,' I said.

'Who's coming?'

'Ingrid.'

His face collapsed.

'I'm close,' I said. 'To figuring this out. You're going to have to trust me.'

'Look, I can't feel what you're feeling or see what you're

seeing. I know it's real for you. And frankly, you can do whatever you want. Sit in the park, own a bookstore, drop out and dial in, whatever. But it's a crime scene back there and it might not be safe in the park today, so come on.'

He tried to take my arm, but I shouted, 'GET OFF OF ME!' and pulled away.

'Look at yourself!' he snarled. 'Look at the people around you – and not just the imaginary ones, the actual ones. There's a dead woman back there!'

'I know!'

'How do you know?'

'I asked what happened and someone told me.'

We'd collected some attention from both the adults and the children in the playground. A guy adjusted his iPhone angle so he could film both his kid on the slide and us. 'Hey,' he called, 'everything all right over there?'

'Everything is fine,' Ian said, looking into my eyes. 'Correct?'

'I'm getting this all on tape, mister.'

Ian said, 'I'm calling Dr Pass.'

'You can call him, I don't care.'

'So let's go *now.*'

'NO!'

He tried to stare me down, but I wouldn't break eye contact with him. What did he know about any of this? What could he understand?

'Go away,' I said.

Ian stepped into the playground and snatched the man's iPhone. 'I'm a cop,' he said. 'I'm erasing this video.' The man protested, but Ian just did it and handed him back his phone. 'They should rip this all up and replace it with something less shitty,' he said, and walked straight out of the park.

SIRENS ECHOED SOMEWHERE distant, like the news of Katerina's death was travelling on soundwaves. The man with the iPhone grumbled to his spouse. I was aware of eyes on me, like spotlights, like cameras. Did the eyes know something? Had Katerina been murdered? Who would *want* her dead? Ingrid, maybe. Maybe Ingrid thought Katerina had said too much, had given something away. Had *exposed* her.

And if Ingrid killed Katerina, was Graham's death a suicide? What if she was killing anyone who'd seen her?

No sooner had this thought entered my mind when something happened in the trees. They captured the sound of the sirens and transformed it into a tone like a violin section tuning itself to A. It went *ahhh* or *awe*. I raised my eyes and centred the tone in my mind.

And my god I was there, I was *right there*. I realized I hadn't looked at any of those thousands of people who hadn't been Ingrid. If I'd let my eyes fall off their faces, I would have seen her, though. Her shoes tossed into the grass, a napkin blowing by with her mouthprint on it. Her voice, identical to mine, mistaken for an echo. The sum of her being was a closed set of everything I'd missed. But if she wanted me, she would have to appear. And now I knew she would.

I lifted my eyes to the southwest corner of Bellevue Square. And I was right, because there she is.

# 2

MY DOPPELGANGER CROSSES THE STREET and enters the park at its southwest corner. It's *her*, in a knee-length blue buttonfront dress. She walks directly toward me, crossing the park on a diagonal. I don't own that dress. I shrink from her, but she's not looking at me. She seems lost in her thoughts, her sleepwalker's eyes staring straight ahead.

The sun changes its angle in the sky to pick her out, and Ingrid glides forward in its follow spot. It's golden hour, which in the park is around eight in the evening now. An early-summer light of promise and memories of childhood. It comes aslant from the west and pushes the shadows of the trees across the grass. Fencelight.

I can't see the rest of the park, but that's because I've slunk down behind the playground wall and only my forehead and the upper halves of my eyes are showing. The kids on the swings behind me are safe from her. She's not after small game. I hold my breath as she walks by. She leaves the park and starts up Augusta under a sky of paintstroke clouds.

I jump up and follow her at a distance of about two hundred metres. We share a purposeful, forward-leaning walk, but her hands are in her pockets, and I'd trip over my feet if my hands weren't free for ballast. Her dress is printed with small white flowers. I guess I'd look good in it. Maybe I should look for one like it. Her thin sandal laces wind up her calf in a helix. I'm not a lacy-calf person. I prefer jeans and T-shirts and the kinds of shoes you can wear in the street as well as in the woods. We have the same bodies, but we use them differently. Yet she is my twin, there is no doubt in my mind now.

Her hair is shorter than mine, like lying Graham said. It's thin hair. All the women in my family have thin hair. It's a curse, but in certain weather – heat! – it's a catastrophe. It's hot today, and Ingrid has had to tame some of her frizz with clips. I wear mine long for this very reason: long hair weighs more and stays put.

She turns right onto Baldwin. I hadn't noticed that she was pulling a wire shopping buggy. Maybe she's just stolen one. Maybe if she's a doppelganger she can materialize or dematerialize physical objects at will. I catch myself beginning to laugh, but I might start crying instead, so I suppress it.

She's going past everything, oblivious, not interested in what's on offer, what's happening around her. Going straight to Spadina with her empty wire shopping buggy. I remember Katerina said Ingrid lived near Chinatown. She turns right again. I have to run to get to that corner, and this time she's turning *again*, left, back out toward Spadina. Maybe she's trying to shake me. If those who know her secret die, then what happens if she turns around and looks at *me*? If she's the harbinger of my death, then she's done for, too. How can you have a shadow if there's nothing to cast it? She goes into Moonbeam. I don't get coffee here because it smells like patchouli inside.

Shhhhhhhhhhhh goes the hiss of the foaming wand; I can hear it. I can see her in the line. I can see her face. She is inside that coffee shop with my face.

Moonbeam's door rushes away, shrinking into the distance. The hiss gets louder. Ingrid stands alone, framed in the doorway, and the doorway is throbbing like a pumping heart. She's tiny at the end of my seeing. I'm paralyzed, but she won't look at me. She knows I'm here, but she won't look at me. Do I have the upper hand? Is she afraid of me?

'Hey!' I call over to her, but there's no reaction. 'HEY! INGRID FOX!'

I can hear my voice, but she can't. She didn't so much as flinch when I shouted her name.

I CAN'T GO HOME YET; I'm too full, my mind is overflowing. I pass Bookshop and look through the window to see what Terrence is doing. It appears the store is empty and Terrence is reading at the cash desk, his eyes lowered, completely still, like he's been powered off. I keep going, but I can't get beyond Ossington – a powerful force weighs me down so much I can't even cross the street. Instead, I turn south, where the Ossington strip turns into a kilometre-long buffet. It's dinner on the Kalahari here. The top of the food chain is lined up on the sidewalk for tequila and pho and they look like they'd rip your jugular out for a slice of pizza. I'd keep walking, but Paula's ringing through on Skype. 'Hold on,' I type. 'I have to find somewhere to sit down. I'll call you back.'

I find a booth at the back of a donut shop and order a coffee so they don't kick me out. I dial Paula's number. 'Listen,' I say, nodding to the dead-eyed geek who drops my mug. 'Something awful's happened. Do you remember me telling you about that lady in the market? Katerina? She was killed!'

'Whoa. By who?'

'Someone shot her!'

'Oh my god,' she murmurs and falls silent. 'That's just awful. Any idea what happened?'

'None. It's possible...' I have to block my face with my coffee mug to keep my emotions to myself.

'Sweetie?'

'I think Ingrid might have killed her. There were people pointing at me when I was at the crime scene –'

'You saw it happen?'

'No. I got there right afterwards. I had to identify her.'

'Poor you!'

I sat sideways and cried into my shoulder, cradling the phone in the crook of my neck. 'She was dead on the ground in a pool of her own blood.'

'Why would Ingrid kill her? You said they were friends.'

'I don't know. But I've seen her...'

'You've seen Ingrid?'

'Yes. I followed her through the market. Paula, do you remember when I was a kid I used to tell you about the vampire that spoke to me? In my head?'

'Hold on! Did she look like you?'

'Dead ringer.'

'Now I'm worried.'

'I'm scared! What if this is something like my vampire problem?'

'The vampire was adolescent existentialism. You were *twelve.*'

'*I am the vampire,*' I whispered. '*I sound exactly like you inside your own head. But these are not your thoughts.* I'm serious. I used to scare the shit out of myself.'

'Oh stop it now –'

'He'd make me hold my breath for long periods. To prevent a disaster from happening.'

'He never told you to hold it longer than you actually could,' Paula says. 'Anyway, Descartes got to this centuries before you were born, dear. Your brain has enough juice in it to pull all kinds of tricks. And did the vampire *really* talk like that?'

'Yes!' We've had this discussion a dozen times. 'He had a better vocabulary than I did! And I bet you misread Descartes.'

93

'René told you what he meant, did he?'

'He meant that because I think, I *think* I am.'

'He left out a cogito.'

'I exist to myself,' I say. 'Not in the cosmos, like matter, but in myself only, the only place I can prove I am.'

'You really miss your students, don't you? You love to lecture.'

'It's true.'

'Get on Skype! I want to see how crazy you look.'

'I'm in a coffee shop!'

My phone goes *boop-bee-booooo gwip gwup beep-boo*.

I answer and put the phone down on the table and her face stares up at me. 'I saw her. Right after Katerina was shot, I saw Ingrid in the park. And Graham is dead, too.'

'Who's –'

'Gavin – you know? *That* guy. I was told it was a suicide, but what if it wasn't?'

'You really think your doppelganger is knocking people off?'

'She could have seen me today if she'd only looked. Katerina said she told Ingrid about me. I gave her a letter –'

'A letter?'

'To give to Ingrid. To come and meet me in Bellevue Square. But she didn't come. Not until both witnesses were dead...'

'If she's out walking around in public, I don't think she cares who sees her.'

'What if everyone who talks to her goes crazy and kills themselves?'

'Slow down...' With effort she lowers her telescopic mount and her face comes close and pixelates. 'You're not having those kinds of thoughts now, are you?'

'No!'

'You've got kids and a good life. A husband who loves you –'

'I'm not thinking of killing myself, Paula! But what should I do?'

'Jesus!' she said, laughing. 'Steer clear! Head for cover!'

'Why are your eyes so puffy?'

She reaches toward the screen and points it down to her feet, which are clad in knitted slippers. Bits of coloured yarn have exploded from them. 'How are my boys?' she asks from off-screen.

'Nick had a nightmare and had to play his six-phase meditation to get back to sleep. He found it on YouTube. A woman's voice, like Sulu. He played it under his pillow lying against me, shuddering. He gets nightmares.'

'What was phase one?'

'"Relax your scalp. Feel warmth flooding your head. Then relax your eyes and your face. Let the warmth travel down your neck into your chest."'

'Mmm.'

'He never makes it to the end of phase two. His breathing changes and Sulu says, "Imagine a light coming from you and connecting you to everything you love."'

'What's phase three?' she asks.

'I don't know. I turned it off when he fell asleep.' I've forgotten I'm sitting in a coffee shop. The coffee is cold. A skin of cream has tightened on its surface. 'Why have you been crying, Paula?'

'I'm not crying, Sis, I'm dying.'

'What's that mean?'

'Look at me. Would you want to live like this? Stuck in a box with windows on the haze, order dinner in every night? I'm never getting out of here. I'm already dead.'

'Stop it. Tell me to come down. I will. Just say the word.'

'You can't. I can't tell you to do that. Anyway, this place isn't for you. It's hotter than fuck. Fuck is the lowest temperature here. And you have your life.'

'You don't want to see me, do you? You want to be alone.'

'I'm seeing you right now. I don't know *how*, I don't understand all these new geegaws. I'm just glad I can talk to you.'

'So I only get my screen looking through your screen on a box of windows. You're like my own personal Russian doll.'

'What will you get when you twist me open and look inside?'

'Us. As happy little girls.'

'Nah,' Paula says, and my screen moirés. 'I'm the one in the middle, kid. The one you can't open.'

When I get home, I'm still doing my breathing: one two three four. My vision is like someone has tweaked the focus and I see, or at least I *notice*, everything. It's a bad high, like the tokes I had in high school that started with everyone else saying *whoa* and *I am so stoned* and ended with me puffing on a paper bag while Nelson Spivak rubbed my shoulders and asked me if I'd be more comfortable with my bra off.

I clean the TV room disaster zone, then the kitchen disaster zone. Focus on the immediate. Half-eaten granola bars are separated from their wrappers by *floors*, a detail that had escaped me before today's sighting turned me into an adrenalin-soaked satellite dish.

Ian appears after I've finished doing the trash rounds. 'Oh, you're back.' He looks at the clock. 'Seven hours later! Wow. Your phantom show her face?'

'No,' I lie. 'And I don't like the way you talked to me in front of those people.'

'I thought you knew all of them.'

I don't give him the satisfaction of a response. 'Where are the kids?'

'At my mother's?'

'Oh, right. Are you going to have me locked up again?'

Ian sits at the kitchen table and lowers his head. 'Why can't you tell me what's wrong?'

'I'm busy at the store. I have a lot on my hands. Just because you have all your time to yourself now doesn't mean other people –'

One palm slaps the table, hard. 'Just hold on! The bookstore?'

'Forget it. I told you I wanted a change from teaching.'

'Did you tell *them* that?'

'Them?'

'Your employers at the college. Where you teach essay structure and creative writing?'

'I go to work –'

'If you want me to trust you… Gary is faxing a prescription to the Shoppers on Dundas. We can talk about *all* of this when your head's on a bit straighter.'

'Are you serious? He's medicating me sight unseen? I don't need to –'

'Yes, you do. And no going back to the market or the park. Will you promise me that? Jean?'

I want to dial this conversation up to ten, but if he's sold on a version of me that's wrong, what can I do? And he's confused, which worries me. I quit the college when we left Port Dundas. I love him and I don't want to lie to him, but I know a lie will salve his anxiety. To show him I'm for real, I take his hand and put it against my cheek. I kiss him. 'I'm sorry,' I say. 'I understand. I really do. I'll stop. Don't give up on me.'

'You'll take the pills?'

'Yes, I'll take them.' I start to cry. I'm actually really sad, but it'll give him a reason to drop the subject, too. We'll make love tonight and the gulf between us will narrow. I can always spit out the pills.

IAN'S MOTHER DROPS THE KIDS after lunch Sunday. They have enjoyed their weekend at the Condo of No Rules. If you want to see what a hangover looks like on a ten-year-old, let him stay up until the middle of the night two nights in a row. Everyone got their freak on at Buby's, but Mother, to keep her promise, has to shut it all down. Today, I'm putting on a Tony-worthy performance as sane mother and wife. Mutually satisfactory connubial lovemaking has righted the balance with Ian, and he's in a much better mood this morning.

'We're eating pot roast and potatoes and green beans like normal people tonight,' I warn them. 'Stop scarfing all that garbage.' Ian takes control of a box of Honeycomb cereal from Nick, who's been popping little wheels of crunchy sugarcorn into his mouth. Now Ian starts popping them into his mouth. Reid is hitched up on the counter, his favourite vantage point on the room, from which he presides over kitchen discussions. He is halfway through a single-serving box of Honey Smacks, a cereal he explains is fifty-six per cent sugar by volume. 'You people are addicts,' I tell them.

'How much of this crap have you eaten?' Ian asks Nick.

'The contents settle.'

'I'm going shopping,' I say. '*Stop* eating that shit. Daddy?'

'Daddy's on it,' Reid says.

'I want to hear from Daddy.'

'Daddy's coming.' Ian accompanies me to the door, and in the kitchen Nick is saying, 'He wouldn't be bad as a baby. Why would you kill him, then?'

'Cuz he's *Hitler*. I'd actually kill Hitler's *parents*. I

wouldn't let them do it *once*.' Reid cocks his finger at Nick, a gesture his older brother detests, and pretends to fire a gun at him.

'Don't blow the smoke away.'

Reid blows the smoke away.

'*DICK*,' his brother says.

From the door we holler in unison the parental HEY HEY HEY!

'Mom would kill Hitler because she knows how to get the job done,' Reid says, stating a pride in me I didn't know he had.

'I don't want this place to turn into a swear party while I'm gone, okay? Keep it civil.'

'You'd kill Hitler,' Reid repeats.

'Maybe I'd try to educate him.'

Ian steps between us. 'I'm surprised you can walk straight today,' he says, leering and winking like Benny Hill.

'You having a seizure, sweetheart?'

'Just grocery store and home, right?'

'Yes. Unless I'm abducted by aliens.' He smiles with all his teeth. I wonder if it'll be tennis or baseball while I'm out. 'See you soon,' I say.

I'm in Bellevue Square by one. It's riotous here on this Day-After-Sighting. There are people swinging soap bubbles around, and a clown on a high unicycle is going about painting the leaves on the trees. He carries a paintbox in one hand and a paintbrush in the other. The paint is confetti.

There's still no Cullen. I'm beginning to wonder if I should tell someone he's missing. What if he's suffered the same fate as Graham Ronan and Katerina?

I want to say it's as if nothing happened here, but nothing has happened here a lot. A murder's not enough to make a ripple in the nothing. I'm disappointed that there's no pong of suspicion in the air, or any hint of despondency. I wasn't the only one who bought pupusas from Katerina. Others should be missing her.

Miriam isn't at her station. I note this walking along Denison Square to Augusta. (It's confusing that they named the street Denison Square, when in fact it's a street, and Bellevue Square is more rectangular than square, and really, it's a park.) I walk up to CHURROS CHURROS CHURROS and find it's been taped off and boarded up. The little yellow flags with pictures of the golden deep-fried pastries are gone.

The brunch crowd is filling the sidewalks. Ninety per cent of them are on their phones. When these pocket computers started getting common, old people like me catastrophized about how bad it was going to be, but we were wrong. It's much worse. We've been looking at each other's faces for a million years. But now you don't see faces anymore. At night on the sidewalks of Toronto people walk around in the dark looking down into tiny lamplit rooms they hold in their hands.

The children in the wading pool rotate in and out of the water, into their mothers' or their fathers' hands. High-pitched laughter. It's a sun-blasted panorama of cherubs in frilly plastic pants, the heavily chlorinated water saturating their diapers, weighing them down. The parents take constant, quick inventories. Babies and the sound of water. Someone tosses a towel, a child vanishes into it.

I do my own habitual scan. I've already completed mental check-offs of the drunks, the painfully pierced, and there have been two iced coffees and a couple sharing a starfruit. Miriam is back in her spot. I go over and ask her, 'If you could go back in time and kill Hitler as a baby, would you?'

'Oh god,' she says, 'do I look like a person who kills babies? I was a *nurse*, you know.'

'It's Hitler.'

'You kill'm,' she says. 'Spin him round by his feet and smack his head against the wall, if you got the stomach for it.' She considers, while I feel like an idiot for asking. 'If I had to get rid of one person, it would be Walt Disney. What a piece of work that guy was. You ever seen *Bedknobs and Broomsticks*?'

'What? No.'

'Well, don't.'

'Did you know Katerina?'

Miriam doesn't answer.

'You knew her, right?'

'I don't keep track of people's names.' She crosses her arms over her big chest and sticks her chin out. 'Someone's staring at you. Over across there.'

I turn around. No one is looking at me.

'The guy in the blue clothes,' she says.

She means a man in hospital scrubs way over on the other side of the park. 'The nurse eating his lunch?'

'He's been watching you since before.'

'Before when?'

'Before today.'

'He's not looking at me.' I wave at him. He immediately throws his lunch into a garbage can and walks away.

'See?' says Miriam.

'He's full.'

'He's not. You interacted with him. He knows you know.'

'He knows I know what?'

'Feh,' she says. 'I'm not matchmaking for you. You're on your own.'

'Wait a second.' I take her elbow as she begins walking

away and she looks down at my hand. 'Did you know Katerina?'

'I know,' she says. 'Of course I know. Everyone knows.'

'Nobody seems to care. What does it take to wake people up around here?'

'Where I come from, there's a saying: "Once you're awake, you can't wake up again."'

I go back to my place on the wall and collect my thoughts. If I saw her here once, she should pass again. After Katerina was shot, I could feel her coming. I have a feel for her now.

When Jimmy learned I paid for sightings, he claimed to have seen her, but now I wonder: what if he actually did? What if Cullen saw her, too? Where's Cullen? Where's Jimmy? If *he* turns up dead, I'll know for sure Ingrid's bumping them all off. But why? To isolate me? To strip me of my protection? For what? How can she kill me if she doesn't even notice me? Maybe she has to kill all the witnesses because she doesn't want anyone to know there's two of us. Once those other eyes are gone, she can kill me and do whatever she wants afterwards. Maybe she wants to have my life, but whatever thing Ingrid is, surely she could have chosen a more glamorous, a more *interesting*, victim. However, if she really wants to be me, I don't know how I'm going to stop her. And maybe I don't even want to. I could use a break. If she wants to be the person who swabs my toilets, she's welcome to them. If she wants to go shoe shopping for kids who need the newest kicks as soon as they appear on the market, she can put the kicks on *her* credit card. She can be the one who discovers under the couch (still sitting on its plate, separated into asparagus-coloured halves) the petrified egg sandwich – the whole sandwich – made months earlier and believed eaten, garnished with three withered carrots tarnished black with mould. She can be the one who elbows the snoring husband at three in the morning, and for that matter, the one who deals with the dawn tumescence.

I wonder if Ian would notice.

The itinerant stand-up comic, Giorgio, is here today. I've paid him for sightings, but so far, Ingrid is letting him live. I wave him over. 'You seen her lately?'

'Naw,' he says. He smells like Sterno and brandy. 'No customers either.'

'You might want to get into the wading pool tonight, after hours. Wash up.'

'It's the material. People don't shock the way they used to. Used to be all you had to do to kill a crowd of nine-year-olds was say, "A poop came out of my bum." Now they see things on their phones worse than I can say.'

'So change your material.'

'You should hear how they talk. "Fuck," "motherfucker."'

'If you see Ingrid, don't look at her. Walk the other way.' I give him a two-dollar coin and he returns to the background, like he's part of an endless line of characters provided by a talent agency.

People are not usually this interesting in real life. They're deeper and more boring and more satisfying than this random collection of passers-through and the dozen or so that get stuck here. I haven't seen a dull person in Bellevue Square this whole time. I just *look* and there's an entire person, with her own clothes, his own hairstyle, her creaky laughter, his filthy dark blue shirt. The way people hold their mouths when they're looking at food – that's always interesting to me, to witness the animal looking out. And the blasted-open irises of the couples on the grass, young people discovering something most of us can't be fooled by anymore. Is it only in this place, in this now, that I notice these particulars?

Maybe it's time to go home, to stop all this nonsense, suggest we move back to Port Dundas and resume our old lives. I need to have a serious discussion with myself. Do you want to go down the long slide? Do you think you can be a rational person? Rational is rules and structure. Everything in it can be made to work with any other part, even if only in opposition, but outside of its math, there's nothing. There's the rest of It. That is where Ingrid has come from.

Maybe it was a trick of the light or the air. Maybe if I concentrate.

THERE SHE IS AGAIN! I open my eyes and she's walking up Augusta with her buggy. Coming from the south. Does she see me now? I dismount the wall backwards and creep to the cover of a large willow. Inside its circle of darkness, I'm sure she won't notice me. Its branches hang down like a geisha's beads. She's back!

She's in her pillar of light. I'm not sure how she does it. Gliding up the road toward the Mexican restaurants, gilded with sunlight. She wears grey pants and a black shirt. With lowered head, she looks lost in thought. Her hair is unwashed. Where is she spending the night? Does she live anywhere? I look down and my feet are a blur of tapping.

Her squeaky wheels roll past and then I'm staring at her back as she turns down Baldwin Street. Does she ever put anything in that thing? I check for traffic and run across. When I get to the corner, she's gone. Baldwin is paved with rose light spreading east to Spadina. A balm? A blessing? She's gone.

When I was seven, I lost my mother in the Dominion in the then-new strip mall at Bayview and Sheppard. I'd been talking to her while she shopped in the canned goods aisle, and I found something colourful to turn over in my hands. When I looked up, she was gone. I went to the end of the aisle, afraid to leave it, and swung my head left and right. She was gone. She must have thought I was behind her. If I searched to the left but she'd gone to the right, the problem would only get worse. But if I stayed where I was, surely more distance would open between us. I chose a direction, I don't recall which; I found myself frantically navigating

106

the aisles up and down, walking quickly at first and then running, and the aisles were *full* of mothers none of whom were mine. We were living in our first house on Dunview. I looked all over for her; we'd been separated for only a few moments, a minute at the very most, but I was electrified. I started shrieking, 'MUMMY! MUUUUMMY!'

Someone's hand clamps down on my shoulder and it's one of the men trimming the vegetables on Baldwin Street. He wears a white apron stained with dirt and smears of green and red. 'Go from here,' he says to me.

A couple sitting in the window of a bakery are staring. My hands are in mid-gesture. Maybe my mouth has been moving, too.

I continue along Baldwin.

Of course my mother found me, and when I later reconsidered that endless minute in Dominion, I concluded that I should have stayed where I was. She would have known to find me, and she did. I went back to the memory of this day throughout my preadolescence and my teenagehood and I think of it still. It was the first moment in which the wrong choice would have been disastrous. It was the first time I knew what terror felt like. A minute of it was a huge dose.

I tell my kids to stay where they are. Someone will find you, or the police will come, or the part of the plane you're in will spring free of the wreckage. I'll find them as soon as I notice they're missing, they know that.

I get to Kensington Avenue. The coffee smell meets the fish smell, the weed smell, and the pee smell. I think I see her right away. A flash of slacks. But it's not her. And she is not among the lanky, loose-panted rastas smoking hand-rolleds, either.

Then I see her again, this time I'm sure of it, crossing

the road in front of a produce store on St. Andrew, the one whose casabas are always overripe. This territory is strictly vegan. Just walking past the Peacefood Lovecafé, I can feel my stool bulking.

I don't know whether to cross the road and speed up, or stop and be satisfied that at least – at last! – I have seen her again. Two sightings! A stupendous thing.

Ingrid glances up the street behind her and I turn my back. Wait a minute. I look again: she's going south. She'll be easier to track from the other side of the street. I cross quickly, afraid she'll look back again.

At Dundas she turns left, and I hurry forward, following the top of her head.

I think the signal memory of losing my mother in the grocery store eventually gave rise to some of the unwanted thoughts I suffered as a teenager. Certain things were impossible to disprove. I believed there was a spirit intruder that could control my thoughts and make me sound like myself *to* myself. I had to fall asleep on my back with the covers pulled up to my chin. I chose this position so it would be possible to see my entire room by opening only one eye.

When I first began to sleep on my back, I imagined that in the dark, forms joined together and came alive. This never happened, owing, I believed, to my mantra, which was: 'That would be *impossible*. I HOPE.' *Hope* was the operational part of the mantra. I thought hoping was supplication.

It was only when I was older that I envisioned the unseen intruder as a vampire, something that had control of my self. I saw what he looked like: an etching of a face with a square beard and slippery lips. I was a silly girl, and I knew other of my silly friends had their own crazy-thoughts.

I left these fantasies in adolescence and forgot about

them, although I didn't change the way I slept. Boyfriends complained that I looked like a Victorian corpse. I knew Ian was the One when he lay on his side, tucked his head into the space made by my shoulder and my neck, and laid his hairy forearm over my belly.

The vampire lost its power over me. In high school the new intellectual scare was a product of my adolescent narcissism. I began to wonder how I could know anything outside of myself was actually real. (I would not have entertained the idea at that age that my 'self' wasn't real.) There was no way to prove that everything I saw and experienced wasn't being performed for my benefit alone or that the things and people I 'knew' blinked out of existence the moment I turned my back. The extension of this was that my entire life was a dream, that I was perhaps a character in a book or in *someone else's* dream, which was extremely frightening. I almost fainted in the cinema at the end of the first *Men in Black* movie, when it turned out that the cat was wearing an entire galaxy around its neck.

The materiel needed to disprove this particular hypothesis – my Blinkout World – I never found. The world would appear to me exactly as it always had, except that when I left a room, or turned a corner, there'd be a void where I'd been. It replenished itself as quickly as I could run and look for it, and it was seamless. That was what my brain had been invented to do: run a program in which I constructed reality by witnessing it.

I was able to disprove this hypothesis by replacing it with a final one. If I believed, in my less overwrought moments, that I was not special or different from anyone else, then the universe being a show for me alone would *make* me special. So I lowered the odds from 0.005 per cent to 0.0001 per cent. But that only means I still believe in Blinkout. On days like this, I can't ignore that about myself. I am willing to believe.

Ingrid's crossing Dundas at Spadina. On the south side, she waits for the light. I miss it and have to spy from a distance. She continues east, pulling her buggy behind her, disappearing into the crowd. I've lost her again.

I still have groceries to buy!

I NEED MORE PERSONAL SPACE than the average person, but I didn't know this until I had children. Once your second child is born, there's always another body on top of you. Sometimes it's your husband, but otherwise it's the constant pawing and sticky grappling of offspring. 'Having you inside me was much easier than having you on top of me,' I said to Nicholas once. 'It only lasted nine months.'

Reid, who's currently regaling me from the countertop with something he's heard, is smaller and lankier than his brother and until he was six he could lie on his side and fit between my breasts with his feet paddling at my knees. He has somehow always been heavier than Nick, as if he's more densely packed. Reid's personality takes up space. Ian says our ten-year-old has an untrammelled ego, but from his point of view – Reid's, that is – he's generously sharing everything he has to offer. He overflows with bad magic tricks and interesting facts – most of which he's gleaned from the internet and some of which are factual facts – and there's nothing he likes more than telling you the whole story of a movie, from start to finish, including the credits if they were cool. This was what he'd started on when I walked through the door. I was thinking about Ingrid's empty buggy and her apparent sadness, but then I heard Reid say, 'Her dad falls out a window,' and I started listening.

'*Whose* dad fell out a window?'

'Eli's, Mom.'

I unpack the avocados, the fish, and the premade salad. 'This is in a movie, right? Did you already say that?'

'Yes, Mom.'

111

'So this isn't someone we know.'

'It's a *movie*, Mom.'

'Stop saying Mom!' He's already opened the nacho chips. 'Did you have lunch? Where's your father?'

'It's Sunday.'

'That's not an answer.'

'He's out. I had some sour keys.' He gives me one of his face-wide smiles. His teeth fill his whole countenance, white and bedraggled. He hops up onto one of the barstools on the other side of the counter. I see the sugardust on the fine blond hairs of his upper lip.

I've been able to make out the resonant thud of Nick's heels, so I know son number one is home, but there's no reply from the husband. Nicholas walks as if his centre of gravity is two feet behind him, landing on his heels and rocking forward. I used to wonder if he did it for comic effect.

'Dad's out getting the Lamborghini waxed,' Reid says.

'You wish.'

'He went to Staples,' says Nick, entering the kitchen.

'Did your brother eat?'

'I made him beef Wellington.'

'Okay, let's make dinner now. Who's mashing the avocados? They're perfect.'

Nick, who is usually immune to requests for help, will do this because it involves using a sharp knife, something he only started doing when he turned twelve. So now Reid has to watch him, for two years, cut stuff. Nick gets to work on the guacamole. I let the little guy melt butter in the frying pan and pat the fish dry.

'What's *that*?' Reid asks, his voice dripping with horror.

'Pickerel.'

'Ew. It smells like dead donkey.'

'It's fresh from an Ontario lake, dork. You can make

little fish tacos if you get the tortillas out of the freezer. We have salsa, too.'

He moves the butter around in the pan on the end of a fork. It begins to melt.

'Okay. So Eli's dad falls out a window.'

'He lets her suck his blood and then he falls out a window,' he stage-whispers, to make his exclusion of his brother audible to his brother.

'Go on...'

'I can hear you, moron,' Nick says.

'Reid, go on with your story. Nick: mash the avocado now.'

'Okay, so she chops off the bullies' heads when Oskar is in the pool. They tried to drown him because he was a pussy.'

'Whoa, what?'

'Because he was –'

'No no, you don't say pussy. Keep moving the butter around.'

'*You* say pussy.'

'For Lefty, Reid. Not for a person. Ever.'

'Ever?'

Nick says, 'Well, not until you're older and you know the other person really really well.'

'What kind of movie was this?'

'A kids' movie.'

'Called?'

'*Don't Let Her In*. It's about this angry vampire girl who makes a friend, but she doesn't have a... a Lefty.'

Nick's laugh is like a plate shattering.

I take Reid's chin in my hand and bring his eyes around. The fork clinks into the frying pan. 'Hey. Did it occur to you that maybe this wasn't an appropriate movie for a ten-year-old?'

'They were talking Spanish or something.'

'So you have no idea what the movie was actually about.'

'Of course he doesn't.'

'Nick.'

'Do you want me to turn this down?'

I don't know what he means until I see the butter is burning. 'Goddammit.' I snap the gas off.

'I *can* read subtitles, you know,' Reid says, bringing the attention back to himself. He'd juggle in a house fire if he thought someone would watch. 'So I knew what they were saying. Instead of a foo foo she had a scar. The boy sees her boobies though.'

'*Fabulous.*'

'I've *seen* boobies, Mummy.'

'Whose?'

'You know. Yours! Other ones too. I saw a monkey with breasts on the internet and they were a lot bigger than the ones in the movie.' Nick is biting his lip, keeping his comments to himself, but Reid plows on: 'Mummy, are all nipples the same size?'

'Did your dad know you were watching a vampire movie with breasts in it?'

'It was a foreign movie,' Reid protests. '*Geez*. Foreign movies got breasts in them, I'm sorry! You want me to watch *X-Men* over and over and never learn about life?'

Nick howls 'BWAAA-HAAAAH-HAAAAH!' and I know Reid's going to lose it.

'Let go of that,' I say to Nick, taking the hand with the knife in it, 'and get out of here for five minutes.'

'Guess what? He pauses the nude scenes.'

Reid shrieks: 'ASSHOOOOLE!'

'Get. Out.'

He goes, but not without first taking a swipe at the back of Reid's head. He doesn't connect, but he makes his little brother flinch, which is all he wanted.

'Nick is nifgit.'

'I don't want to know what that is.'

'It's a dangler hanging outta your –'

'*Enough.* Go wash your hands.' He goes to the sink and washes his hands with the dish soap. 'For your information, all nipples are not the same size.'

'Do they only get as big as the baby's mouth?'

'I don't know if anyone's ever asked that question. You should have a chat with Mr Google about it. But if you ask me, I think it's a random thing, how big a person's nipples are.'

'Ladies' nipples,' he corrects. 'Men all have the same size nipples. Their nipples are nickel-sized nipples.

'Stop saying nipples!' I say, but I'm laughing because I'm a soft touch. 'I can't believe you were down here, unsupervised and unfed, looking at vampire breasts.'

'You're a bad mother,' he says, deadpan. 'Are you at least going to cook dinner? And wouldn't frozen waffles be faster?'

Later, after I have both kids fed (fish tacos), Ian makes an appearance.

'Reid watched a Swedish vampire movie,' I inform him. 'Did you know that?'

'No. But so what?' His lips glance off my cheek, but he waits with his lips hanging in the air until I kiss him. 'He has to learn about Swedish vampires sooner or later.'

'Where were you?' His hair is cap-shaped. 'Did you go somewhere in your uniform?'

He offers me an irritated look and puts two bags down

on the stairs. They don't say Staples on them. 'I found some sheets on sale.'

I look in one of the bags and indeed, there are two zipped-up plastic packages of queen-size fitted sheets and covers in deep purple and bright yellow. Wamsutta, half off. 'Sweetheart,' I say. He hasn't done anything this thoughtful for some time.

He shucks his raincoat and shoes simultaneously, and then slides into the slipstream of domestic chaos. There's a cluelessness to boys and men that must be very pleasant, an ignorance of the peripheral that women are aware of every waking hour. Maybe not all women have a sense of hints and shadows, but I gather there is some biological, evolutionary role for it. 'Men defend, women protect' is one of Ian's memes, a motto rather than an idea. But he may be right. The one who defends already knows his enemy. The protector knows the enemy can take any form it wants. Pedophile, peanut, gunshot in the food court.

Only Nick can detect that I'm off. Beneath his shell, he's a feeling boy. I go into his room at ten to turn out his lights.

'You okay, Mum?'

'Of course I'm okay.'

'Your face is white and shiny.'

'I had a Filet-o-Fish for lunch.'

'You ate fish twice today?'

'I guess I did.'

'On purpose?'

'It's lights-out now, so let's finish with the questions. Scooch.'

He wriggles toward the foot of the bed and I pull his covers up.

'Can I ask you one more thing?'

'What?'

'Do you have cancer?'

The question shocks us both. 'Why on earth would you ask me that?'

'Cause you look sick.'

I kiss his forehead. 'You're a good boy.' I worry about what goes on in their heads when they're alone. 'Everything is fine. We're all together. We're safe as houses.'

'Some houses fall down,' he says.

I NEED TO UNPLUG, TO shut out the voices. It takes three episodes of *Antiques Roadshow* to settle me down. Some of the world's stock exchanges are open by the time I go upstairs, as evidenced by the fact that Ian's in his third floor lair, clacking on keys. Sunday nights, he doesn't like to miss the Monday opens in Asia and India; apparently they set the tone for the week to come. Sometimes I think we should just have an old-fashioned ticker spitting out tape in the living room. I climb the stairs and sit down behind him with one of his policing association magazines. This one is called *Canadian Police Chief Magazine*. Very niche. 'Why do you still subscribe to this?'

'Because I'm the chief of police?' He's watching stock prices speed by under a silenced hockey game. 'And I don't subscribe, sweetheart. They send it to me for free.'

'Ha,' I say. He never used to be facetious, but that was back when he was employed by the OPS rather than just getting their magazines. 'What's eating you?' I ask him.

He looks beyond me. He says: 'Hey, what are you doing out of bed?'

Reid is standing at the top of the stairs. 'Are you guys doing sex?'

I scoop him up. 'Back to bed, cakiepie. It's almost midnight.'

'Who won the game?' he asks. Ian tells him the Kings 'blanked' the Sharks, and with sleep in his voice, Reid asks, 'Have they taken a strangehold on the series?'

'That's exactly what they've done,' Ian says.

Reid wraps his legs around my waist and we go down

the stairs. He's all boy, gangly and scentless, while Nick has little filaments turning black in his armpits and his shoes smell like death. I put Reid into his bed.

'I had a bad dream,' he says. 'I dreamt I got lost in the woods and you didn't look for me.'

I tuck him in, using brusque movements under his ribs to make him squirm. 'I'll always come looking for you. And there's nowhere I wouldn't find you.'

I wait in the hallway silently for a couple of minutes and listen for him to turn over and arrange his blankets, which can take up to two minutes until he gets it right. Nick fell asleep the second I left his room, this one has nightmares. The hallway between his bedroom and ours is hung with family photos. The lights are out, and the wall looks hung with darkened screens.

Reid sighs. I creep back upstairs. On one of Ian's monitors I see the welcome screen of the Ontario Police Services website.

'What were we talking about before?' I ask.

'I don't remember. You don't either.' His phone rings. I peer over his shoulder: Unknown Number.

'Who's calling you from an unknown number at this hour?'

'Hold on a second. Hello. Hello? I'm fine, thank you.' He listens. 'What's the name of your company again? Uh-huh. Okay, I'll take it! No, that's fine, I'll just take it. How much is it? You take credit cards, right? I can send a money order, too, in Canadian funds, euros, pounds. A week for rubles. I can *bring* you my money in a taxi if it's urgent. Pardon? No, I trust you, why wouldn't I trust you? You *have* my personal phone number. Uh-huh. Uh-huh. What will your boss say if he finds out you're turning down a sale? You don't trust *me*? Well that's something. By the way, I have all of this on tape.' He looks at the screen. 'He hung up!'

'That guy's getting paid four dollars an hour.'

'Fuck'm. I save the numbers and they run them in batches for me down at the station. Speaking of which, sit down for a minute, okay? I need to tell you something. One of the officers at the scene in Kensington Market canvassed that food court your friend works in. He asked about the victim's friends and relations. A few people gave a description that matches you.'

'How the hell would you know that?'

'Cops share with each other. It's routine. They want to talk to you.' His eyelid twitches. He's hiding something, seeing how I'll react. 'When you're feeling a little more yourself, they want to ask you a couple of questions. It was your friend, wasn't it?'

'What's the victim's name?'

'They're not releasing her name until they find her next-of-kin. Probably that's all they want to ask you about. Maybe you can help them with that. I called Shoppers, by the way, to check if your prescription was ready and they said it was. So do you want to go get it, or should I?'

'I'll get it.'

He laughs. 'No you won't.'

I retreat to the bedroom. Tonight has felt like a step in the wrong direction.

WHILE WASHING MY FACE IN front of the mirror, something happens I can't credit. I lean down to rinse the suds off, and when I rise, I'm in the mirror, but I'm certain I'm not in the room. I see what I think is my reflection, but it's actually someone standing in another bathroom, an identical bathroom behind this one. I look down, afraid there'll be nothing below my head, but my body is still there. I lift my eyes back to the mirror and my double also looks up. I reach for the light switch and snap it off. In the dark, there's profound silence even from other parts of the house. I feel for the mirror. I find its featureless cold surface and hold my fingertips to it and wait for my eyes to adjust to the junk light seeping in from under the door.

Crazy is normal. I've been crazy before and I'll be crazy again. It's everyone's biggest secret: those times they wondered if they'd lost it and those times they knew they had. Memories of choking on tears, alone in a dorm room three time zones from your parents. Driving way too fast after losing a job. Cheated on. And you must be crazy if you can't love the baby. But then, one day, you love the baby. There are so many books with crazy main characters, too. Don Quixote is not the only one. Ahab has borderline personality disorder; Gregor Samsa, persecution mania. The Cat in the Hat is clearly batshit. And of all the characters in the Bible who supposedly hear directly from God, Noah gets the craziest task. Unless, of course, God never spoke to Noah and Noah had reasons other than divine inspiration for building the ark, like schizophrenia or OCD.

My eyes begin to adjust. I can see the grey box of the bathroom in the surface of the mirror. It's empty! The other one has gone to bed!

I WON'T GO TO THE square today. It's a new week and I'm in Bookshop. I put on a good pair of slacks and a dark blouse with bits of shiny thread in it and I open the store at ten. Before I left, Ian asked me again about going in for 'your interview.' He's trying to trip me up. Or he's scared. He tells me he doesn't want it weighing on me; I should get it over with. But nothing is weighing on me except him being sneaky. Do they think I killed her? He was with me the whole time. Except for when I went down the alley, but she was already dead by then. I couldn't have done it.

The shop is the only place I feel safe right now. I told Terrence not to come in. There is work to be done, and thank goodness for it. I've got half an hour to sweep and straighten, do some bookkeeping.

The part of the bookstore that was supposed to be the café is blocked off by bookcases on wheels. They slide apart to give access to the office and unshelved inventory, as well as the bathroom and the door to the rear of the building. My overhead went down when I closed the café, but I can't do readings or have people gather and talk over one of my amateur flat whites. (The Pavoni would take an hour to heat up right now.) If I keep the bookshelves open I can see all the way to the street.

I've been making money. That's what Excel tells me. Money goes in a pattern like the Krebs cycle. 'Everything about money is imaginary,' Ian is fond of saying, as if there were *no* luck involved in his schemes, the ones he is suddenly in denial about, and he's actually an expert on money. 'Capital does what people will it to do. But they're

123

not meeting under a tree on Wall Street anymore. They *send* the idea of money over the internet to a bank, or a lender, or a debtor. Mood decides what happens to it, whims. Nothing real is happening. We are using computers to trade something that doesn't exist.'

Oh shut it. I still like the rows with the numbers in them that are supposed to relate in a direct way to my actual wealth, or the things that wealth could buy. I could buy myself something nice, says this electronic bookkeeping program.

It's almost ten thirty. It's a gorgeous day. I need normality. Time to put the trolley out with the dollar books, turn the sign. I leave the door open to let the air in. Books create must.

This is a neighbourhood of young mothers and gay men with small dogs and people with blue hair in miniskirts and stars of professional sport. Terrence says he sold a copy of *The Feminine Mystique* to R. A. Dickey last week. Bookshop is in a stretch of businesses that bring what used to be a barren strip of Dundas to life. There is a butcher here, who specializes in salamis and sausages, and a baby apparel store and the standard-issue coffee shop with people bent over laptops. But people come, bless them, and I have a vocation of sorts to keep my mind off what is going on around me.

Most people who browse don't buy anything. But you still bring in two hundred dollars a day, no matter how dead it is, and that's plenty to stay afloat and that's all I want. I want to keep coming into my shop whenever I care to and to afford a hand like Terrence.

Weekday afternoons in the early summer go like a blur. People have questions. Someone brings in a box full of stuff and you have to disappoint them. Or you buy a little. The boxes in the back room are all full of volumes waiting to be shelved. I close at six although the sun won't set until after eight.

At the end of the day, there's $420 in the till.

IF I HAD BEEN LOOKING closer, I would have seen something that only began to pull at my attention as it got late. A sped-up version of the day, taken by a camera pointing out the front window, would have shown steady flashes of pedestrian traffic and shadows lengthening to the east against a blur of vehicles. Every second a streetcar would blink in the frame. I'd have seen a stillness behind it if I'd known to look for it, a red stitch flashing in the middle ground. Briefly absent mid-afternoon, back until close. That's what I took unconscious snaps of all day long: my doppelganger standing on the opposite sidewalk in a red flannel coat. She stood there for eight hours. But when the day was over, she was gone.

SHE RETURNS THE FOLLOWING DAY. In her red coat. Are you ready to murder me now, Ingrid?

I stay in the back half of the store. I can pull the rolling bookcases closer together and hide behind them. I'm more convinced now that she doesn't mean well. She's cleared the way, removed the witnesses, and there's only my living body standing between her and a new life. She'll be able to fill up that buggy of hers. If I see her begin to cross, I can go out the back. She looks pitiable, though. She's been crying: her face is streaked with white mottles. It's perfectly dry outside, but her hair is astraggle, as if she's cried so much the tears started coming out of her follicles.

I have a good view of her from here. I get out Ritt's lotus-pond picture and study it. I look across the road to the weeping Ingrid Fox. I can't remember being there because I wasn't.

You can look at yourself in pictures or even on video, but you still don't have the experience others do of you in the world. Now I see what others see. And would I look at that *thing* over there and think it contained multitudes? Look at her! She's unremarkable. I wonder what's really under her imposter's skin. Muscle and bone, or stuffing? Maybe a hundred tiny servos operate below her face.

A man appears at the cash desk. He looks around and sees me peeking through the space between the bookcases. 'Oh, hello. If you could just –'

I put the photo away and walk stiffly to the front. 'Inventory never ends.'

'Sorry?'

'Three dollars.' *Macrobiotics for Dummies*. Some of the titles in that series are a bit on the nose. He unfolds a five from a bundle of bills and drops it on the counter. When he leaves, he crosses the street and takes Ingrid's arm and...
... he touches her!

I HAVE THE STORE CLOSED up in less than thirty seconds. I stay on the north side of Dundas, crouching and running along. They're holding hands, Ingrid and the man who bought the book. Is this the husband? Why didn't he freak when he saw me? Did he even look at me? Now I can't remember. Did I look at him?

They're a hundred metres ahead on the other side of the street. He looks nothing like Ian; he's maybe average height, but he's so stout he looks shorter than he would if he were thinner. Good luck on the macrobiotic diet there. Or maybe it's for her. She's gripping his hand hard; his arm is stiff. Ingrid walks with her head down, listening to him speak. One side of his face shows his emotion and his love. His lips move. She nods.

We continue across Bathurst Street, pass below the Toronto Western Hospital, where I have come twice this year to get my retinas stitched back on with laser beams by a doctor whose identical twin also does eye surgery. This seems significant now, if only because the set of things that could be significant grows by the moment.

They lock into the route Ingrid took when I lost her at Spadina and Dundas, and they cross at the same corner and go into the heart of Chinatown. Only on tiptoes can I see a flash of her red crying coat down the road. I slip in and out of the crowd, high-stepping it and dodging people. I smell five-spice, overripe banana, duck fat. At Huron Street I run across on the yellow. Before Beverley Street, they turn right. I slalom through humanity to get to them and they're way ahead now, walking south on a side street.

I check the name when I get there: Pine Street.

I'm a stone in the river as people flow past me. The old Chinese ladies make a rustling sound when they brush by, like they're made out of paper. From behind a postbox at the top of the street, I watch them unlock the door of a house on the east side of the street. She's still crying. He takes her hand off the knob and holds her. I can't see his face but I think he's crying, too. My tongue thickens in the back of my throat.

I return to Dundas, where the swarm swallows me and I'm singular again. I have to look at myself right away. I find a Starbucks bathroom and I stare at my face. I'm on both sides of the mirror now.

I inspect the prominent vein under my left eye. My teeth are off-white with the front ones atilt one way or another, like stones in an old graveyard. My skin is not as pink or fleshy as it once was, the way the kids' faces are. It's tending to translucent.

I remember standing in the mirror as a child, staring into my own eyeball. I lined one eye up against its reflection and shut the other. I saw a slippery black void but that's where I was: in that void. My face was wrapped around muscle and bone. Before Ingrid, it was my face alone. Now I exist as myself only inside my own dark eye.

THE WEEK CREEPS ON. Ingrid doesn't return to her post at the top of the park, but I feel trapped when I'm in the bookstore now, almost as though she can see me better for not being present.

I've resisted doing much doppelganger research because I haven't wanted to know. Now I think I need to. Clearly, she still can't see me. Neither could her husband.

I have a complete set of *World Book* from 1965 on top of Reference. It's twenty volumes long. A set of encyclopedias seems more antique than a Gutenberg Bible now. I've decided anyone who actually wants it can have the whole set for a dollar, but no one has ever enquired of its price. I pull the stepstool over and get down the D volume.

Dop pel gang er. Apparition of a living person. From the German: double walker. Sometimes sports an umlaut. Said to presage death. Abraham Lincoln witnessed a double image of himself in a mirror on a number of occasions, and each time one of the faces looked like him, while the other was aged and sick. The first Queen Elizabeth saw her own corpse lying in state when she was getting into bed one night and *she* died soon afterwards. And Shelley's doppelganger visited him on a terrace and asked him: 'How long do you mean to be content?' Two weeks later, he drowned at the age of twenty-nine.

The Egyptian Ka has the same thoughts and feelings as its counterpart. The Irish fetch presages long life if seen in the morning, death if seen at night. La Llorona cries for a lost child and goes in search of one it can steal away...

I return the volume to its place, feeling no better for having deepened my knowledge.

THE STREETS ARE EMPTY AT midnight as I drive along Dundas under a fine rain. Electric lights make colourful bouquets of fireworks in the wet road. The parking is free up at the corner of Pine, though not all of the spaces are available. There are speakeasies and gambling holes in the Chinatown malls shut up for the night, but much of the neon is still glowing and there are cars in small bunches all the way back to Spadina.

The west side of Pine Street is given over to a narrow park that backs onto a high brick wall: the back of a church. Its window casings are made of stone. In one of them a sign reads: VR Studio for Rent. A bench sits back in street-lamp shadow under a tree almost directly across from Ingrid's house. She's at 36. Ingrid lives close to the Art Gallery of Ontario. I can see some of it across the street beyond the rooftops.

The houses along Ingrid's street are dark except for a few lamps and a bunch of televisions splashing light. Sometimes when you see an actual TV screen through a window, from a sidewalk or as you pass in a car, you realize how many layers you look through every day to connect with others. Through a window, see a show in which a character is seen in a mirror watching a television show. Navigate a world where half of everything you know is a reflection, a refraction, or a memory. Working theories are almost always incomplete or dead incorrect, including all the important ones you're operating under. No brakes, no map, off you go.

Ingrid's house is dark. I've sat for half an hour, studying every aspect of it. There is no way to the front door except by crossing the driveway, and in approaching the house you become visible, eventually, to seven of 36's windows.

Two hours later, I feel the chill and stumble up to the car, my joints unforgiving, and get the hoodie that's in the trunk. When I return, I'm rewarded with a light in a third-floor window! A yellow light, a bathroom light. A shadow on the wall leans in. It's her; her short hair falls forward. She stands and tosses her head back, hand cupped to her mouth. She washes her face. The box of light winks out. I imagine I can hear her footsteps in the upper hallway and I cast my own house as hers and see her bare feet on the runner and then the cool wood in the bedroom for a few steps before the soft white shag rug that leads her to her side of the bed.

Then I imagine myself sitting in a shrink's office. Diplomas and a rubber plant. Do you think anyone else can see her? he asks me.

Her husband can see her. He bought a book in my store and went right over and gave it to her. He took her arm.

But if you're seeing her, maybe you're seeing him as well, do you know what I mean? Do *you* think you're seeing things?

If I'm delusional then you could be part of my delusion, Doctor, so how can I answer that?

Well, you're right. Not all of my patients are as insightful as you are. The problem for you is that you could talk yourself into anything.

So what's your diagnosis?

Well, there could be any number of reasons why a person perceives something that isn't there. Amputees frequently have pain in their missing limbs, did you know that?

Are you suggesting we were once Siamese twins?

No. I'm saying that there are a surprisingly large number

of *somatic* conditions that can cause realistic hallucinations. But how do you know she's not simply a very good likeness of you? Have you spoken to her?

No. But I'm sitting across from her house at two in the morning.

Ah. Do you do this a lot?

Not yet.

Why are you doing it?

I want to see her again. I want to talk to her.

So why don't you? Go. What are you afraid of?

My phone says *plink*, snapping me out of my inner therapy. It's a text from Ian. *Where are you?*

*Long walk. I'm coming home.*

*It's the middle of the night. People don't go for walks at two in the morning. Where are you?*

*I couldn't sleep. I thought the air would be nice.*

*I see the car is missing.*

*I took it.*

*To go for a walk.*

*I drove to the walk.*

*You're in the park.*

*I'm really not. I just wanted to get out of the neighbourhood.*

*You're at the market.* I don't reply. *Where are you?*

*Walking. To the car. I'm coming home.*

However, I'm not hurrying home on his say-so. I sit for another half-hour. I want my patience to be rewarded with another sighting. I'll take any part of her: a wrist, a shoulder. But the house remains dark. I cross the street with silent, mincing steps, a cartoon mouse on the prowl. I have to go halfway down her driveway and flatten myself against the side of her house. I slip along in shadow, around the corner to the door. Three wooden steps up, each with its own creak. I put my hand on the cold chrome handle and depress the latch and it slips down in its slot without catching. It's locked. I pull my hand away and a lace of steam seeps out of the keyhole.

MY DREAMS ARE BAD. Although I slept in my bed, I also watched my body sleeping, from a vantage point in an upper corner. I hung above myself, looking down. I saw a distortion simmering in the air beside the bed, and it expanded and then contracted until it disappeared, like something slithering into an invisible hole. I saw my body struggling. Something or someone was on top of me. I felt it up against me, too, pressing me to the ceiling. In my bed, I took shallower and shorter breaths and strangled for air. I tried to speak, I tried to say, *Don't let her in!* but I couldn't make a sound with my phantom mouth. I don't remember the rest of this dream. I don't know if I made it back into my body.

IAN IS STILL ASLEEP WHEN I leave the house at eight, and this time I walk all the way to Pine Street. At this hour, the pong of yesterday's garbage is still a layer of air with undertones of diesel, bile, and turps. I walk along Dundas and pass a phalanx of vegetable pruners and choppers in front of a produce store, the elbows of hairnetted women churning, their feet buried in trimmings.

I go down Pine and stand at the end of the church wall and watch number 36, my heart pounding. The husband comes out at nine on the dot and stands at the bottom of the driveway, a leather briefcase held in front of him. He's the man in Ritt's lotus-pond photograph, the one in focus. A black Corolla drives up and he gets in. It could be the same car that took Cullen. I write down its licence number. It's one of those vanity plates that cost an extra $310. It reads: SCTMSG.

Then nothing happens. Voices from other streets. A prickle of fear creeps over my back and shoulders. A plane flies by in the street's upper windows and I look behind myself and see it in the sky, pointing east.

At ten, I cross. I walk up Ingrid's driveway with purpose, like I have something to leave in the mailbox. I mount the steps, which go *eek, ack, ohh*, and knock on the door. I hear the knock echo inside the house. I wait. I knock again.

No cars going by, no neighbours on stoops. I try the handle, but the door is locked. My palm leaves a sweat stain that vanishes into itself. I go back down the steps to the driveway and look down the alley between 36 and 34. A grey-painted gate opens onto a small backyard. At the end of a concrete patio there's a vegetable patch with the first of the summer's green tomatoes. Sliding glass doors look in on a kitchen. On the other side of the glass is an oak table with four chairs around it. The kitchen is spacious, with new cabinetry and a rolling butcher's block. I like it. I can see them moving around each other in that space. She ducks her hip, he lifts a tray into the air. She says whoops, he says pardon. The kitchen is empty. There is nothing on the counters.

I walk down the concrete steps to the basement door. The handle won't turn a millimetre in either direction, but the door feels loose. I nudge it toward its hinges and a crack opens on the latch side. On TV, detectives and criminals jimmy doors with credit cards, and I get out my driver's licence and slip its knife-edge into the crack and work it down until it meets resistance. I push the card in further and angle it to get purchase. If the bolt's curved, I can depress it by pushing the card in hard against the door. If it's a deadbolt, I'm SOL. But it's going in. The card scrapes metal and I press the door against its hinges. Then the card vanishes as if it's been snatched away, and it takes me a moment to register that the door has swung open. My face stares up at me from the floor. I'm going into her house. I'm breaking the law.

I close the door behind me and stand inside the house of Ingrid Fox.

So who is she? She's a woman with a washer and dryer set in her basement. Take note of that, *washer and dryer set in basement*. She also has a small unfinished bathroom, a furnace, some raw-wood shelving with paint cans and tools scattered on it. She illuminates it all with a forty-watt on a pullchain. It's not enough to light the corners of the room. I see stacked suitcases, a headless dress form, an unplugged generator, a couple of stashed radiators. I have none of these things in my house, although of course I have luggage, black luggage like Ingrid's by the look of it, but I don't keep mine in the basement. There's nothing here of interest, or at least anything that might tell me what she's capable of, or who she thinks she is.

A door at the top of the stairs opens into the kitchen. I allow my fingers to drift over the slightly oily surface of the butcher's block. In the sink, there's a coffee cup with an inch of cold coffee in it and the buzz of fear begins to sound again. A faint pink lipstick smear on the rim.

I come out of my body. I see myself in the kitchen from the corner of the room, looking down into the sink at the coffee cup. I leave myself there and go into the hallway, where, through reverse-telescopic vision, I see the front door six miles away. I'm unsteady on my feet, vertiginal. The living room curves into place as I turn my head. Its shelves line one wall, floor to ceiling, full of books. The sight of this multiplex of spines makes my eyes strobe uncontrollably. I have to get back to my body. I hold the wall and close my eyes. Through a squint, I navigate to a wooden chair. My back teeth send bolts of electricity directly into my eyes, and there are venetian blinds on the back of my neck, opening and closing, scraping me with their cold edges.

My kitchen self joins me and we breathe and count and count and breathe.

When I can lift my head, I look around at the living room. At the front of the house, through a pair of open French doors, is a small office. Its window gives out on the church wall across the road, as well as the tree and the bench beneath it.

Around me, the house sighs and hums like a living thing. After a few minutes, I can breathe normally again, although I'm cold all over. I walk along the shelves with my arms behind my back, one hand clenched tightly in the other. The books aren't alphabetized and mystery shares shelfspace with poetry. Of course I've seen a lot of her books in my store. Marilynne Robinson, *Housekeeping*, U.S. hardback edition. *Secret World of Og.* Ditto. Hard book to find in original hardback. I still have one in my glass case of unmoveable first editions.

I run my fingertips over the spines. A vein in the top of my hand is throbbing.

Raymond Carver's *Cathedral; Collected Poems* by Adrienne Rich. So she has taste, Ingrid Doppelganger. I have seen almost all of these editions, either on my own shelves at home or in the bookstore. Why should I be surprised if we have the same taste when we already share so much?

One shelf is stocked with art and photography, and I don't have to scan it too long to determine that Ingrid's modest art book collection contains all of, and only, the art books I am currently stocking. A bead of moisture rolls down inside my hand and collects on the end of my pinkie. I look at the other books again, muttering under my breath. Her first edition of *Time's Arrow* is signed by the author. I call Terrence at the store, my voice as low as possible. 'Do we still have that first edition of *Time's Arrow* signed by Amis?'

'Who is this? Mrs Mason?'

I have to repeat the question.

'You want me to look?'

'Simple instructions, Terrence.'

Silence, and then he returns. 'Yeah. Should I set it aside?'

'That's great,' I whisper and hang up.

I creep past the reading chair into the little office behind the French doors. There's a desk and a couple more bookshelves. I put my phone away and enter the room with a feeling of deathly reverence. This is Ingrid's office.

I recognize my handwriting on a pad of paper. That's my handwriting. *Jesus.*

A professional portrait of Ingrid and her husband stands in the recessed windowsill. I pick it up and bring it close to my eyes. That is, truly, my mouth. The expression is mine as well. It's my take-the-picture smile. It's everywhere in our photo albums.

The glass captures the reflection of another picture, a young girl, hanging on the wall behind me. 'You're home early,' it says, and I involuntarily pee. *'Mummy?'*

'You're up?' I ask.

'Duh,' she replies. She cranes her neck to see my face. 'Are you going back?'

'To what?'

'Work!'

Her mother can't keep looking away! Is the girl sick? Maybe she's home-schooled. We look at each other. Her expression doesn't change. At a glance I can see the fever in her eyes.

She says, 'Can you make me a gorilla?' and bounds away.

I follow her like I'm being called to my execution. She sits at the kitchen table. 'Sweet... heart? I didn't hear you.'

'A gorilla?'

'Right. Just one?' I see a picture on the fridge of Ingrid and this child. I scan the fridge for name-clues and there's a diploma for circle-drumming presented to Dana Fox. A feeling of terrible grief washes over me.

'Just one.'

'Anything else? Dana? On the side?'

'Just the gorilla. *Mother.*' Her legs are long enough to reach the floor when she sits forward on the seat, but when

141

she pushes back they dangle like clappers in a bell.

'Why don't we make it together, then. It'll be fun.'

She sighs and slides off her chair. Why does *she* have to do everything? 'Fine. I'll get the bread. You get the cheese.'

Gorilla cheese sandwich. I hunt beside the stove for a frying pan. The cheese singles are in the fridge door. The child and I move around each other and I steal glimpses. Her hair is stringy and a little damp – fever hair. Like her mother's hair looked in her red coat. Dana's blue eyes have a gloss of red in the whites. I pour her a glass of water. 'Drink that,' I say. 'You'll feel better. When's the last time you had any medicine?'

'You gave me grape Motrin before you left? Why are you using *that* cheese!'

Two slices of American droop off the side of my hand. 'Sorry. Maybe I'm getting a touch of what you have.'

'What do I have?'

'It's nothing serious! It's nothing! A touch of flu.' There's only one other cheese I can find in the fridge and it's a hunk of real cheddar. I slice thin squares of it onto a cutting board under Dana's careful gaze. She coughs into her shoulder.

I fumble about pretending to look for stuff and Dana butters the bread. She's beautiful, with tiny feet and toes. I'd always wanted to have a daughter. She's so delicate in her illness, but I can feel her will pulling at me like a river current. How is it she doesn't know I'm not the one she thinks I am? That I might be her mother's Llorona?

'Mummy – ?' Her hand slides into mine. Cold, soft. My stomach cringes. She puts the sandwich into the pan and it hisses like it's recoiling in pain. 'I heard you and Daddy crying.'

'Oh. I thought… we thought you were asleep.'

'You have a bo-bo in your head. You said you're sick.'

'Oh, sweetheart.' I take her into my arms, I can't stop myself. 'Sometimes adults have problems,' I say. 'And they cry. It's not the end of the world. Don't you cry?'

She pushes away from me. 'Flip it.'

'What?'

'My gorilla.'

If Ingrid has my looks and my books, then why doesn't she have two sons? Why doesn't her husband look like Ian? Is she at Bookshop right now, greeting my customers? Terrence would have said something. Unless he's in on it. Unless everyone is in on it.

The girl takes the sandwich out of the pan with her bare fingers.

'Careful,' I say. 'Do you think... you'll be all right on your own this afternoon?'

'You left me all morning,' she says. 'I think I'll survive until one of you gets home.'

'One of...?'

'You or Dad? Holy wow, you're goinked worse than me today.'

I have to get out of here.

'Are you going back to work *right now?*'

'I'm sorry.'

She directs a steady stream of ketchup onto her plate. I reach over and touch her hair as she wanders past me, heading into the TV room with her sandwich and a glass of milk.

'You called me Dana, like, *twice*,' she says. 'Maybe you should go back to your feelings doctor and talk about your feelings some more.' She searches my eyes for knowledge I don't have. 'Hello, Mom? I'm Jean? Dana's the dead one.'

I HAVE TO WALK, AND walk, and I have to stay in motion as long as possible, and not go in the direction of Bookshop or Bellevue Square, although I feel like eating a huge hunk of meat, raw red hamburger if I have to. But I walk away. I walk down into the old garrison part of the city where the streets meet at right angles. The buildings on either side of me in the old core crowd the street and make a person lose their sense of direction.

Little Jean, sick, sweet Jean lost a sister and Ingrid lost a child. Was that why Ingrid was crying? Is the bo-bo in her head grief? I don't share this with her. I have no grief. I'm happy. Right now, in this part of my life, except for a few bumps such as seeing things, I'd call life peachy. Ingrid has grief.

The faces of buildings repeat and repeat until I lose track of which direction I'm facing or what time it is. I feel safer among others. I feel compassion for them, certain of their sufferings and courage. But maybe they are bad people. Is this why Ingrid's grief is happening to me? Am I a bad person?

WHEN I GET HOME, IT'S in time to make like mother and wife again. Both children are stupefied in front of the TV, not necessarily looking at it, but abiding with it, their attention downward as usual, peering into the only real windows they look through anymore, their fingertips moving over the glass.

I collect the empty plastic bags that contained whatever they bought at Bulk Barn on the way home from school. Sugar crystals. They say hello in unison.

I look in the fridge and try to imagine the dish that can emerge from its puzzle of ingredients. My mouth is dry. I drink iced tea straight from the bottle. I could make grilled cheese sandwiches again, these guys could live off of grilled cheese, and it's easy, and no one will complain if it's American cheese.

As I assemble the ingredients, I have the sensation that I'm underwater, complete with the inability to breathe. The air has thickened. The presence that pinned me to my bedroom ceiling is back. It's everywhere now, a current or a wave. I go out into the living room and it's there too, going through the room like a braid woven through the space, filling in the nothing. It's not Ingrid at all. It's deeper than Ingrid. It's an invisible fortification holding everything in.

When Ian gets home, he wants more than grilled cheese. He encourages the kids to go downstairs and play a board game. This is like asking them to wear top hats, but their father has a convincing way.

I know there's no hiding from him anymore, my husband and sometimes confidant, the father of our two children,

145

our genes stirred together in them. Today is he my friend?

He tells me that he had a conversation with a Detective Sanchez, who told him that a woman named Ingrid Fox identified the body behind the food mall.

'So do you believe me now?'

'Sanchez described her to me. It was you. He had you down to the part in your hair. You disappeared from me for ten minutes and that's where you went.'

'Don't you think if I had a doppelganger that she'd part her hair in the same place? That's how identical things look: the same.'

'Why did you tell Sanchez you were Ingrid Fox?'

My silence is uninterpretable.

'Are you still going to the park?'

'Yes,' I tell him, because he's relentless. 'And I've gone to Ingrid's house, too. Okay?'

He changes seats at the kitchen table to be beside me. He puts his arm around my shoulder. 'Jean? Please talk to me.' He shakes me, gently. 'Were you in a relationship with that woman?'

'Oh my god.' I push his paw off my shoulder.

'Was there a fight?'

'We were friends. Only friends. How can you even ask me that?'

'Which part?' he asks, his eyes tearing up. 'If you're cheating on me, or if you killed that woman?'

The doorbell rings. He doesn't break eye contact.

'Expecting anyone?' The second ring is more insistent and he rises from his chair. 'Wait here,' he tells me.

I get up and turn on the little countertop television and watch with my arms crossed over my chest, shifting from foot to foot. Through my socks, the floor tiles are cold. Katerina and I were only friends. She was in love with

Ingrid. Or Jimmy. Or Miguel. And she was already dead when I got there. But why do I feel Ian knows something I don't?

I want to stay here, in front of the TV, and watch this man in the traditional garb of his country play a woodwind instrument for his po-faced king. I want to be here with my plans for dinner, and night falling, and getting into bed. What's so difficult about that?

He returns alone. 'Some woman wants to talk to you. Don't be long, we're not done here.' The ringing in my head starts before I leave the room. I reel into the front hall knowing it's her. She's going to be standing on the other side of the screen door under the glow of the porch light. And she is! It's her. Ingrid Fox stands at my front door. But how did she find me? Well, of course! She's already been in my bathroom mirror.

The light spills over her, shadowing her eyes, but it casts her smile in phosphorescent pink and white. She clasps her palms to the base of her throat, as if she's having trouble breathing, and I open the door for her.

'I knew you were back,' she says. 'I'm ready now.'

3

I HEAR THE SOUND OF gas in a tube. It hisses a hollow note. Ian's voice says: 'Her eyes are open.'

His voice comes closer, but it distorts in what I think must be an operating room because the light is immense and tear-inducing. I hear him through this medium of light, which is like being under the surf with the sun just inches away from the surface of the water, except I don't know how far away the surface is.

If this is death, it's confusing, but it doesn't hurt and it isn't frightening or sad. Then something changes and the light recedes like a drug wearing off and then I remember – for I am still myself, I can feel that I am here – that at death, the brain releases natural opiates, to calm you, to give you a final dream and then after that there's nothing. It's a trick, after all, a merciful trick, but a dirty one just the same because the last thing that ever happens to you is untrue. I don't want to stop being myself –

(Jean falls into a sleep so profound that only I can tell you she loses sense of what she is and shades into no-mind and not-time. She's starry potential and dead signal. She 'sees' her mother's face. She 'sees' 'light' beyond a 'door.')

Luminescent lines speed down cometlike behind my lids. They've hooked me in this black ocean and I feel them reeling me in.

'She's crying,' Ian says.

**NOW I AM AWAKE.**

I'M IN A PRIVATE ROOM at what used to be the Clarke Institute but then someone started calling it the Jurassic Clarke and now it's just CAMH. Centre for Addiction and Mental Health. Spoken like a person's name: Cam Aitch. This is Jimmy's sometimes home. The trees are in full summer leaf. I look out over an ocean of green. I'm high up, looking toward the campus of the University of Toronto. I see its treetops in the distance.

The TVs they have here lean down from the corners of the rooms, so you have to crane your neck if you want to see anything. It looks like the little boy running toward the camera with his arms spread is actually up there, in the corner of the room, about to leap from the ceiling into my arms.

I guess I've been here for a couple of weeks. That's what they tell me. I have to get my strength back before they send me home, and for now, I'm not even allowed off the floor.

I'm still having seizures. They want me to stay in bed, where it's safe if it happens, but lying in bed starts to make you feel crazy. I've walked around the ward. Nothing to see. I don't need to make any friends, because I'm not going to be here much longer. I'm not like these people.

After I collapsed in my front hallway, they couldn't wake me up. Ian says I wasn't in a coma, because I responded to pain. But I was asleep and I wouldn't wake up. It's frightening to think of being unconscious for as long as I was – five whole days. I don't remember a thing from my sleep, not a flicker of a dream, but since I've been awake I've begun to wonder if those long nights were so dark because my dreams had already escaped into the world.

The doctors say I might need an operation. They're taking a wait-and-see attitude. Some bad wiring is the culprit. Ian seems very relieved. The boys have been to see me a couple of times now. Ian had to bribe them with Happy Meals because they were scared. I understand. I don't want them to see me like this, but I want to see them. Reid is playing with his plastic toy at the foot of the hospital bed. The toy says, 'Always alert, to save our dirt!'

Ingrid leads me away from the house. 'He calls you *Jean*,' she says. 'Come with me! I have to show you something! This is just… it's *absolutely* fucking incredible!'

'I should tell my husband where I'm going.'

She strides toward Dundas, looking back as if to check I'm real. 'Come on! *Jean*!'

We're going to the bookstore. When I catch up to her, she's standing in front of it, shivering, although the air is not that cold. She jiggles the knob impatiently. 'Come on. Open it!'

I unlock the store and she goes in first. She pulls the window blinds down, blocking the street lights and dropping the store into a gloamy dark. I get as far away as I can from her in the little space. In the lunarglow, her skin is tinged blue. 'Turn some lights on,' she says.

'Stay over there.'

'Where's the switch…' Her hand feeling along the wall makes a faint hissing sound. 'I can't believe you have a bookstore. This is fantastic.'

'What's going on? Explain who you are! And don't touch my lights!'

'Oh, here's one.' She's revealed standing in front of the Pavoni. 'Does this work?'

*She wants a coffee?* 'Can it wait until you're done blowing my mind?'

'Oh sweetheart,' she says, her eyes tender, 'you're blowing mine.'

'Please, I'm begging you – don't come any closer.'

'Our voices are different,' she says. 'D'you hear it?'

'I don't know what I sound like.'

She points at her lips and makes a circle. 'You don't sound like this. Can you whistle?'

'No.'

'I can.' She does. I've heard better. Whatever this is, I'm just going to have to go with it. 'And this is *your* bookstore?'

'Yes.'

'When did you open it?'

'I rented –'

'Two Aprils ago.'

'Yes.'

'April 2014.'

'Yes. Why does it matter?'

'I was diagnosed that April. I get seizures. They alter my perceptions. Specifically, I hallucinate.' She looks to me for a reaction. I shrug with my eyebrows. 'First I started having trouble recognizing myself in the mirror. I could take a photo of myself and I'd know it was me when I looked at it, but if I looked at the photo in a mirror, it looked wrong.'

'It looked wrong.' She's got me trapped between Travel and Psychology. 'Stop moving! Wrong in what way?'

'I made Larry cover all the mirrors. Out in the world, if I saw myself in a reflection and there were other people in it, I couldn't find myself. I'd have to make a peace sign and see who made one back. Larry says, "I'm living in a permanent shiva house and no one's dead!" "Yet," I tell him. That's our little joke. Too dark for some people, but you gotta laugh, right? I started seeing you that fall, last fall,' she continues.

'I hadn't looked at a mirror on purpose in months. I was doing fine. I was working on my book –'

'You're a writer.'

'I shouldn't presume you know everything about me. Hold on a second!' She vanishes down the back of the store. From there, she calls: 'You're pretty good looking! You dress like you think you're not, though. We look good in long, simple print dresses and solid colours.'

'I don't take fashion advice from phenomena.'

'Is there a light back here?'

I flick a switch behind me. 'So you think you can read my mind or something?' I ask her. 'What am I thinking right now?'

'Not much for alphabetizing, are we?' She stands straight, her head cocked. 'You don't know everything, but you understand before I've even explained it to you.'

'Explained *what* to me, Ingrid?'

She keeps hunting through the shelves. 'Looking alike isn't the half of it. Oh! There's one!'

I whip out my cell and text Ian. *I'm here with her now. We're at the bookstore.* I put it on vibrate.

'You have two of them!' She comes back with a couple of trade paperbacks and puts them down on the cash desk, turns their covers toward me. They're titled *Utter* and *Murder Plot*. I have no memory of buying them, but Terrence does his share of buying now.

'Huh.' I run my finger over the shiny raised type. 'Ingrid Fox.'

'Not my real name.'

'No? What's your real name?'

'You don't need to know that. I also wrote *A Kept Woman* and *Sown Bones*. Do you ever see them?'

'I don't know. Why do you use a pseudonym?'

'I like pretending to be someone else. Although you probably think I'm overdoing it.'

With the desk between us, and the initial shock wearing off, I want to know more. 'Go back to the part where you hadn't looked at mirrors for a while.'

'Mirrors?'

'You said you couldn't –'

'I lose my train of thought so easily.'

'You stayed away from mirrors, until one day...'

'I remember now. It was the fifth of April. The nones of April. Some months it falls on the seventh. The ides have always been tied to brutal murder, but the nones are just about phases of the moon, did you know that? Anyway.' She moves a couple of books off a display table and sits on it. 'I was in Kensington Market and I thought I'd passed a mirror, but then my image walked away – and it was you! You were sort of dressed like you are now. I was stunned, I didn't even think to follow you. And after that, I'd get a glimpse of you driving past in your car, or through a window of a restaurant. I lost my nerve on a couple of occasions, but I almost went up to you.'

'I thought I was going crazy.'

'You're not. There's nothing wrong with you.'

It feels like a meat locker in here. I click the heat on. 'How is it possible we didn't run into each other? I spent hours and hours in that park.'

'What park?'

'Bellevue Square.'

'Is that what it's called? I see it from my shrink's window.'

'Katerina must have told you about me. I told her that if you were looking, that's where I'd be. I gave her a letter for you.'

She looks concerned.

157

'What? She didn't give you the letter?'

'I don't know who you're talking about. No one told me about you and I didn't go looking for you, either. I just kept seeing you.'

'Katerina? *Your* friend? My friend?' I'm about to use the word *murdered*. 'So what are you, then? What is going on?'

'You're *my* doppelganger, Jean. You're here because I'm dying.' The fluorescents over Romance make a clicking sound like bugs trapped in a jar and go out.

'WHERE IS THIS BOOKSTORE?' IAN'S voice. I'm awake again. 'You talked a lot about a bookstore in the spring, but you know you work at Ryerson University, Jean. Right? You're a teacher. You had an accident, but everything's okay now.'

'I have a headache. Why does my head hurt?'

'You've had a procedure – don't touch that.'

There's a tube going into the top of my hand. 'What is this?'

'It's just saline.'

'Ian, Ingrid doesn't know Katerina. She's never met her. So who was Katerina seeing?'

'I'm sorry, sweetie, I don't know who you're talking about.'

'Why am I here now? Where are the boys?'

'Try to calm down, sweetheart. The surgeons warned us that you would lose some memory. You knew you were going to have this operation. I can show you the consent form you signed.' A nurse enters. 'I think she's in pain,' Ian says. 'The doctor said she can have up to two hundred milligrams an hour.'

The nurse smiles down at me like she's hiding something. 'Hello, dear. We're awake, are we?' Her hand goes to the top of my head, but I don't feel her touching me. 'How much so far?' she asks a machine. 'I can push fifty.'

'When did I have an operation? Ian? Where am I?'

'There it goes,' says the nurse.

'It's September ninth, Jean, 2016, and you're in the ICU at Toronto Western. You're just waking up. It won't make sense to you for a – should she be touching those bandages?'

I AM HAVING A HARD time with systems. Now that I'm awake more often, they've explained how after a surgery like mine things like numbers or grammar and colours or even the parts of my body may not make complete sense. They give me blocks and ask me to put them in order. There are numbers and letters and the blocks are different colours. I may not know what order to put the blocks in, but I know they're different, I *see* they're different sizes and have different symbols on them, but I can't transfer this information to my hands. Touching the blocks changes them. Dr Morbier says I have functional delusions, as opposed to the delusions people have who are not aware they're operating under incorrect perceptions of the world around them or inside of them. In other words, I'm not crazy. Hurrah.

Dr Morbier, after he agreed to take my case, warned me that my recovery would be lengthy and difficult, but that he had treated a number of cases of autoscopy successfully and that sometimes all it took was pills. Surgery first to snip the bad wires, then pills. He's warned me I'll probably need a 'multi-modal' approach, but 'a motivated, intelligent woman such as yourself has the power to make a full recovery.'

Morbier is tall and bald and there's a half centimetre of gum above his front teeth when he smiles, which is often. He has soft pike-grey eyes. My appointments with him are twice a week, on the weekdays that fall on either side of the middle day of the workweek. All of the visits so far, he wants to start from the moment I opened the door on Ingrid and go as far as I can, telling him as much as I remember, although now, in my own memories, scrambled as they are,

160

I'm not with Ingrid the way I was before. In my mind, I have new perspective: from slightly above, looking over my own shoulder. Morbier encourages changing what he calls my camera angle. I see both of us. I see things I couldn't have seen when I stood behind the cash desk and flipped the lights on for her, like the dust bunnies that had collected on the tops of the shelves. I can see the back of my own head.

'What happens when you go to the door?' Morbier asks. 'Take me through it again.'

'I went to the door and she was there.'

'Remember, we speak in present tense here. So we can be in the moment as much as possible and really see what was there.'

'She says "I'm ready now."'

'And then you go with her.'

'We go to the bookstore.'

'Does anything happen on the way?'

'She leads me there. I feel a… painful buzzing at the top of my spine, between my shoulder blades. It's scary, the whole experience, but she's making me… What are you thinking?'

'Go on,' he says.

'I open the door and she follows me in and pulls the blind down in the front window. I say to myself that whatever happens next, I'm just going to have to go with it. She stands in front of the door and I go to the cash desk and sort of wait and she stares at me like she's falling in love.'

'Do you touch?'

'Not yet. She went, I mean she *goes* to look for her books. She's a writer. Her books are schlocky mysteries.'

He writes on his lined white pad. I like it when he writes because it means I've said something interesting. I imagine him behind a lectern at an international symposium on disorders of the temporo-parietal junction saying, *Patient is a Caucasian woman of forty-two who collapsed in the doorway of her home. First diagnosis was stroke, but an MRI revealed hundreds of seizures within the temporo-parietal junction as well as in the parietal-occipital cortex.*

'Why do you think Ingrid writes mysteries?'

'Probably because my unconscious wants me to solve my own mystery. Good answer, eh?'

'Top-drawer. But you don't recall ever stocking her books. I find that interesting. You own a used bookstore, but you've never heard of her books – four of them, am I right?'

'Yes.'

'You have a huge mystery section and there's lots of turnover, but you've never seen her books. Why *didn't* you stock them?'

'Well, it turns out I did!' We share a laugh about my imaginary bookstore. 'I figured Terrence must have bought them.'

'I guess so,' he says. 'Okay, so you arrive at the bookstore.'

'Yes. She tells me she'd been seeing me herself, but it was hard to catch up with me on busy streets, or she'd only catch sight of me when I went by in a car or in a cab. And then she says she doesn't know who Katerina is. And she's never been to Bellevue Square.'

'Maybe she has something to hide,' Morbier suggests. 'Maybe she's not telling you the truth.'

'She says we should sit down and talk. She says she'll put the kettle on if there is one and then she offers me one of my own chairs.'

'SO,' INGRID SAYS. 'HOW DO we do this thing?'

'This *thing*?'

She passes me a cup of tea. She's made it exactly how I take it. 'It was just sightings before. This is a pretty significant increase in symptoms. I'm actually talking to you.'

There's something amusing about her (I tell the doc) because she's almost out-of-her-mind enthusiastic, manic even. 'You know,' I say, 'I didn't think things could get any stranger than having an actual doppelganger, but to have one who doubts *my* existence? My kids would say "amazeballs."'

'But you are my doppelganger, Jean.' She prods her own chest with splayed fingers. 'You must see it now. Think. Almost all of your books in here are on *my* bookshelves. And why are you a bookseller?'

'Why?'

'Yeah, *why*?' She doesn't pause to let me work out a response. 'You're a bookseller because I'm a writer. Of course you would have a bookstore! Who else would sell my books?'

'Your books are published by a large German conglomerate, Ms. Fox. I can see the colophon on the spine from here.' I point at the two books sitting on the cash desk, about a foot from her. 'Make haste slowly. Did you know that's what it means? Every bookstore in the city has your books.'

'How do you know all the bookstores in Toronto carry me? *You* didn't know you carried me! This bookstore wasn't even here until I hallucinated it.'

163

'So you're hallucinating now? That I believe.'

'Do you?'

'A little,' I say. 'I definitely think one of us is not well.'

'That's right. It's me. I'm not well.'

'Where did you grow up?'

'Willowdale.'

A valve in my heart starts fidgeting. The area's old postal-village name hurts to hear. 'I grew up in Willowdale.'

'Get real, of course you did. I grew up in your house, Jean. I even had a doll with a porcelain head that I named Jean after Billie Jean King. I know everything about you. Anything I said about you would be true. Even if I made it up.'

I put the tea down. 'Do you know how crazy you sound? You're already off the scale, but trust me, you're not making me up as you go along. I'd probably be a lot more interesting if you were. But *I'm* making me up as I go along.'

She studies me. No, admires me.

'Stop looking at me like that. Are you proud of yourself or something?'

'It's easier than I thought it would be.'

'What is?'

She only smiles. 'What's happening to me gets refracted through you, changed into something similar but different. Like your husband.'

'He's imaginary, too?'

'He's based on two ex-husbands. Martin, an NHL agent who gambled and lost the way most people breathe. I had Jean with him. Marty was a risk taker and a very bad card player. But always chasing the next new kid coming up in the Canadian and American leagues, hustle hustle.'

'How many husbands have you had?'

'Three. The second one was Shaun. More smart than good looking. Meth-head. He worked for Wood Gundy. In fact, *I* worked for Wood Gundy. That's where we met. Is Ian in money?'

'He was a meth-head?'

'Math-head. What does Ian do?'

'Cop,' I say. My fingertips are freezing cold. 'Did you lose a child?'

'How do you know that?' She jumps up and disappears down a rank of shelving again. My hands are shaking. This is the panic-feeling I first felt in childhood, perhaps even as an infant. When I feel like this, there is no imperative but to run. I have the urge to wash my hands and I run scalding water over them at the sink and wash them twice.

'Look at this,' she says, returning with another book. 'Guy de Maupassant. *The Horla*. Have you read it?'

'I haven't.' I remain by the sink, my hands still dripping, as she sits and begins to read silently to herself, flipping pages.

'*The Horla*,' she says, 'or, *Modern Ghosts*. Shall I read it to you?'

'Just give me the short form.'

'It's the journal of a man who goes mad when he realizes that his mysterious illness is not physical. He's been possessed by the Horla, a being that can control his thoughts and even his actions. Very dramatic.' She riffles the pages, and the book blurs into a little accordion. 'The narrator is never named, but he writes in the style of de Maupassant. He does an experiment. When he thinks the Horla has been coming into his bedroom at night, he leaves out food and drink, like wine and fruit and milk. And by morning the Horla has drunk the milk and left the rest untouched.'

'Why?'

'Because the Horla only drinks water when it has to, and milk when it can. The man won't believe what is happening until he has proof, and he devises a test to prove that *he* himself is sleepwalking and that he is the one who drinks in the night! He stoppers up the water jug and the milk jug and ties a white muslin cloth over the stoppers. Then he draws all over his lips and mouth with a lead pencil and goes to bed.'

She's found the passage she's looking for and starts reading. '"Irresistible sleep seized me, which was soon followed by a terrible awakening. I had not moved, and my sheets were not marked. I rushed to the table. The muslin round the bottles remained intact; I undid the string, trembling with fear. All the water had been drunk, and so had the milk! Ah! Great God!..."' She closes the book. 'I love that. "I undid the string, trembling with fear." I can see the stiff hemp twine coming off the bottle neck. You know what happened after he wrote this?'

'Do I want to?'

'He went mad and killed himself.'

'So you're Guy de Maupassant and I'm your Horla,' I say.

'Something like that.'

'You don't seem upset by it, though.'

'Well, you don't control my thoughts. That's what's different. I control yours.'

'Maybe you do. I like the one you're coming up with right now, about getting out of my store.' I go lift the blind in the front window.

'I tell you I'm dying and you kick me out?'

I open the door. 'You can do it somewhere else.'

'When I die, Jean, you die, too.'

'Get out.' But Ingrid is unbuttoning her blouse. 'Oh – god. What are you doing?!'

'You might want to close those blinds again. Take off your top.'

'Get the hell out of here!'

166

'I'm taking it off.' She removes her blouse and begins to undo her bra. I close the door and drop the blinds, which race down with a violent clatter. She stands topless under the cruel white light. A recent scar, one with the red dots still visible on either side, describes the curve of her sixth or seventh rib, on her left side. It resembles a cave drawing, a primal red in the shape of animal tracks. 'In one of my surgeries, I lost our mole,' she says. 'They needed some bone.'

I can hear sounds from the street as if they're being piped directly into my head. I have a mole below my left breast. About halfway along where her scar is.

She brings her body to me. 'Take your top off,' she says. 'I won't bite you. Unless you ask me to.'

I pull my shirt up over my head. She flips up my bra, nudges my breast aside and puts her finger on the brown bead of raised moleflesh. My heart thrashes behind her fingertip.

'See?' she says. 'Now get a load of this.' She bends away from me and spreads the scar with her fingers. The very edge of the mole pops out. 'When the Horla drives his victim mad, you know what he does? He burns down his own house and everyone who's in it. Just to kill it.' She reaches out tenderly to flick my bra down. 'Get dressed, sweetheart. We don't have a lot of time left.'

'YOU'VE MADE SOME EXCELLENT PROGRESS, Jean.' Dr Morbier flips a page in his notebook near the end of our session. Much writing this time. It helps to believe, as I unspool this story, that he is at least impressed by its originality. Then again, he has probably seen and heard everything.

'Did you tell me your father was an alcoholic?' he asks me.

'I don't know. Did I?'

'Was he?'

'Yes. But I don't think I talked about it.'

'I thought I'd written something down, only I can't find it now.' He waves the notebook beside his head as if it's somehow at fault.

'Maybe I exhibit some tendencies of children of alcoholics.'

'What kind of drunk was he? What was his behaviour like?'

'Not very friendly,' I tell him. 'He had sulks. He screamed at our mother.'

'*Our* mother?'

'I have a sister. Paula.' He opens the notebook again. 'She lives in Phoenix now. You might find this a little too coincidental, but she has a tumour in her ear.'

'You don't have a tumour, Jean. Tell me more about Paula.'

'She's older. Sick with this thing in her head, but she's been a huge help to me through some of this.'

'Have you seen her recently?'

'She lives in Phoenix, so no. We Skype all the time, though.'

He writes on his pad, for what seems a long time, and then puts it away in a drawer in the desk. 'Well, we really do have to stop,' he says. 'We'll see each other again on Thursday.'

'Yes.'

He rises.

'Doctor, when do you think I'll be ready to go home?'

'Why don't we revisit that at our next session, Jean? You're having another CT scan tomorrow?'

'I can't remember.'

'I'll check with Miss Maufrinuz and she'll let you know before the end of her shift today. All right?'

THE HALLWAYS IN THE WARD are hung with art made over the years by some of the 'clients' of CAMH. A lot of it is drawings or paintings of faces, presumably self-portraits, done in various media. Some of them are excellent. They draw themselves looking into the mirrors they've been supplied with, along with the paper and the paint and the pencils (blunted 3B pencils), and if the eyes look alive enough you can feel the person who's looking into the mirror.

You don't see many eyes on a psychiatric floor. People are really into themselves here, staring out windows onto eternity, or looking down at the floor in shame or terror. If someone actually looks at you – and you learn this in the first week – you'd better shuffle along. Those of us still capable of rational thought were warned that there's a number of inappropriate touchers on the ward. Not all of this touching is sexual; some of it is comfort-seeking. Some patients revert to childhood or infancy. It's hard to know what to do when a weeping sixty-year-old man comes to curl up in your lap. If necessary, a doctor can prescribe something to quell too much zest for life.

Time goes differently in a place you can't get out of. When Ian and the kids visit, I'm often wrong about how long it's been. I get a lot of 'Mummy, we were here *yesterday*.' I can't imagine it's any easier visiting your mother in a locked mental ward than it would be to visit her in jail. At least we're free to walk around, as long as we don't leave the floor. Because of the (small) risk of relapse in the first weeks after the surgery, best practice is keeping the patient safe and near medical professionals familiar with their individual case. Unfortunately, the locked psych ward is considered the safest place for people recovering from or prone to autoscopic hallucinations.

The surgery was ten days ago. The last thing I remember was Reid showing me a toy. It had been the summertime, but now it's early autumn. There must be fifty get-well cards, some of them dated August, but I don't remember opening them or reading them. Ian's shown me some video he took of people who came to see me. A couple of my colleagues, my friend Brenda, (whose calls apparently went unreturned for three months), and my *mother*. But I can't remember any of it. I see myself in the videos, laughing, talking, making jokes about doing my time. It's as if it never happened. The surgery erased two months of my life.

Ian is in police uniform when he and the boys visit one day after lunch. I know this is Morbier's idea, that it's reinforcing to see Ian in his work clothes. I don't care what he wears, I'm just happy to see him.

Daddy has clarified that Mummy isn't crazy. Mummy had a little accident in her brain and nobody knew until she started seeing things. Kooky things, like seeing herself walking through parks in different clothing, shelving books in an imaginary little shop on Dundas (where it turns out there is a pet store).

Nick wants to know what it feels like to see something that isn't there, if it's like dreaming. It is like dreaming, I tell him. 'You know how in a dream, you're convinced that the craziest things are real? Like you're talking to your best friend except he has your father's head and it's normal in the dream? You don't even question it.'

'You saw your own face.'

'I saw a lot of things. I thought I was running a bookshop. And Daddy had made two million dollars on the stock market!' They laugh at this, nicely, and Ian laughs because, really, what cop quits the force to make it rich on pot stocks?

(Ian: That's the only thing you thought was strange about it? What about when I went to work every day in a uniform?

Me: I don't know how I didn't see that, but my mind edited it out.

Ian: It got cut in a seizure?)

'Anyway,' I continue, on this visit or some other visit another time (they've long ago blurred into a smear of sameness), 'It wasn't like a dream. It happened when I was awake. I didn't realize I was seeing things because the stuff I wasn't seeing, I mean the stuff that was real, kept it camouflaged. I mean *almost* everything was real, so I didn't know. I'm pretty sure.'

'Like us,' says Reid, with confidence. His tongue is stained orange with Popsicle. 'We're real. Orrrr... are we CGI?'

'Computers are amazing,' Ian says, 'but the human brain can still come up with some doozies.'

'Can I have another Popsicle?' Reid asks. He's irked by how unimportant he is right now, how little his needs count.

'You both go get another one,' Ian suggests, and the little one is gone in a flash. His brother follows morosely. After they go, Ian takes off his cap and lays it on the bed. He sits beside me and squeezes my thigh. 'Are you okay?'

'I'm handling it. What are they saying at home?'

'My mum is at the house right now cleaning it from top to bottom –'

'I mean the boys.'

'Not a lot. They want normal life as much as possible, so there's the regulation amount of bad words and name-calling. But I think they're very scared.' He moves his hand up my leg.

'I was, too. Morbier says I can come home in another week.'

'Good. That must mean you're better. And you look better to me. You look like someone I know.'

I let him touch me. His hand on my belly. 'We were rolling in it.'

'We're rich in all the ways that matter.'

'And you were... different sometimes. She told me you were made up of her ex-husbands.'

'The real thing is better, I hope.'

'I'm relieved.'

He leans down to kiss me, but on the forehead. The chaste kiss contradicts his vaguely sexual touching. I need to be fucked now like I never have before, not since before the kids. But who wants to fuck a mental patient? He goes to collect the children from the staff kitchen where the treats are. Later, when we're lined up for pills, Corine (a bipolar coming down from a manic break) tells me how good it was to see children in the ward. 'So sweet,' she says with a weak smile. 'They have no idea.' She's been in and out of CAMH for twenty years. I'm going home in a week. Morbier has promised me.

MORBIER IS A FRENCH CHEESE. I've been given access to the ward's computer for an hour in the evenings. Morbier is made from 'evening' milk and then covered in ash before 'morning' milk is added to it the next day. The cheese has a thin black line in the middle, separating the layers. Apparently the evening milk is fruitier and the morning, nuttier. I wonder if 'Morbier' is a pseudonym, adopted in order to communicate this complex metaphor to autoscopy patients.

There were some concerns with the recent CT, but I am not being told what they are. They are things 'not to be worried about' and I only need 'a bit more observation.' A few more days, which makes the promised week two weeks now. 'You don't want to leave until you're ready, Jean,' Morbier says. 'We want you good and strong when you go. I'm going to up your dose of oxcarbazepine. We're almost there.'

IN WEEK SIX, STILL ANOTHER week later than scheduled, and still on the maximum dose of oxcarbazepine, I walk into the wrong room. My mind has softened in the last couple of weeks, as though the drugs are massaging my brain into a smooth lump. I'm sleeping a lot. I'm half-asleep when I go back to what I think is my room – 308 – which is on the left, across from the nurses' station and three doors past the mag-locked exit to the outside. I *think* I've opened 308, except in my zombie state, I've come from the other end of the hall and I've walked into a room on the *same* side as the nurses' station. It's also a private room, set up like mine, but there is already someone in the bed and I can't help thinking: it's her.

The door whispers shut as designed (imagine slamming doors on a locked ward). I freeze and attempt to camouflage by holding my breath in the dark. It takes a minute for my eyes to adjust. The room sharpens into being like a photograph in developing fluid. I know the person in the bed. It's not her – it's Jimmy! He told me the last time he was in they had to knock him out for a week. It must have been curare, to judge by how anaesthetized he is. He lies under his covers, breathing very slowly and very deeply, curled toward me with his dirty beard tucked between his knees.

I creep forward, right to the bed, and kneel. If his eyes fly open, I'll scream. But he's so deeply asleep that they've sunk into his head. I imagine them pointing backwards, staring into his own frontal lobe, where his illness flows out from its source. This is the first time I've seen him this close

175

up. The lines along his cheeks and beside his eyes look like dry riverbeds from the air. What do you dream of if you're beset by demons? Nothing if you've had a couple shots of phenobarbital for dessert. He's so still he could be dead.

I see greeting cards on his bedside cabinet. I can see some of the brief handwritten messages in the faint light. The one signed *Dad* reads, *You will always be my son and I will always be your father.* The one signed *Karl and Wendy* says, *Get better and come party motherfucker.* A third one is addressed to Daddy in a child's script, and I look away.

The society of the mad contains primarily other sick people, as well as doctors and nurses. Some family if you're lucky. I've learned that many of the people here have been here before and will return again. Out in the world they're burning fuses, a danger sometimes to themselves or others. In here, they shamble, their legs confused on anti-seizure drugs; they wince at their thoughts; their lot in life is revealed to them over and over. They are poor and sick and shabby and hungry.

I back out of Jimmy's room unnoticed. I heard that he had a job last year driving a forklift. Even had a girlfriend before the summer, the first one since losing his kid in the divorce, but he went off his meds because they gave him blurred vision. He hid his returning symptoms at work until he couldn't control them anymore and then he took the forklift for a drive on the QEW and they canned him.

IN THE MIDDLE OF WEEK eight, Dr Morbier announces that my latest test results show great improvement and he has put me in for Sunday release. He begins to taper the oxcarbazepine. I'll still have to take it for another couple of years and be monitored regularly, but he calls my recovery excellent. For two days I get a half dose, then for two days I get a quarter dose. On my last night, I dream in the ward for the first time.

It's a simple, straightforward dream. I'm on a ladder passing books down to Reid, who is putting them into boxes. I look around and I see this is a house we lived in when we were kids, a house that was sold decades ago. These are my mother's books. Reid tells me we have to go because the plane home is in two hours and we have to be at the airport an hour before. I come down the ladder and tape up his box and put it with the suitcases by the door. The suitcases are full of books, too. From upstairs comes the sound of footfalls and a rumbling voice. 'We better get out of here,' Reid says. 'Before it comes down.'

'Why is it here?' I ask.

Doors open and close somewhere in the house. The footsteps come nearer.

Reid is pulling my hand. 'It's in the room, Mom! You have to get up! Get up!'

I awake from the dream and see a form at the foot of the bed. It's come to claim me. I hold my breath, my mouth open.

Then it speaks: 'You were in my room.'

'Jim-mee?' I say, through fear-hiccups.

'I saw you, but I was asleep. They shot a daylong nap up my arm. But I knew someone was there.'

'I'm going to turn on the light,' I say. 'Okay? Don't moo-hoove.' The light has a urinous cast, but it's really him. He's in the pyjamas they supply you with if you don't have your own. White with grey dots, button-up top with lapels. The pyjamas hang off him. 'It was an accident. I didn't mean to go into your room.'

'But you were there.'

'Yes, I was. You're totally right.'

'Good. I thought I was going crazy.' He twirls the air beside his ear with a finger.

'You were curled up in a ball.'

'I prefer paranoia to death. My room smells like diapers.'

'I didn't think so.'

'There's no sushi here.'

'That is one of its detractions. Can I ask what you're doing in *my* room?' I hiccup so hard I belch.

'We need to talk,' he says.

I sit up, alarmed by his swaying, shuffling movement toward me. My pulse dances in my temples. 'Okay, Jimmy. Let's talk.'

'Look at me, okay? I'm sour in kopf. But before, you should have seen me, Jean.' The light picks his eyes out above his dirty, multicoloured beard. 'I was a person.'

'You're still a person, Jimmy.'

'In a villainous vessel.'

'You're not so bad.'

'I was married. We had a boy of my own, we called him Tommy. But I haven't seen him in a long time. I don't know if he even lives here anymore. I worked as a bartender in a nice hotel downtown, made dirty martinis, made bourbon sours. Tommy'll find me. When he learns about his mind, though, look out! He'll say: Who put *that* in me? Was it my father? Was it my father's father who put my terrible self in me?' He leans in and I pull the covers up. 'Are you afraid?'

'Of what?'

'Me?'

'No,' I say. 'I know you can't help it.'

'What are you afraid of?'

'Really? Spiders.'

'Which ones?'

'All varieties, all sizes, from any country or time period. And stucco.'

'Eructate!' he says and slaps his forehead. 'I couldn't remember. Animals are afraid all the time, but they don't know what it is. The only difference between my brain and a dog's is that I think there's something I can do about it. You're nice.'

'Thank you.'

'When I'm on my Seroquel I'm as dull as a Mountie. Can I sleep with you?'

'You hoo what?'

'I have low oxytocin levels. It's good for both of us and anyway, you say you're not afraid of me. I'm asexual. Shiva touched my lingam.'

I weigh my options and arrive at a decision based on the behaviour of early humans. Because of the caves we once slept in for warmth and safety, I let him into my bed. I'm better off than the cave-women of the paleolithic, anyway, who had nothing but Neanderthals to keep them warm. I open the blankets and he slides in. His thin stubbled legs make scritch-scratch noises on the sheets. I shudder at the feeling of his beard painting my shoulder as he pulls me down into the bed and folds one leg over me.

'Turn off the light,' he says.

I can just reach the switch. His breath comes in rattles, smelling of red Jell-O and tooth rot. He sounds like an old tom with a broken purrbox. 'Can you try to calm down? Just try to breathe – not in this direction, though. When's the last time you brushed your teeth?'

'Have you been to Nepal?' he whispers.

'No.'

'If you don't get better soon, you'll want to go. I want to go. I can't concentrate very well and that's what they recommend: go to Nepal. Cullen is going to give me my no-mind.'

'Cullen from the? You've seen him?'

'I've seen him. If you do no-mind, you can get out of yourself. Be in the *ultimate* present. Jean?'

'Yes?'

'Would you try no-mind if you could?'

I don't know what he's talking about. It sounds like a medication. 'Are you... on it right now?'

'Can't get any. Still in beta because it broils your liver. But,' he says, clamping his leg more tightly around me, 'I think it's the way to go. You scrub out time and then you can see everything.'

'Sounds like something I'm not ready for. Maybe not you, either.'

'One day everyone's gonna be on it. It'll be in the water. Tasteless, odourless. Coming to a major city near you.' He inhales slow and deep. The staves of his ribs spread open along my side, a threadbare bellows. 'It's just a matter of time,' he says into my ear.

IT SURPRISES ME HOW EASY it is to don the clothing of a normal person and go to work. And how good it is: simple, splendid work. You get up and connect the day to come to the day that was. Whose file was open on my desk? When is my first appointment? Bathe. Kiss the husband, kiss the kids. Coffee on the way, coffee when you get there. Soon after, someone brings you coffee. Meetings, lunch. Discussions, leave-taking. Eat as a family. Argue, play, fuck, sleep. In bed, you think: what is it again I have to do in the morning?

I am on the path of routine and it is glorious. But the machinery that gives it its texture of lived life is a watchworks. I'm aware of the mainspring keeping the tension.

'It will take a long time before that feeling of being in danger passes,' Morbier says. 'That's its nature. To make you doubt. But in the meantime, you carry on! With some enthusiasm, even!'

My first days at the bank, I felt eyes on my back every time I turned it. We – Dr Morbier, Ian, and myself – decided I should backburner any ambitions I had of getting back to teaching and focus on a job with simpler parameters. (When I finally checked the emails from the university – emails Morbier suggested I had filed in a psychological spam folder – they revealed an increasingly hysterical one-way correspondence from the splenetic man who had hired me and was dealing with students asking for refunds.) Morbier suggested a part-time job somewhere brightly lit, where my tasks would quickly become routine. I thought a bank would do it. I put my resume out, and in a couple of weeks, I landed an interview at the Royal Bank at College and Bathurst. The manager called me back as I was walking out of the interview and told me I could start the following week.

I didn't mention my health issues and answered the question about the long gap in employment by telling him about my bookstore. At least it was half-true, in the sense that on some level, it had happened to me. Morbier couldn't explain why my memories of the hallucinations were so strong. 'They should fade, like dreams, shouldn't they?' I'd asked him. 'Why can I still feel my wooden cash desk under my fingertips when it never existed in the first place?' He didn't know; he couldn't explain it. My syndrome was too rare, few people studied it, and subtle differences in wiring and chemistry in patients produced wildly differing effects. There was no baseline.

'And where was I? When I was 'at' the bookstore? Was I standing out on the sidewalk? Was I just wandering around?'

'You were in a fugue state, wherever you were. I bet you spent almost all your time on that wall in Bellevue Square.'

No one at the bank should have known about my problems, but it felt like everyone did. It wrong-footed me from the beginning. I went out of sync. I banged my knee on a doorframe and said *holy fuck* too loud. I developed a strange, nervous body odour. I got locked in the safety deposit on my second day. I earned the nickname Boom-Boom, which I hated, but I smiled and tried to play along.

The hardest part of getting to know new colleagues is figuring out which ones you can talk to. People keep their pasts to themselves at the bank. The ones who don't might trigger me out of the blue, like Meaghan, who confided that her brother had a psychotic break in Peru after drinking an herbal tea. 'He's still not himself,' she told me, 'after fifteen years.' Karl with a K tells Carl with a C that his sister's kid has to be on mental health tablets and his opinion is that some people are born broken and society shouldn't have to pay their medical bills.

I figure it out after a while, and that leaves me with a small group of people I can confide in, people who are not on automatic pilot. Some of them have also been places they'd rather not talk about, and a kind look from one of them can put the day right.

At home, Ian and Reid have worked out a new routine to an old joke. 'You know, Reid,' Ian says, 'it's not entirely uncommon that people lose their minds once in a while. For three long years, I thought I was a chicken.'

'How come you didn't get help any sooner?' Reid asks him.

'My father owned a pillow factory and we needed the feathers.'

'Thank you, Wayne and Shuster,' I say, 'but I haven't lost my mind. I had a microangioma and some bad electrics. But look at me: I'm a new woman.'

By the time the Christmas jingles are poisoning the air, I'm no longer thinking that much about what happened in the summer-time. It's last season's flu. But it's hard to accept that what I experienced didn't happen. The fade never comes on: what I saw and did occupies a part of my memory where the experience remains stubbornly intact. I can bring to mind in the smallest detail the things she wore, the feeling of sticky sidewalk beneath my feet, her voice, my thoughts. I can smell the carpet in the bookstore.

I continue to see Dr Morbier, but in his own practice, which is in his house, ironically on Denison Avenue, below the park. I take Dundas, walking if the weather is good, but always on the south side. I only cross when I'm at Denison. I can see a snowy wedge of Bellevue Square at the top of the street, but I have cause to look away quickly as I come to Morbier's. I haven't been back and it's going to be some time before I can step into that space once again. I use a side door and a bell rings. I have already come to associate the sound of this bell with a feeling of sanctuary.

I've done plenty of my own reading by now and I offer Morbier the observation that memory is not located where my seizures occurred. I love watching a doctor's face when you start quoting what you've found on the internet. 'The brain is not divided into sections like a side of beef,' he says. 'And your whole brain is active all the time. Not just ten per cent.'

'That's bullshit?'

'Total.'

He wants to continue seeing me because there are only three cases in the literature of autoscopy at a distance, which Morbier calls asymmetrical autoscopy. Now that I'm cured, he wants my assistance in exploring the psychological side of the phenomenon. While my memory of it is still fresh, he wants to see if the contents of an autoscopic response – to physical injury, to electrical issues in the brain or seizures, to trauma states – reveal anything about the construct we call selfhood. His theory is that our experience of 'first person' might be encoded in that cleft, between the temporal and parietal lobes.

'Why imagine seeing *yourself*,' he asks, 'when that part of the brain in particular has been damaged? Why not see unicorns or tiny people running up the walls? It's very specific.' Sometimes I wish Morbier smoked a pipe. 'I believe if you went in here' – pointing to his own head – 'with a hot wire and poked around, you could lose your entire personality and still carry on with all manner of activities and functions. You might even have a job and be married and have kids. But you'd be unaware of yourself because you'd have no self to be aware of. Do you follow?'

'It sounds like autism.'

'*Yes.*' The tip of his pen does a paradiddle on his pad. 'Maybe autism and autoscopy are along the same spectrum. Interesting.' Much writing. 'Can you imagine, in real life, a person without a person in it? Such as you interacted with while you were ill?'

'But Ingrid had a personality.'

'I mean in a more… meta sense. She was manifest only to you. Therefore Ingrid had no person. Do *you* think she was self-aware?'

'It felt like she was. She felt, to me, like anyone else, like there was something going on behind her eyes. She even had a scent.'

'Of what?'

It comes instantly to mind. 'The inside of a chest freezer.'

Sometimes I follow the motion of the top of his pen and try to winkle out what he's putting on the pad, but everything looks like the letter O to me. 'It was quite an opportunity you had,' he says. 'Meeting yourself. I wonder, if I could bring Ingrid into this room, what would you want to ask her?' He sees the look on my face. 'Don't worry! I can't produce her.'

'I would ask her what she remembers about her mother and compare it to my own memories.'

'Like which memories?'

'I can't think of any in particular right now. I'm not sure how much I remember happening and how much of it is memories of seeing pictures or hearing stories. It took so long to live through and now I can barely remember it.

Maybe Ingrid remembers more than I do.'

'Is she your personal backup disk?'

'I don't know what she is. Apart from her inoperable brain tumour, she seems to have her act together. It's weird that everyone in this story has something wrong with their head.'

'Who's everyone in this story?'

'Me, Ingrid. Paula. Katerina.'

'I know what's wrong with you and Ingrid, but what's wrong with Katerina?'

'She has a hole in her head?'

'Right. I forgot about her.'

'How can you forget?'

'Jean, Katerina doesn't exist. You met her in the bookstore, right? She walked in one afternoon and told you –'

'Oh,' I grunt, like I've been struck. 'Katerina… but whose pupusas did I eat? Who was my friend?' A panicky feeling begins to fill me. 'I can't tell what happened and what didn't. Will this go away?'

'It's a lot to digest. It's going to take time to tease the strands apart. Tell me about Paula. What's wrong with Paula's head?'

'I told you. She has an inoperable tumour. Almost exactly where you say my seizures originated. They don't know what it's going to do next. I'm afraid she's going blind. I'm afraid the tumour is going to affect the part where she speaks from. That's all we have right now. Her hands shake too much to type.'

'She sounds trapped.'

'Yes. She won't let me visit her. But we Skype at least once a week.'

'So you've Skyped her this week.'

'Not this week.'

'So a couple of times a month?'

'Right.'

'She must be pretty concerned about what happened to you.'

'I'm sure she is.'

He leaves a silence. 'So you *haven't* spoken with her lately.'

'I have. We talked about the boys. She knows what I'm going through. I told her about seeing Ingrid in the park.'

'But that was months ago,' he says. 'That was May or June. It's December now. Did she ring you in hospital?'

'She doesn't *ring*. She likes to see my face. I must have talked to her a couple of times before I had my operation, but I don't remember everything from before.'

'You've really been through a lot, Jean.'

'Why are you so interested in Paula?'

'I'm interested in what you say to her. If she's your sister, you must share a lot with her.'

'What do you mean, if she's my sister?'

'I just mean I wasn't aware of her until you mentioned her, and I'm not clear on what kind of closeness you share. Like, was she there for you after you lost the baby?'

How does he know that? 'That was a long time ago.'

'It sounds like you've been there a lot for Paula. Why hasn't she been in touch since your surgery?'

I'VE BECOME A BRAIN MAVEN! As I have these thoughts of myself, the thoughts are also tiny impulses and electrical charges and neurotransmitters squirting over the wet machinery of my brain. My thoughts, which are things I 'have,' undergo translation from one set of symbols to another, the way ones and zeroes turn into colour pictures on a screen.

And I realize, going in to visit Jimmy the day before Christmas, that I have lost all my fear of – even my dislike of – mental illness. Not in myself, where I may not detect it, but in others. My prejudice is gone.

Jimmy says: 'This afternoon, stock values flashed a warning.' He spoons rice pudding out of a Ziploc bag. Cary, the triple-nicotine-patched erotomaniac, had an hour pass and came back with a litre tub of Kozy Shack, but there was nothing to share it in because all the bowls were being washed. 'And,' Jimmy continues, 'Chinese sounds like English spoken backwards.' He offers me some of his pudding; I decline.

'Where are you going to go if they let you out of here over Christmas? It's fifteen below.'

'They won't let me out. I serve at his satanic majesty's pleasure. But I might go to my sister's place after the new year.'

'You have a sister?'

'Nada.'

'No siblings at all?'

'No. I have a sister. Her name is Nada. Tell me who names their kid Nothing?'

'Your parents must have felt differently after having you. James is a noble name.'

'James is the usurper. The understudy. Can we turn that goddamn thing off?' The television overhead in the common room is tuned to a yule log. Someone turns it off. The only two adolescents left over Christmas are sitting in the window hutch with their bags of Kozy Shack, huddled up against each other. They've snipped the corners off their bags and are sucking the pudding out, as if from plastic teats.

'Is your mum still alive?' I ask Jimmy.

'She's sick.'

'With what?'

'Whore disease.'

'Hore –?'

'She hoovers pills and fucks strangers for fun. She was run down one night stumbling out the highway exit, glue dripping from her nose, and it took five months in hospital to rebuild her vagina.' He slaps the tabletop hard and I almost leave my shoes. Flecks of wet rice fly. 'It was just *fine* to begin with, but now it runs like clockwork!' Through the windows, Spadina Avenue stretches in a string of flashing colours south to Queen. I feel his hand feebly squeezing my forearm. 'Santa, can you help me?'

I run down to the station to get the orderlies. Christmas is hard. It makes people think of family.

189

ALTHOUGH I HAVE TO PASS the site of 'Bookshop' once on the way to Morbier's and once on the way back, I am no longer afraid to. He's suggested that I don't go into the pet store that occupies its space in 'this' reality. I have no desire to look at goddamned puppies. Part of my treatment is a cycle of 'exposure and response prevention,' and apparently just being able to walk on Dundas, across the road from the pet shop, is progress. I have to reclaim streets and then neighbourhoods one at a time. We both agree that I'll leave Bellevue Square for sometime in 2017. But I am becoming impatient. 'I feel the need to go there,' I tell him on our last session before the new year.

'Why? What's there?'

'I know people. I want to see how they're doing.' Technically, I want to confirm that they exist. 'You know that some of the people I met in the park I've seen on the ward.'

'I'm not surprised. The park is close to the institute. Who have you seen there?'

'A guy named Jimmy.'

'Are you friends?'

'Yes. I've been visiting him.' He starts writing. 'It's surprising how much of a, you know, what you'd call a real person is there, under his symptoms.'

'That surprises you?'

'I guess so. I never thought about it very much, although you see people with mental illness every day in a big city. They're out on the street, they're poor, I would guess most of them are self-medicated. And people see them as their symptoms. I did. When Jimmy's really sick, I can't see anything except his illness. The way he looks, what he does, what he *says*. Like there's no room for Jimmy.'

'Self-medication isn't an inherent part of homelessness or mental illness. Just saying.'

'I know. My point is, I feel different now. Medicine has helped me, it's helped Jimmy. And more people should recognize that if you can treat it with medicine, it must be like every other disease and no one should be ashamed to have it and others shouldn't be afraid of it.'

'This is excellent self-talk, Jean. You must have done some CBT after you lost the baby.'

The baby again. 'I saw some doctors, read a few books.'

'Are you uncomfortable talking about this?'

'No,' I say with conviction. If I have to talk about it, I'll talk about it. 'It was a huge shock and then after it happened I couldn't feel anything at all for the longest time. I was convinced Nick would never be born. For the last two months, I was really sick. Then I had more trouble afterwards.'

'Postpartum depression.'

'No,' I say. 'Psychosis. Postpartum psychosis.'

'That must sit heavy.'

'Oh yeah,' I say 'The postpartum depressives look down their noses at us. I heard voices.'

'How did you feel about that?'

'It was very scary. I knew they weren't real, but I still heard them.'

'I wonder if you were already suffering from seizures that far back? Could have been a complicating factor.'

'Maybe. It doesn't matter. It happened.'

'What did these voices say to you?'

'Oh god. Well, they didn't like me much. They told me I

was a bad person and that even the baby knew it and the baby was going to die because it would prefer being dead to having me for a mother.'

'I bet that was just for starters. But you didn't see anything? No hallucinations?'

'I don't know. How would I know?'

'Right,' says Morbier. 'Well, it's entirely possible that these were early manifestations of your bad wiring.'

He's so fixated on the etiology of my disease that he's not paying attention now. 'This isn't that,' I say.

'What isn't?'

'I thought we weren't going to do therapy. Why are you asking me about my feelings?'

'Your emotional life, if it remains within what I'd consider a wide spectrum of normal – including brief relapses – is a good way for us to measure your progress. When I asked you how you felt about hearing voices, you gave me a rational, balanced answer that included naming the feeling. This is *not* the answer, I'll hasten to add, that you might have given me if you were still traumatized by your experience with psychosis.'

'Us?'

'Hm?'

'You said a way for *us* to measure your progress.'

'I mean your caregivers, including me.'

'How many caregivers do I have? Are you all talking to each other?'

'You're misunderstanding me. You and your husband signed documents admitting you to Western for surgery. Then you were transferred to the Clarke and into my care, which meant I had to know what the issue you'd been treated for was, of course. How else can we coordinate your care? This is about your recovery. Although we can do up other papers that restrict everything that comes up in here to *this* room.'

'Are you a shrink?'

'No. Not really. I'm a specialist. You're safe here, Jean. Can I ask you, have you heard voices at other times in your life? Before Nick?'

There are certain problems that cannot be solved and one of these is the liar. Whether for strategic or emotional reasons, the liar who is convinced of the necessity of his lie will adapt the defence that he never lies. And a person who is trying to convince you that they are not lying could be lying about never lying, *exemplum* Morbier's slick explanation of who *us* was. The liar is an example of Schrodinger's cat: at all times half-true and half-false.

'Jean?'

'Not the way I did after Nick was born. But I'd had issues before. I played mind games on myself. To freak myself out.'

'Ah,' he says, but he's writing again.

'I imagined a voice was telling me to stop breathing, that I wasn't allowed to breathe and that I would never be able to breathe again. But obviously I never died or even fainted – I'd always have to breathe in finally. And the voice would say: *This time, I let you live.*'

'You were how old?'

'Eleven. Twelve.'

'Your voice never told you to hurt yourself or anyone else?'

'No. It was a trick I played on myself. To see how scary it would get if I pretended some kind of paranormal thing was inside my head, like a parasite, and it had taken over my thoughts. I'd have to prove to it that I was myself and *it* couldn't exist.'

'Did you prove it?'

'I must have. It went away.'

'Or you just got used to it.' He smiles and his eyebrows seem to lift off his face. 'How did you get over it?'

'Oh god, I don't remember. I called it the vampire and pictured it as this dark, square male face covered in hair. I told him I could *make* him stop talking to me just by trying, and then I would. But an hour later, he'd say, *I stopped talking so you'd think you were free of me. I might stop for ten years and come back!* So then I'd tell him as soon as I get distracted by something, you'll disappear. *No, I'll just be watching*, he'd say. And so on.'

'So far his case is more convincing than yours. I didn't hear a proof in there.'

'I told him if I'm hearing him in my own head then he's reaching me through my own consciousness, you know?'

'Uh-huh?'

'So he's inside of me, no matter where he thinks he came from. No matter how much he wants to pretend he's separate.'

'Beat him at his own game. How did he like that?'

'He tried to tell me that one day I'd want him to be in charge. That there were things I couldn't or wouldn't do on my own. But I told him he'd have to show himself in person if he ever planned on taking over. And I've never seen him.'

'Maybe Ingrid is a more sophisticated version of your vampire?'

'It was a logic puzzle, like an existential one. I think a lot of people do it. To prove to themselves that they're really there.'

'So are you really here?'

'I better be. Or you're wasting your time.'

He laughs. A person's laughter tells you a lot more about their trustworthiness than their reassurances. He's okay, is what his laugh says. But maybe he knows how to laugh in a trustworthy way...

He asks: 'Do you think Ingrid would have visited Jimmy in the hospital?'

'Ingrid? I don't think Ingrid knows Jimmy exists. I was the one keeping a vigil in the park.'

'I'm asking, given the little you got to know her, do you think she was the sort of person to visit a stranger in a hospital? Is she as kind as you?'

'Well. If a doppelganger is the exact same person as the doppelgangee, then I guess she would be. But if she's different inside, how would I know? She'd had a surgery, one that I haven't.'

'You didn't mention that.'

'A recent scar, over her ribs.'

'Show me where.'

I put my hand under my left breast. 'Here.'

'What was the surgery for?'

'To harvest some bone, she said.'

He turns the little black clock on the stool toward him. He does this instinctively within three minutes of the end of our sessions. 'Maybe she was telling you she's Adam to your Eve.'

'Turns out to be the other way around.'

'I have faith in you, Jean. You've battled demons before and won. And so you have this time. Because Ingrid is gone.'

When he speaks of her in the past tense, I get a little shock. She's gone and I'm still here.

'Time,' he says. 'Let's continue this in the new year.'

JANUARY 2ND, WHICH IS THE quietest day of the year, I find myself haring around the basement, looking for pictures of Paula and me from when we were kids. I've had dreams about my sister since matters have regularized. Normal dreams that feel like memories as well as their extensions into fantasy. Usually they're similar: a scene from our childhood backyard, the one on Dunview with the two big white sidewalk slabs just a step down from the kitchen's sliding door. Dad found them in a grassy lot and dragged them home behind his Volvo in a tin wheelie bed he made himself. Easier, he said, than going to Canadian Tire. The backyard has only a few elements in it, and these are the same elements I can bring to mind when I try to remember it: those two uneven, tilty sidewalk pieces, sitting atop glinting white gravel the size of acorns. Square shrubbery on three sides with birches rising behind them.

When I was ten, I broke a bottle of vitamins on one of those white slabs and I can feel the fear as I pinch up each tablet in trembling fingers and try to collect the glass pieces without making a sound. It was a miracle he didn't come booming down the stairs at the noise of the big bottle shattering. I couldn't put it into the garbage where it would be discovered, so I swept it into a paper bag and crept down the street to the mailbox and dropped it into the chute.

That's the backyard Paula and I are sitting in. In the grass, playing with our trucks. I'm seven or eight, she's ten or eleven. It could be an accurate recollection, except that the vitamin tablets are lying here and there in the grass, glowing orange within green. I have my own point of view,

196

which is to say, I don't see myself, I see my surroundings. I'm inside my childhood body.

I get up and start collecting the tablets. The more of them I pick up, the more appear, as if they're multiplying through being seen. They are strewn around the base of the birches. I glance up to the house and see my father's shadow behind the upper curtains, pacing. He throws a window open and looks right at me, sees what I'm doing, and his red face bulges out of the frame like a parade balloon, his huge eyes inky black.

Paula makes a run for it. A woman wearing a beautiful black dress comes into the backyard and scoops her up. I don't see her face, but I know it's not our mother. Paula goes with her and they disappear through the gate. In this, and other dreams like it, the woman who takes Paula appears over and over until I begin to 'understand' that this is Paula's new mother. And that is *my* father whose face bursts from an upstairs window. Paula's new father is in another house, but we are sisters! Are we not sisters? Our house, squatting on its foundation of broken stone, starts to shake and come loose of its plot.

I don't put as much store in dreams as Dr Morbier would like me to. He says talking about them lubricates real memory, but I tell him there is much I would prefer not to lubricate. I don't want to know what the vitamins in the grass mean. I don't want to know why Paula has a different mother whose face I can't see. Just because you can (try to) interpret a dream doesn't mean you should. It's like getting your fortune told, I tell him. You don't really believe in it, but once you hear what the palm reader has to say, you can't forget it, either.

Morbier backed off. He seems more interested in Paula now than he is in Ingrid. Why does my sister have another mother? How can she be my sister, then? And where is *my* mother, he wants to know. The woman in black is not her – this I seem sure of – but my real mother does not appear in these dreams.

Our lived lives end up feeling compact in retrospect. Some periods grow together in memory and become one, while others, important or not, vanish like they never happened. My experience of my life is the same as my experience with books: so vital when I'm present, forgotten afterwards. I can barely recall the names of the main characters in my favourite novels. I feel their longings and I might still fear for them in a specific way, but I can't remember very much. I couldn't bring to mind the way Virginia Woolf wrote a sentence well enough to make even a feeble imitation. I can't hear her in my mind, nor the rhythms of any poems I have ever read. I don't recall, but for a few very significant exceptions, the most stirring lines from the most moving plays I have ever seen.

Where does it go, all this happening? The books that took root as pictures and sounds in my mind – sensations sometimes absolutely like life – are gone as soon as the book is finished. Same as my days. It's like a fuse is burning just steps behind me, reducing my lived life to ash.

While Ian is with the boys at the rink, I get down a few of the old bankers boxes from their shelves. After the first one, I vacuum up a dozen years of settled dust, and then change the bag and suck up some more.

I find the baby pictures of Nick. We didn't take as many of Reid. He's chided me for that, for expunging him from the official record. But after the first baby, when you see there are nine thousand photographs you'll never have time to organize, you go easy on baby number two. And baby one is making it hard to snap photos spontaneously because he is stuck to you like the monster from *Alien*.

Still, I can't find any photos of Reid by himself. He's in many of the family photos, the majority of which show him with an expression as demented as he could come up with the instant before the picture was snapped. An earlier box contains albums from the wedding and our first couple of years dating. These take some time to work through. It's only from this distance that I can see how good looking I really was. God, to have that skin again and those legs, which seem longer on my younger self. I had dimensions Pierre Trudeau would have appreciated. Now I have fifteen extra pounds and a gravity-induced ratio problem.

I can't bring back a single memory from our wedding except the images I encounter in the albums. Before we had Nick, I looked at these pictures regularly. It was just Ian and me, and for some years, the wedding was the highpoint of our lives. Then I got pregnant, but only for seven months. Afterwards, I had my troubles and put the wedding albums away, as if to punish myself for thinking *that* was happiness. A living baby was happiness. When Nick arrived two years later, I was grateful he was a boy. I was afraid of giving birth to a girl. That I might have to love and grieve her all at once.

After my miscarriage, I didn't feel the emotions my wedding photos had once roused in me, and for years I've left these albums uncracked. When I look at them now, the people in them are so foreign. They're as generic as the photos that come in new picture frames. The bride covers her mouth as the groom withdraws the cakey fork. A blur of arms below a garter frozen in mid-air. Some of the people are dead. There are dead people at my wedding. I can't think of a thing I said or did that night. Nor what I ate (salmon mousse?) or if we made love or not (I'm sure we did), or what happened the next day.

Strangely, of Paula there is nothing. She is in one wedding photo, surrounded by people who were my close friends at the time. She thinks nothing of broadcasting her couchbound self in real time now, but perhaps then she disliked being photographed. I don't remember. We fought at times, maybe we fought that night. She could go weeks cutting me in the hallways of our childhood home. A famous period after her first boyfriend broke up with her was when she went silent on everyone she knew for the better part of a year. Then came accusatory emails and phone rants that sounded nothing like her. I look back on it and wonder if it was the earliest hint of the schwannoma.

It's worrisome now that I can't locate any pictures of myself before I met Ian. They might be in a box with only pictures of me in it. Self storage. There are albums at my mother's house, but if I begin asking for them, she'll want to know why, and you can't lie to our dreamproof mother. Standing in the basement with open boxes all around me, I try to think of where else my older albums might be. I go check in Nick's room. We keep extra pillows and blankets in his closet, along with unused candles, a humidifier, a painting I hate, and an ironing board. I feel along the blankets and remove them. The closet is deep, and once the clutter's been moved, I encounter two more boxes. One of them is full of silent Super 8 movies still in their orange Kodak containers. The other has a projector in it.

Ian won't be home for another hour, longer if there is a stop for treats on the way. The projector is simple to set up, and a diagram engraved on the metal side of the motor housing shows how to loop your film through the gates and set the sprockets onto the spindles. It's got a handle and weighs almost nothing. I plug it in and test the bulb; it works. In the middle of Nick's room, I hold the thing and point the lens at a bare spot on his wall, between a José Bautista poster and a poster from the movie *Rogue One*. I flip the switch. The film chatters through the insides of the projector and a box of dark grey shudders onto the wall. Cracks splatter to a burst of light and then our mother's face appears. It jumps up and down because I can't hold the projector steady. I have to drag Nick's side table around and put it down.

My mother is talking to the camera. She's sitting at a table and the ocean moves over her shoulder. They're on the *Queen Elizabeth*, the first one, when it was still the Cunard Line – their gold laurel shines on her wineglass. Then a hard cut and the view is of the ocean all the way to the horizon. It pans over the railing to where my father is standing, staring into the lens with his bright, evil eyes. I can smell the burning soot coming from the liner's funnels, but it's dust on the projector bulb.

It's their honeymoon. Before they knew much about each other or what they wanted from their lives. For my father it was already booze. Later came the women, the pills, the car wrecks, the bad paper. I didn't attend his funeral and felt no shame about it. He was his fourth wife's problem. The third was the one he broke his fist on. The first and second were my mother. Here he seems undiluted. A man no one called father or fiend yet, looking at a woman he believed was the answer to all of his problems, chiefly his loneliness and his rage. I never asked him for the truth about anything. But I don't want to know the truth. I don't want to risk feeling something for him.

Another of the films shows a wide expanse of park with willow trees at its edges and two children in identical outfits romping in the grass. I stand with my shoulder against the wall and try to get a close look at their faces. It's us. We're really little, capering under a lemony light. The camerawork is shoddy: someone is stumbling down a hill as they film. The cameraman must have called to the children because the two girls stop and look back. Their faces lose their graininess as they trot toward me. I see her now, darling Paula. I want to reach into the wall and put my arms around her. A wave of grief washes over me and passes. Why did they dress us alike when we weren't twins? Suddenly, the lens faces the treetops and the sun bleaches the picture.

I put on the next reel. Same location. Off we go. I can imagine what he said: 'Don't waste all three minutes acting like idiots. Do some cartwheels or something!' We do cartwheels in the grass and our dresses fly over our heads.

From somewhere off-screen, two women appear and chase after us. They're pretending to be monsters, stalking us with huge clumsy steps, their hands formed into claws. We run away until they catch us up in their arms. Our mother has scooped me up, and the other woman grabs Paula.

I stop the film and rewind it. The women leap backwards. I turn the switch to 12 frames per second and they run in again, more slowly this time. There is real fear on our faces, as well as delight. We peel away, tumbling slowly. The first time I watched the sequence I didn't see that Paula's captor had stopped and turned to look at the camera. The light is high behind her, and sundogs swell and obscure her face, but it's Paula's mother from my dream, and she's looking into my eyes from inside the stilled frame. My heart makes a sound like an axe on wood. I turn the film off and rewind it back onto its reel, panting with fear, the skin on my neck buzzing.

I return that reel to the box. Some of the other containers have labels on them. Many have lost their descriptions:

where a label had once been glued down there is only a tracery of white dust. I'm threading another through the projector when all three boys burst into the house. I hear the skates and helmets and pads crash to the floor where later I will grumble while picking them up. They start braying for me: Mummy! Mummy! Hey, Jean!

I wonder how long they'd look for me before beginning to worry. What would they do without me? I'm the hub and the spokes, the vessel and its contents. Matryoshka!

I call them up and the thumping approaches. 'I scored on Nick!' Reid shouts from halfway up the stairs.

'It went off the back of my pad,' says Nicholas, running into the room ahead of his brother. 'It's not like you shot it and it went in.'

'But it did go in!' Reid enters, his eyes glassy from the cold.

'I also scored on Nick!' comes Ian's voice from downstairs.

'You're so hard to score on!' I say to Nick. 'They must have got lucky.'

'It *was* luck. And Dad did a slapshot! On a kid!' he shouts. 'I'm not going to try to stop a two-hundred-mile'n-hour frozen puck with the second-hand crap you bought me!'

'Watch it.'

He flops onto the bed. He hasn't noticed the projector or the fact that I'm doing something in his room without his permission. He isn't paying attention to anything but his own humiliation. 'Goalies get scored on,' I explain. 'Otherwise no one would ever play! You should be happy for these guys that they had a good skate. I bet they didn't score many and they probably took a lot of shots.'

'I was dekin'm out comin' in with the puck,' says Reid, also indifferent to the strange old-fashioned machine on Nick's side table. 'I was just lookin' through his mask, like at his eyes, lookin' at where his eyes were lookin' and –'

'Aw shut up,' Nick warns him.

'I dangled and pulled him to the left and just as he was slidin' over, I jammed it through his five-hole!' He blows imaginary smoke from his fingertip and a red Hot Wheels Corvette bounces off his head. 'You ASSHOLE!'

'Nothing but net!' Nick snarls. Reid is on top of him instantly, pounding away. 'And anyway your move wasn't a dangle, cock-booger.'

'BOYS!' I shout.

'It was dumb luck because you whiffed on the wrister I was ready for but you pussied it into the net by accident!' Nick's got his younger brother flipped over and pinned to the bed and Reid is getting red in the face, getting ready to change the temperature of the whole encounter. I grab Nick off him just as Reid horks a gob of foamy spit that goes up, pauses, and returns to his own face. Nick's laughter is cruel. 'Can't even aim your own goober!'

It's about to become a massacre when Ian walks in with hot chocolate. Both kids freeze. They aren't tamed by the appearance of the drinks as much as their fear of their father. He is a cop, after all. Me they'll carry on endlessly for, but Ian they don't mess with. 'What's this?' he asks, seeing what's actually going on in the room. 'You watching old movies?'

'Yeah.' The boys are shooting looks of murder at each other, but sugar is at hand to narcotize their animal urges. 'Get the light.'

'Oh god,' Nick moans. 'Please tell me it's 3D gay midget porn.'

'You want to know what kind of ice you're on now?' I ask him.

The lights go out and I switch the machine on. The reel

is a costume party for children. Gypsies and doggies and pirates gambol about in a dimly lit basement with a low ceiling. I see myself and Paula again. Dressed differently now, older. It's my birthday. At one point I can make out an '11' on the cake. 'Oh jeez, there's Stephanie Brunson,' Ian says. 'She lived at the corner. I had a crush on her, even when we were really little.'

'Uh, sorry,' I whisper to him, 'this is my eleventh birthday party. These are my friends and my sister. That's not your Stephanie Whatserface.'

'What are you talking about. That's Steph Brunson, and this is my eleventh birthday. That's our basement on St. Spiritu.'

'What? This is me.' I put my finger on myself on Nick's wall. 'That's Paula. This is Adam Selby who died, that's Nialle Tyler.' The boys have become quiet. 'And that's me, blowing out the candles.' On the wall, my childhood self blows out all eleven candles.

'You think I don't know what I looked like?' Ian asks. 'And I knew Nialle.'

'You grew up in Saskatchewan, Ian. There weren't the same people at your eleventh birthday party.'

Behind us, lying in the bed with their legs stretched out, our sons blow on their mugs and watch us *and* the movie. The kid in the blindfold turns with a stick in his hand; we watch, too. He spins in and out of the frame and back in.

'You're right,' Ian says. 'I just thought I recognized everyone.' He starts to leave the room.

'Hey. But you see that's me now, right? And there's Paula.'

From the hallway: 'Yeah. There's Paula.'

THEY'VE STARTED LETTING ME TAKE Jimmy to the tenth floor, which has a south-facing lounge looking down Spadina Avenue to the lake. We drag the comfy chairs to the window and stare out. He's glum because I've told him I'm going back to Bellevue Square this week, the first time in over seven months. Dr Morbier thinks I'm ready. Jimmy wants me to wait for him. But he's not likely to be out any time before spring, and I have to go. I must go.

I come by to see him weekly now. As winter grinds on, how hard it must be to have to live in a place more drab than the weather. He at last consented to a haircut and a shave, so long as I was present. I came in late one afternoon in early February, and watched his face in the mirror as Mherill cut his hair and lopped off his knotted black-and-grey beard. Little dreadlocks bounced around on the floor. She put a hot towel on his face for a while, took it off, and sprayed foam on his cheeks. When she drew the razor through it, he said, 'Looks like you're shovelling snow.'

When Mherill was finished, she'd brought his face back into the world. His head appeared squat for losing eleven inches of hair – three on top and eight below – and his brown eyes lifted away from their orbits. She wet a cloth and washed the rest of the shaving cream off and the three of us said, almost in unison, 'Holy shit.'

Jimmy ran his palms over his cheeks. 'I wanna date myself.'

He hadn't shaved in ten months. He told me whenever he got clean-shaven, it meant he'd reached the height of recovery and soon they'd have to turn him out.

Sitting by the windows, we share our four weekly donuts. I've offered to go to the schmancy place on Queen with their bacon & Cap'n Crunch donut, but he wants Tim's.

Jimmy takes the apple fritter, the Boston cream, and the chocolate-glazed. I take the maple dip. Now that we're friends, we know each other's favourites. I always leave the chocolate-glazed for him, even if I pick first. I can get one any time. He looks down at it, deciding where to chomp.

Spadina is strung with curtains of multihued blinking neon. Headlights and taillights are red and white going north and south. The wet surfaces catch reflections from everywhere and all the cars and people float upside down in it, inside a continuous psychedelic throbbing.

He eats his donuts in three bites each. He's two-thirds of the way through the apple fritter. He asks me if I'm scared to go back to the market. 'Since you're not going to wait for me, you should at least go with someone. I bet Mherill would go with you. She's a supergiver.'

'I'm going alone.'

'That's cool. You can't wait forever. This is part of your therapy, it's gotta take precedent. I understand.'

'Thank you, Jimmy.'

'I can't gain weight, you know. I burn calories all day having thoughts. I don't think they feed us enough. Thank you,' he says, holding up what's left of his fritter.

'You're welcome.'

'Obviously, *your* meds are working.'

I acknowledge that they are and reassure him that his will too. I remind him that I'm cooperating with my doctor and keeping my appointments so that I *stay* better. I've heard him say more than once that they're never letting him out of here. They're just going to keep him locked up until he withers away.

'You might have to break me out of here if they don't let me go,' Jimmy says, lifting the Boston cream to his mouth. The first time I brought donuts, he offered to demonstrate how he eats a Boston cream in one bite. His method was disgusting, but effective. He thinks it's funny. The sound of him eating it is bad enough, but it's the kind of thing you can't not watch.

'You're going to choke to death one day.'

'An honourable deaf,' he says through the mash. 'You ever fink it frew?'

'Think what through?'

He swallows. 'Ever tried to see the whole situation from her position? Could you work it all out, you know, how your life could actually be a bunch of symbols for hers?'

'What Ingrid's hallucination about *me* means?'

'Yeah. When Ingrid gets her diagnosis, she goes into shock. She sees her alter ego in a park! She's going to die and the universe is going to replace her and no one will ever know!' He's heard the whole story now. You don't skim here. If you want to make any friends in the bin, you have to spill. Otherwise, no one will trust you, not even the paranoid schizophrenics.

'Ingrid never saw me in Bellevue Square. I saw her. She wouldn't even look at me.'

'Right. So you're something she can't look at, can't face. She's not ready to accept what you mean. You can see her, because you don't know what you are –'

'I'm *her* replacement.'

'You are. She could see you if she looked, but she's in no hurry to confront you. She just keeps watch out of the corner of her eye. One day, she sends her husband into your bookstore, and when he comes out he doesn't appear to be a man who's just encountered his wife's doppelganger. She's reassured: he didn't see you. It's all in her head.'

'Then I break into her house and make her child a grilled cheese sandwich in a demonstration of transdimensional cookery.'

We pause to laugh at ourselves. He's on a sugar high. 'Finally, Ingrid confronts you at your home. She tells you she's ready. And then *you* wake up.'

'You should stay on your meds, Jimmy! The side effects are useful. So why's she dreaming *you*?'

He makes a shrugging face. 'I don't know. The chorus? The footnotes?'

'You're not a footnote.'

I can't finish my donut. He picks it off my napkin and polishes it off. 'She lived down there?' he asks, pointing with his chin at the window.

'Her house was on a street that doesn't exist. But it was down near Dundas and Beverley. I saw it.'

'You're the sickest person in this place and they let you go.'

'I got better,' I tell him, and I add a wink.

MY FAMILY TREATS ME LIKE an invalid even though I've been at work for ten weeks and it looks good on me! Their solicitations come out in little acts that are ostentatious, given the actors. Beatrice bought me a copy of *Celebrity Recipes* and a flagstone-sized slab of orangey peanut brittle and told me she knew there'd been something wrong with my colour in the summertime. I know she's concerned. You don't want the mother of your grandchildren to go off the actual deep end, or even die! She's not that bad, for god's sake.

Reid has put himself in charge of the toaster. In the after-school specials he watches, sick people are forever being given toast. He has made some variations on the theme, which include butter-and-sugar-and-cinnamon toast; linzer torte toast, which is two pieces spread with cream cheese and red jam, cut into one-centimetre strips and arranged in a criss-cross fashion; egg-in-the-hole in rye bread and egg-in-the-hole in cinnamon-raisin bread, the discovery of which put paid to his rye version.

Lately, Nick has been giving me looks of frank fear. My illness has scared him straight and he's upped his game at home. I have seen him put dirty dishes *into* the dishwasher, and once I had to leave the kitchen to keep from gasping because he was sweeping crumbs off the countertop into his hand. When I see his anxiety, I take the opportunity to have a quiet talk with him. It's 2017, it's Canada, it's Toronto. Good people are looking after your mother. And these things happen, they keep happening the longer you're around and the more people you care about. But look at me

(I'll put in a grand curtsey here): I'm in one piece, feeling better every day, and eating like a horse.

'If you die, I'm going to kill myself,' he says.

'I'd feel the same way if anything happened to you. Look, it's awful to feel scared, but so what? Being scared means you're part of something you care about, and that's a good way to spend your time on Earth.' If the lights are out and I'm in bed with him, he'll talk to me like he used to, when he was littler, about what scares him, and he's willing to hear his mother tell him something not untrue and not unkind. 'Life is like this. We don't know how good things will happen, how bad things will happen. We just know they'll happen.'

'Not if you're dead. Things don't happen to you when you're dead, right?'

'If anyone knows the answer to that question, they haven't been able to pass a message back.'

'I bet if you die, all three of us will kill ourselves in horrible ways.' His tone of voice acknowledges he's being ridiculous. I go along with his idea of lightening the moment.

'How you gonna do it?' I ask him. 'I mean, if you're going to make a big symbolic gesture like that, I hope you have a plan.'

'We'll stand on the front lawn and drink all the stuff that's under the sink until we collapse on the ground, twitching and gushing blood from our eyes. People'll come and try to rescue us, but then they won't be able to, because we'll be *dead* from drinking poison.'

'You should have a sign that says HONK IF YOU'VE LOST SOMEONE.'

'That's nice, Mum. I wonder when people would realize something was wrong. Probably when the diarrhea started shooting out of our noses.'

'I wouldn't stop for that,' I say, getting out of his bed and tucking the covers around him. 'I'd throw you a quarter, though.'

Ian is not his usual self. He follows me around the house as though I might veer off course and walk through a wall. There have been nights of attempted normality while we both pretend to watch television, but in bed, I feel him not sleeping, his body stiff and alert beside me. I wonder how far the effects of my illness will extend. I imagine my sickness like a layer of smoke that crawls along the floor and goes into the boys' bedrooms and under their beds.

My husband is tender with me. Does that feel right? Is this okay? I can tune his thoughts in and he's wondering how he's going to raise two kids alone.

And then the days start to go by again. The roses he gave me for when I came home have lowered their bloodblack heads and time shows on the inside of the vase in powdery white lines. At the bank, the trucks of new cash roll in through the back.

I never told Ian what Nick said to me. I've just kept my eye on our now thirteen-year-old. For his birthday, we got him a phone and an electric razor. 'I'm not old enough to shave!' he protested, but Ian ran the back of his hand up his face and said *ouch*.

BELLEVUE SQUARE IS BRIGHT WITH snow. I come up Denison, passing Dr Morbier's home and office without so much as a glance. My eyes are trained on the corner of the square, white and shiny as an unlicked envelope flap.

Tomorrow is Valentine's Day. It's a welcome break from the monotony of repetitive thoughts that grow on you from the middle of January. *Will this ever end?* is one of the thoughts. Others are *I want to kill* and *I want to die*. Of course, Valentine's is only a pleasure if you have someone to love, and I doubt the collection of misfits I used to know in the park have anyone to love them. I doubt the greeting-card companies have included them in their budget projections.

I recognize a couple of parkies right off the bat, and feel thankful. Ritt is still lurking around the snowed-over wading pool. I don't remember if I ever paid him the remaining money I owed him. I'm sure he's too shy to ask. I don't have enough on me.

Miriam is staking out her territory beside the Kiever. New faces sit on the bench beside the white-capped Al Waxman statue. Bronze is a cruel material. It makes you look that little bit deader.

I cross to Miriam, crunching deep through the thin icy layer on top of the snow. The six inches of wet pack beneath it grabs my boot and tries to keep it.

She doesn't recognize me at first. She gives me a hard, unfriendly look. 'Can I help you?'

'It's Jean.'

'Jean. Lord. From St. Mike's.'

213

'No. We know each other from here. We've talked before, but I haven't been around for a while.'

'Sorry, dear.' She glances off. 'I believe you, but I'm not focused on names or dates anymore. Are you parked near here? There's a recessed hydrant.'

'I'm on foot,' I say, and she looks down and notes my snow bound Blundstones. 'Are you sure you don't remember me? I was friends with Cullen and Jimmy. And Ritt over there.'

'I know Jimmy.'

'You do know Jimmy.' What would Miriam be in Ingrid's dream? 'Jimmy's in CAMH. He's been ill most of the winter.'

'Yes,' she says. 'Poor boy. He's missing a gene.'

'Is he –'

'When he gets drunk he produces masterpieces in electronic music, but by nature he's a teetotaller.'

'I don't know if we're talking about the same Jimmy.'

'I'd be ashamed to be him, though.'

In the summer she was a keen-eyed opportunist with a talent for gab and a heart full of charity. She once told me she made forty dollars an hour in the summertime. She owned a boat in the port and slept there. It doesn't look like she's making a living now, though. Grey stuffing made of a synthetic material leaks from her parka.

'I mean thin Jimmy with the beard. Grey-and-black beard, although he – they – shaved it off. It's okay if you don't remember him. I was just coming over to say hi. Do you want a coffee?'

'Yeah,' she says. 'Triple double. Come back I'll give you something for him.'

I trudge up Augusta looking for coffee. So far it's not too difficult being back here. Jimmy and Morbier would both be proud of me. Maybe if it were the same season when I first came here it'd be more frightening. But the cold and the monochromatism dampen the place's power.

Kensington Market has the last bank machine in Toronto that dispenses five-dollar bills. I get five of them. I go all the way up to Pamenar to get Miriam an americano. They pull the best shot in the market. She's told me on a number of occasions that she's Turkish, so I believe her. She says she can't get Turkish coffee in the market, but I doubt she's ever looked for it. 'You don't want to meet other Turks,' she says. 'If you see two Turks sitting beside each other and they don't start arguing within ten minutes, it means one of them is dead.'

I give her the hot coffee. 'How many years have you been here?'

'It's 2015 now?'

'2017, actually. Happy New Year.'

'1985, I came.'

'To Kensington or Canada?'

'Canada. You mean here outside the *shul*? Only fifteen or so. First I was a nurse, in neonatal units. At night, I drank to sleep. Then I drank in the day. I worked over there on University Avenue. Sick babies, happy babies. They came and went.' When she purses her lips to suck at the coffee, fissures appear in them, reminding me of my own grandmother, her red-lipsticked mouth pursing to kiss me and those lines appearing in a darker red.

'You don't drink anymore?'

She shakes her head. 'Oh no. No. It's a very very very toxic dance.'

'Are you still giving out milk?'

'I have my people. I don't have room for anyone new.'

'I can get my own milk. You don't have many customers today. From the look of it.'

'Ritt drinks my milk. Cleone drinks my milk. As long as I'm here: milk.'

'Have you seen Cullen?'

'I don't know a Cullen.' She goes up the steps of the synagogue and disappears through one of the doors. She returns with a couple of books in a plastic Loblaws bag. 'Give these to Jimmy,' she says. The two books are *Peer Gynt* and *No More Curried Eggs for Me*.

'He lent these to you?'

'He did.'

'What did you think?'

'*Peer Gynt* was funny.'

The door to the synagogue opens, and a woman in a long black robe emerges. She looks like a drawing by R. Crumb, hair in tight black rings and a Sphinxy nose. She stops behind Miriam, leaning in to make herself known. 'Hello!'

'Rabbi!'

'Sorry,' she says to Miriam and quickly to me, 'Hi,' and she makes eye contact for an instant too long. Then she returns her considerable charm to Miriam. 'Love, you're blocking the entrance. Can you find somewhere else to collect your tips?'

'This is the sidewalk,' Miriam says, firmly planted. 'It's city property. Rabbi Shoshana, this is my friend.' She takes my arm in a show of solidarity I haven't agreed to. 'I'm giving her some books to give to a friend who's sick. Which is one of the Ten Commandments...'

Rabbi Shoshana looks at me again and twigs. 'Ingrid Fox!' she says. 'I thought I was going crazy for a second –' She takes me in her arms! 'Where have you been? I thought you were dead.' She half spins me back to Miriam. 'This is the *author* Ingrid Fox. She talked to our writing circle, gosh, three years ago? Best talk we ever had. But of course everyone's writing these days. So, listen – ' she says, but I can't hear the rest over the high-pitched squeal in my ears. She called me…

I'm going crazy. I've imagined this park, this synagogue, this lady rabbi, all of it! Or… there really is an Ingrid Fox, and Katerina is actually dead, and… Morbier? 'You know August Morbier, don't you?' She's not listening. 'Hey!'

'I'm having a fundraiser in five hours and the tables aren't here and it turns out we don't have some kind of certificate –'

'Do you know August Morbier!'

'– from the fire department, who?'

'Doctor. August. Morbier.'

'She's from the park,' says Miriam, apparently in my defence.

'Mirrie, my kishkas are sweating from the stress. Do please be nice and go around the side.'

'Give these to Jimmy,' Miriam says, pushing the bag into my hands. She vanishes around the corner of the synagogue to stalk her quarry on Bellevue Avenue.

'Are you sure you're okay?' the rabbi asks me.

'I'm fine,' I say.

'Who's August Morbier?'

'No one.'

'There's a fellow right here on Denison Square, a Dr Mourguet. Do you mean him?'

'No. I made a mistake.'

Shoshana waits a beat, leaving space for me to keep talking. 'Well, it's nice to see you again!' she says at last. 'When's your next book coming out?'

'Soon.'

'You should visit us again – the group loved you.' She opens the synagogue door.

'Hey, wait. You know, I have some jumbled memories of my afternoon with your group.'

'Evening. And we're a *circle*. A writing circle.'

'Right! I know this is going to sound fishy, but I don't recall that evening very much. I had a bump on the head a year or so ago, and – ' My mind is swimming.

'But you're okay now...'

'Oh yeah. Much better.'

'You should come visit again. Except we do themes these days, instead of individual authors. You should come to Voice Appropriation in the springtime.'

'Yeah. Maybe I will.'

'Oh lord, here they are again. You fellas are back too soon, I don't have the certificate!' She's off to talk to a couple of palookas in a truck.

I walk briskly across the park, my legs stiff. By the time I get to Dundas, I'm half-jogging. How can she know Ingrid Fox? I'm out of breath running across Bathurst on the yellow, but I keep going. My thighs burn. I have no time to work this all out before it changes shape on me again.

The name of the pet store is Pet Project. I go in and set off a round of barking. I pretend I know what I'm looking for and start down an aisle of rabbit bedding. The rows correspond with the position of the shelves in Bookshop. Above me, the lights are the same. The switches are in the same places. A solid wall with two large windows in it occupies the space where I'd had sliding shelves. A door in the middle leads to the puppy and kitty room behind. Hopeful animals look out at me. Can't help you.

'Ma'am?' someone says. 'Looking for anything specific?'

The speaker is a handsome, middle-aged man in a collared Pet Project shirt. His nametag says Terrence. 'Oh, for Christ's sake,' I say.

'I'm sorry?'

'Was this a bookstore?'

'I don't know. Not since I was here.'

'Which is how long?'

'Is there anything I can help you with?'

I look at him long enough to make the silence uncomfortable. Then leave without a word.

THERE WERE TWO STORIES ON my Facebook feed this morning that seemed to be in cahoots with each other, and could have something to do with my condition. In one, a link to an article in the *Guardian* that went through the evidence in support of something called the 'ancestor simulation,' which proposes there is probably a civilization in the universe with enough computing power to run a simulated reality with self-aware simulants, i.e., us. It's real only to those inside the simulation; outside, it's a form of entertainment or education.

In the other story, three media outlets, including a gossip website, sued the FBI for information on how they hacked the iPhone of a husband-and-wife terrorism team. Under this story, the comments were split. Half thought the media was obligated to report on how government powers hacked a phone, the other half figured the media just wanted to learn how to do it. If everyone knows how to do it, it's not exactly hacking, is it? It's first past the post, to the first hacker go the spoils. It's the end of lying, the natural conclusion of the end of privacy, and the beginning of an evolutionary leap in which humans find new and different ways to hide from each other.

The second story makes the first so much more plausible. For what am I now but a hacked mind?

WHEN I'M NEXT AT THE hospital, they're busy putting up their spring decorations. Because they're a non-denominational public hospital there are no large pink cardboard eggs taped to the windows, nor addled bunnies dealing candy, nor, for that matter, the paschal lamb. Instead they've drawn flowers on all the windows and some are even coloured in, reducing the amount of light that reaches the lobby. Still, it's a light of springtime intensity, nourishing and spirit-lifting everywhere it falls. Walking to the elevators, I slip on a wet teabag and pull a blue-gowned man to the floor with me. I apologize profusely and ask him if he's hurt. 'I'm not that sensitive,' he says, disentangling his hand from my hair.

I take the elevator up to three and sign in. They know to give me the key to the tenth floor because they trust me and because Jimmy is supposed to be discharged, finally, at the end of this month. I'm secretly relieved because I don't want to have to keep coming back to this place.

'Longest inmate,' he proudly calls himself now. He's been here seven months. After forming him a half a dozen times, they got a special order to keep him at their discretion. I can't say he's been thankful about it. He's compared himself to a man on death row.

On my way to Jimmy's room, a big man in a white overcoat comes around the corner. And holy god if it isn't Cullen. I stop, stunned. 'Cullen? Hey! Cullen!' He's got a badge pinned to his overcoat pocket with the name DR JOSEPH MACDONALD. The photo is not of Cullen. 'I'm so relieved to see you! What are you doing here?'

'So good to see you as well! How have you been?'

'I'm good.' He doesn't recognize me. 'We know each other from the park. Jean.'

'Jean!'

'I was worried about you!'

'Oh, I've been buried in work.' He scuttles into a room and emerges with a clipboard. 'I better finish my rounds. Are you being checked in?'

'No. I'm visiting Jimmy, actually. Have you been in to see him?'

We're interrupted by one of the orderlies. 'Is Mr Gossage bothering you?' he asks me.

'Who?'

The orderly takes the clipboard out of Cullen's hands and puts it into an acrylic holder screwed to the wall. Then he's on to untangle the next mess.

'Are you a patient here?' I ask Cullen.

'Yes. Well, not always. I have a lab as well.'

'You told me once you'd worked as a chemist at U of T. You sounded like you knew your stuff.'

'Oh I know my stuff. Just because I'm off my tits, excuse the egyptianism, doesn't mean I don't keep working and I don't keep learning. The learning never ends. I'm learning here, too.'

'What are you learning?'

'To take my meds!' He laughs and then starts coughing wet, deeplung coughs. 'You visiting Jimmy?'

'I was coming to see him right now.'

'Hey... you have ward privileges, don't you?'

'No. Ah, *no*. I can only take Jimmy. And that's to the tenth floor, not outside.'

'Shit.' He beckons me toward the common room. One of the shopping channels is on. I count no one watching it. 'Remember that thing I told you about in the park?'

'You told me a lot of things, I don't remember all of them.'

'I have a couple lab assistants upping their dose today. They'll feel better if I can be there with them. I've levelled out. I'm good now.'

'Just slow down. A dose of what?'

'You don't remember.' The look on his face: I've really let him down. 'This is the anti-Heisenberg drug. We're in testing!'

I recall this, but I thought we'd been talking about *Breaking Bad*. 'Are you making meth?'

He laughs heartily. 'No, dear. It's called – are you ready for this? – dimethyltryptaminetetrahydrocannabichomene. Uploaders call it No-mind.'

'There really is a No-mind?'

'Get me out of here after you see Jimmy. They'll let you sign me out. And you can try some.'

'Why are you wearing someone else's badge?'

He lifts it up and inspects it. 'No, this is me. Look again.'

I look again. It's a black man, and it's not him. 'That's *not* you.'

'It's my lab name. You think they'd still give me my funding if they knew I was insane?'

'I'm not sure I can help you. See you later, Mr, uh, Gossage.'

His look sours. He follows me down the hall. 'Wait, wait. You know the Large Hadron Collider, the LHC? Big steel donut under the border of France and Switzerland?'

'I've heard of it.'

'You know what they're doing down there? Detecting the smallest particles in the universe by looking for their *waste products*. They're astrophysical turd hunters! They can't *see* what they're looking for, so they've got to infer it from degradation. When you get to the point where you're hunting for garbage by inference, you might as well measure the inside of a soap bubble! You know what they're looking for?'

'I thought they found it.'

'The Higgs boson? That piece of shit? That's a swine's tooth compared to what they're really digging for. But they're not going to find it with the LHC. The Chinese are building a collider *three times* the size, and they're not going to find it either. But I can find it. You just have to get me out of here for a few hours.'

'What is *it*?' I've had to stop walking. I don't want to take this conversation into Jimmy's room because I don't know what kind of mood Jimmy will be in. And I'm still trying to figure out if Cullen is a genius or a lunatic. 'You expect me to believe *you've* found something more important than what all those people underground have?'

He turns shoulder-to-shoulder in collusion, starts drawing lines on an invisible surface in the air. 'You know how in the game of Clue you go from the conservatory to the lounge by a secret passageway?' Diagonal line. 'And the study to the kitchen by another?' An up-and-down line in the air. 'Imagine all the particles in the universe connected to each other like that.'

'Quantum, baby. Can I go?'

'You can map all of spacetime onto a single point – it's true – and when you do, you can send a signal through that point and whatever's on that signal will be carried everywhere all at once. It's the intra-universal organic web, the transmission layer, I call it. But they need a particle accelerator from here to the moon just to see *waste products* from it, you know? Are you following now?' I am, sort of, with regrets. 'This is where Heisenberg comes in. What if we cancel out the observer effect? Get rid of the looking but keep the seeing?'

'Oh, right. You did tell me about this.'

'See, you change the frequency of the observer's perception with consciousness-altering drugs and yoke them to computers fitted with steady-state quantum microscopes,' he says, like he's stating the obvious. 'No-mind is administered in small doses at first. That allows the subject to acclimatize to super-high doses before they get any of the negative side effects like death or sporing. We're trying to get to the exact balance of compounds needed to *effect* upload without degrading data or killing the uploaders.'

'Who are uploading to the transmission layer.'

'Yes, Jean, yes! To the *hard drive* of the cosmos. We put all of, of, of human culture and history, all of the experience, the expertise, the art, the science, the music –'

'Our blogs.'

'By gum, anything! It's quite a commitment. I mean, they're wet-hooked right into the computers. Gives us slingshot clock-speed that uses *today's* internet to build links!'

'You're insane. What future civilization is going to want to read our blogs?'

'And our comic books, bootlegs, cures, operas, our spoken word performances, how to read Braille, every formula science has ever come up with, episodes of *China Beach*, all of Mervyn Peake's *Gormenghast*. All of our pictures! Kept permanently available to anything that comes after us, whether on this planet or some other. It's the remaking of the library of Alexandria!'

The man whose badge Cullen is wearing strides toward us with a blank look on his face. Cullen removes the lanyard from around his neck and hands it over without a word. Dr Macdonald goes back to wherever he emerged from and Cullen says, 'We have to keep things on the lowdown, totally confidential. Here.' He digs in a pocket and removes a small silver pillbox. Inside are half a dozen tiny pink tablets sitting on black velvet. They are the exact size and colour of children's Aspirin. 'It's better if you chew it. Work it into your epithelials.' He pops one in his mouth and chews it up. It even smells like children's Aspirin. He holds the case out to me. 'Take a couple.'

'What is it?'

'It's the thing itself – No-mind! I trust you, Jean. You're labile, you're honest, and you're *flexible*. To do our work, that's very important, to wit what is and what isn't and what's now and what's not. It won't hurt you. It will *help* you.'

I take two of the pills. 'Maybe for later,' I tell him. I might be getting a headache.

He clicks the case shut and puts his finger beside his nose. 'I believe you will come to see "later" as a very rather particularly elusive concept, Jean. I really believe you will, Jean. I will see you later, although I'll also be here for a while. Thank you very much for our talk.'

'Thank you.' I carry on down the hallway, feeling I should tread carefully.

'Oh – do you have a good credit rating?'

'I don't know,' I call over my shoulder. I open the door to Jimmy's room. Cullen is approaching and I make quick to get behind the door and lock it. It's lucky Jimmy is asleep. I can hear Cullen breathing on the other side of the door and I remain still and silent. After another half minute, he walks away. The problem with manic depressives is that you can't wrangle with them. Mania is an airtight argument. I hear Cullen out there haranguing others, addressing their concerns with even more ornate reasoning.

I worry, though, that his basic theory makes sense. Wasn't Isaac Newton bonkers?

When the coast is clear, I go down the back stairs and return to the park. I didn't speak to Jimmy, but I know he clocked my presence, from whatever in-between place they'd put him in.

A light snow falls on College Street.

I'M NOT AN ADDICT OF anything, although I will admit to compulsions. Not bad ones, just certain things I have no control over. I have to check the mailbox when I'm walking into the house, for instance, even if I collected the mail four hours ago. Ian joked about it for years (he wasn't above sticking the day's mail back into the mailbox), but he eventually lost patience and I had to make a case for something I knew I couldn't stop doing. I told him that there was sometimes a special delivery, for instance from FedEx, or someone might drop off a handwritten note *after* the mail had come.

When I told Dr Morbier about this, he asked me if I could remember the first time I found something unusual in my mailbox, and I easily could, because I still have what I found. On my ninth birthday, I found an envelope with my first name on it in the mailbox and there was a five-dollar bill in it. It had the serial number A/Z 00000011.

Morbier of course wrote this all down. What does the A/Z mean, he wanted to know. But it means nothing. It was just the series designation. Maybe you are the first and last of something, he suggested. He wanted me to figure out what A/Z meant, but I haven't and I won't. Not everything means something, I told him. It doesn't matter. If there is anything strange about me, I'm still me.

During that session I could have told him about the current compulsion I'm dealing with: that I cannot stop thinking about Rabbi Shoshana. If I told him about her, though, I might be putting myself in a dangerous position. Because if Shoshana knows Ingrid, then Morbier is not who he claims to be. And Shoshana knows Ingrid. I owe it to myself to listen to the compulsion, or I might do the wrong thing. Shoshana is the mailbox with the hand-delivered letter in it.

I go back to Bellevue Square. The crusty snow is long gone, replaced by a slush with the texture of quicksand. It goes shklort when you walk in it. The top layer is a dump of grey wet snow an inch deep over a mantle of hardpack five months old, now mid-thaw. It's treacherous. It's cold.

I don't see Miriam, but Ritt is lurking by the public washrooms. The usual drug deal is endlessly unfolding behind the locked bathrooms. The money and the drugs go round and round like an Escher drawing.

Ritt comes to where I'm standing, across from the Kiever.

'I never paid you,' I say, getting out my billfold. I only have twenties. I give him one.

'I don't have change.'

'Keep it.'

'I want a piece of cake.'

'Well, you have twenty bucks now. Go up to Wanda's.'

'I'm gonna go up to Wanda's.'

'Better hurry before they close.'

'Remember in the olden days,' he says, 'there was cake everywhere and everyone had a piece of cake after supper in a time of prosperity when people ate richer desserts?'

'I don't think you see things as they are,' I tell him.

'That's why I take pictures of them.'

'Pictures don't see things the way they are, either.'

'But they *can* see what things are not,' he says.

He goes up to Wanda's.

I walk down the side of the synagogue, past the recessed hydrant (and really, why put it there?), and go behind the building, where I have never been. The back door, made from planks, doesn't have a handle, just a brass disc with a keyhole in it. It's a sinister door.

It opens and a man in a worsted vest and a leather kippa stands in the doorway. 'Can I help you?'

'I was looking for the lady rabbi.'

'Shoshana? She was a rental. You looking to rent?'

'No. I was looking for Shoshana. Do you know where she is usually? Which temple?'

'She's more of a travelling salesperson than an actual rabbi. Far as I know she's the same lady who used to live in the park. Was a long time ago, but I don't think she went to rabbi school. Just the same, she's got a lot of followers. On Twitter, I mean.'

'Ah. Do you know how I can reach her?'

'She uses the handle @rabbishoshana.'

'I mean, do you have a phone number?'

'That's all I know, sister.' He looks past me, as though the street might be full of possible synagogue renters.

Within an hour, I have managed to install Twitter onto my phone and made an account (@ingridftoronto), all on two dots of reception while sitting on the playground wall, my legs pressed together, shivering. It's having two kids that convinces you you can handle anything, but while I was watching the screens load one after the other, step by step, and then inputting the verification code that took more than six minutes to arrive as an email, and so on, I became lividly angry. Why am I still a part of any of this? I haven't seen Ingrid in months. I can stop seeing Dr Morbier any time I want, and I am *happy*, to be exact I am *much happier than I was*. And yet, I cannot stay away from this place. I need do nothing more than continue as I was – in my *normal* life. I can have that life.

But what if it is not the truth? Could I not easily make a Coles Notes of my whole life, as Jimmy, a schizophrenic living in stir, was able to do? A reading of the phantasmagoria that I experience as my life? But rooted elsewhere. Beside or beneath my conception, beside or above my feeling. Only as real as felt. How does that make me different from any other person on Earth who worries they're sleeping through their life? Reinforced in the witness of others, grounded in repetition, the Me that is out among other Me's. Good afternoon, sir, I confirm your existence. Sweetheart, your tongue in my mouth is confirmation of the existence of an Other. Have I got a lovely bunch of shibboleths.

You can probably take apart every detail of your life and make it stand as evidence in an unreal pattern. Why do I and my husband have the same name? We are both called John in English. Why did the entity that provided that detail do it? Why Bellevue Square?

The most obvious association to the name Bellevue is the hospital with the famed psych ward. I close Twitter and go to my notebook app and type:

Bellevue. New York City. Madness.
Ingrid the original elle, the A/elle. Jean is the B/elle.
Vue/Look.
The only consonants in Bellevue: BLV. Believe.

I save it and go back to Twitter, where it takes more swearing and furtive glancing around to figure out I have to use the 'at' sign to write to someone.

**@rabbishoshana** When will you be at the temple again?

I have the superstitious feeling that I can't leave the park.

If I do, my message will be lost or her reply will never come. It begins to snow, an instantly melting, substanceless snow that adds to the base of slush. The folded *NOW* magazine I'm sitting on is beginning to soak through.

Forty-five minutes pass and the last of the light fails. I'm the only sign of life in the park, and although the streetlamps up Augusta are glowing in different colours, here it's nearly dark. A perfect time for a mugging, but it's too cold to mug anyone.

My screen lights up.

**@ingridftoronto** There's no minyan tomorrow, but come Saturday. We get the most people on Sat, you'll be invisible. Some members of the book circle might crash it though, gotta warn ya!

**@rabbishoshana** It's not about the minyan. Are you busy right now?

RABBI SHOSHANA, A COFFEE IN front of her, is waiting for me in a booth in Steele's Tavern on Yonge Street above Dundas. The bar is almost empty, and there's a single chair and a mic stand on the tiny stage in the front window. The piece of white cardboard leaning against the chair says in red sign paint, LONNIE JOHNSON ELECTRONIC VIOLIN 7 AND 9 PM.

We barely have a moment to say hello before the server comes. His nametag says STEELE. A grey pushbroom moustache sits on his upper lip. I order a glass of red.

'Red what?' he asks.

'Red wine?'

'I have beer. You eating?'

'What's good?'

'The breadsticks are free,' he says, snatching a drinking glass full of sesame-seed-speckled breadsticks off the table beside us. 'Apart from that, the hot hamburger is good, the boneless fish steak, and the shad roe with bacon.'

'The what?'

'The shad roe with bacon.'

'We don't want any of that,' Shoshana says. 'Can you make chips?'

'Liver'n chips?'

'Just the chips.'

'Sure,' I say. 'I'll have… chips. I'll have mine with the liver?'

'You bet,' Steele says. 'Grow hair on yer chest.' He returns to the bar, splitting the light spilling in from the front. The walls are upholstered in a velvety red fabric and

233

hung with scuffed mirrors. The menus are tall enough to hide behind.

'Is that the owner?'

'I think so,' says Shoshana. 'I don't come here that often.'

Steele returns with a beer for me. 'Oh, I didn't order –'

'Yeah, all right, whoops!' he says, spinning around with it and expertly containing the suds. He puts the beer down in front of a man at the bar.

'So, why did you need to get spiritual advice at this hour? Or is this about something else?'

'Remember I told you about that bump on my head? Well, it's a, it's worse than a bump. I have a brain tumour.' Her eyes go wide. 'It's okay for now. But it's affected some parts of my memory. And... there are phenomena.'

'Phenomena?'

'Hard to describe. What you said, my talk to your book club? I don't remember that at all.'

Shoshana puts her hand over mine. 'Oh, Ingrid I am so sorry. How bad is it?'

'They're doing everything they can. I want you to tell me about that night.'

'It was three years ago!'

'Try.'

'It was a smallish group. There were three of our ladies. One guy. Fella who comes and listens. Never speaks a word. One of the ladies gave you a rough ride!'

'What about?'

'Oh, gosh. She thought your detective had never been to detective school, to judge by her methods.'

'Was *she* a detective?'

'Just a cranky lady who reads a lot of books. She comes to all the meetings.' Shoshana's phone goes *A-men!* and she checks it. 'Shoot, I have to take this.' She goes and stands by the phone booth at the front. I hear plates clacking. *Two chips one no livah.* I watch Steele come down the length of the restaurant, shearing the light again, a tray aloft in his right hand.

He sets the plates down. 'You two students? Taking the stewardesses' course at Ryerson?'

'I'm a writer,' I tell him. 'She's a rabbi.'

'A writer, huh? What kind of stuff you write?'

'Oh, this and that. Mysteries, mainly.'

'Like crime?'

'Like crime.'

'You base any of it on real stuff?'

'Sure,' I say.

Now he sits down, pointing his knees out of the banquette. 'I bet real-life stuff happens allava time and you crime writers just change the names. 'At's what I'd do. You know what takes balls, though? You write the fictional novel. That's what the smart money says. I got this idea about a guy who climbs a mountain, and I'm thinking there's an avalanche.' He drifts away into thought. 'Anyway, he finally gets to the top of the mountain and he looks, and he looks, and there's the sunrise.' He shows me the sunrise with wiggling fingers. 'But guess what?'

'What?'

'He's undead!'

'Wow! When did that happen? On the way up?'

'No, he was always undead.'

'And that's how it starts?'

'No. That's the whole thing. I'm just giving you the broad outlines.'

'Can I have some ketchup?'

Rabbi Shoshana is now outside the tavern, still on her

phone. Steele returns with the Heinz. 'You're right. It's boring,' he says.

'No, no –'

'It's *lacking* something. Hey, I'm being rude. I'm Clark.'

'Clark Steele? Not Kent or Man of Steel, but Clark Steele?'

'Ah, Superman. No one's ever pointed that out before. Maybe there's a novel in *that*. Hey!' he says, as if he's just come up with the unified field theory, 'I betcha there's a novel everywhere you look. So what's your new one about?'

'Aw, it's too far-fetched. And I'm still working on it. I like to keep it private while it's gelling.'

'Wanna hear a joke? A writer and a rabbi walk into a bar –'

'*Okay*. Okay. Basically, there's this woman. Her name is Paula. She's a normal Torontonian, living and working in the city, good marriage, solid guy, two kids. So it's like the story starts out and she's just doing her thing.'

'What's her thing?'

'Oh, uh, she works for RBC.'

'Who's Arby C.?'

I squint at him. 'Her boss. One day, she starts feeling like she's being watched. She doesn't have any proof, but sometimes she senses that something is watching her, an eye or a camera. At night, it's like there's someone in the room, looking at her.'

'Yeah?' He leans in, a fist under his chin.

'Then people start to call her by the wrong name. She's drawn to Kensington Market because there have been repeated sightings of her.'

'Of Paula?'

'No! Her identical *twin*.'

Steele slaps his hands together. 'Except! She don't *have* a sister! Am I right?'

'Yeah. Her twin is named Jean. They finally meet. And, uh, Jean tells Paula a story that is hard to believe.'

'And?'

'And I don't know.'

'What's the story she tells?'

I have to make something up. 'That they're clones of each other.'

'Clowns?'

'Yes. It's all just a silly joke in the end, Mr Steele.' I cut into the liver. It's wet in the middle, the way I like it.

'I thought probably at the end they'd wake up and it'd all be a dream.' The grey moustache above his smile fans out. 'You want hot sauce?'

I decline. He takes his charming self away to the bar.

'Sorry,' says the rabbi, sliding back into the booth. 'I bounced a cheque on the frummy who own the synagogue.'

'Go back to my critic. At book club. What else did she say?'

Shoshana zigzags ketchup over her fries. 'I just think she hates everything. But listen, that happened a long time ago now. Don't worry about her. You need to focus on your health, Inger. Is it okay if I call you that?'

I'm suddenly swoony. She leaps up and comes to sit on my side, pulls me against herself. She smells like hand cream.

'What's wrong?'

'Why would it be okay to call me Inger?'

'You told me your name,' she says, her eyes wide with worry. 'Ing –'

'Don't say it! Write it down.'

With a trembling hand, she writes a name on the inside of a Steele's matchbook cover. I look at it and put the matches into my pocket. 'I have to go see my doctor.'

'Right now?'

'Yes. Help me up.'

She supports me around the waist and leads me to the door. Steele comes speeding around the bar. 'You want I should call a cab?'

'I think an ambulance,' Shoshana says.

I try to wrestle out of her grasp. 'No. I need some air. I need to walk.'

'I'll come with you.'

'Do you know,' I say to her, 'if something changes your brain – like a flowerpot falls on your head or you get meningitis – afterwards, sometimes, you turn into somebody else. The person the flowerpot fell on is gone.'

'Should I be worried about you?'

'But when death comes, who's died? The person before, or the person after?'

She gives Steele a look that makes him go away. 'Your soul is inside you and it leaves your body, sweetie.'

'Whose soul, though?'

'Let me take you to the hospital.'

'No! I'm good! I'm good now!'

She lets me go.

THE SNOW HAS CHANGED. IT was spitty and damp; now it's feathery and insubstantial and melts on your tongue like communion wafers. It makes me think of the pills Cullen gave me and I get one out and start dissolving it on my tongue. It's been a long time since I've had a kid's Aspirin. I'd forgotten the aftertaste of metal.

I speed-walk to Morbier's along Dundas, keeping my head down. I know Ingrid's here, somewhere close. I can feel her eyes on me.

It's getting dark. There's something I'm supposed to do: an image flashes in my brain's Fotomat. I see Ian and the kids. Their faces, and then their eyes.

I buzz at Dr Morbier's side door. There's no response. The flakes have begun to join as they come down. An infinitesimal change in temperature at four thousand feet or a shift in electric charges attracts them to each other. They fall to earth in the shapes of anvils, barbells, skaters with their arms out, turning and turning. I buzz again. There's an intercom button. It makes an electrical hum when you press to talk. 'It's Jean Mason,' I say. 'I'm standing at your office door. Can you open? It's an emergency.'

Release. No response.

I go around to the front. The entrance to your shrink's house is a portal between kingdoms, between realms. Below, in the office, he's my help and confidant; on this floor, he's another person. But I have to ask him what he knows. He has to talk to me.

I knock on his front door. No answer. I knock again.

I stand back on his front lawn in plain view and study

239

the house, looking for light within. But what is inner light and what is reflected from the incandescent bulbs fixed atop poles at thirty feet and what is the angle of the watcher – my internal observer effect – I can't tell.

It's too early for a spring dress, but I'd put it on in an act of encouragement to the weather gods. The cumuli snow was their answer, but it was coming from a dim, cloudless sky, a snow blown in from another weather system, hatched in clouds too far away to see.

The inside of my dress generates an icy draft that clings to my skin, tightening it. But Morbier won't answer, no matter how cold I get. I put my hand against the front door frame. I feel nothing against my palm. I crouch and put my ear to the door. I hear the furnace chug a couple of times. Then maybe voices speaking in a low register. Not mechanical or singsong. A thump comes through the frame of the house: someone moving a chair.

I fly up to look down through the roof. Dr Morbier stands right behind the front door, his arms held out from his sides like a gunslinger, except all he has in his hand is a steak knife. In the kitchen, they've already cut into their meat, his wife, I presume, and his two children, I presume. Motionless as gophers on hills, their little hands folded up in front of them.

I hear footsteps coming heavily to the door and I run down Morbier's walkway and crouch on the sidewalk behind his hedge. Through its panoply of leaves, I see the door open, and August Morbier is framed within it.

'Who's there?' he says, squinting into the night. 'We're at supper, you know!' There's anger in his voice, a tone I've never heard in his basement. 'And furthermore, I don't buy things through the *door* to my *house*!' I stand up so he can see me before he slams the door. 'Jean?'

'I'm sorry. I tried the side first. I have an emergency.'

'Jean,' he says and fumbles for what to say. 'Jean, I wish I could help you right now, but the line between my personal and professional life has to remain sacrosanct. For the good of us both. I'm sure you can understand. I'm eating dinner with my family.'

I approach him, showing him my empty, unthreatening hands. 'I'm dying,' I say. 'Or going mad. Or I'm mad already. Or already dead. You have to help me.'

'Oh god, okay... come in.' He stands aside and lets me into his house. 'Go in there,' he says, directing me to a half-open door. I go toward it, but I'm also frightened of it. I haven't considered what will happen if Morbier *is* behind all of this, and here I am in his house, in a room, alone with him. He's saying something, not to me. 'Go back to the kitchen right now. I mean it.' There's fire-flicker inside the room. And a child, a boy of five or six, is standing behind Morbier. I'm paralyzed where I stand.

'Who's it, Papa? Who is that?'

'Jean, please. Wait for me in the den, would you?' I go into the 'den' and close the door and recommence breathing. The fire is in a black pot-bellied stove. 'That was a friend of Papa's,' he says. 'Now you go back and eat your supper.'

'She has long hair like Mummy.'

'Go back to the kitchen, sweetheart,' he says.

The room is furnished with a sofa and a couple of chairs at either end of it. The pouf that ties the room together is a gathering place for magazines and remote controls. It's all upholstered with very soft brown corduroy.

'Sit anywhere,' Morbier says, closing the door behind him. 'What's the problem? Please sit.'

'If you don't mind, I'd rather stand. I have to ask you directly... I'm sorry if this sounds crazy, but I need to know if you've involved me in some kind of an experiment. Am I a, a test of something? Did you drug me, am I being drugged?'

He searches my eyes, back and forth, one at a time. 'No. I haven't drugged you.'

'Am I the subject of an experiment, Dr Morbier?'

He sits down on the couch and crosses his legs. 'Jean. I'd like you to sit down. You're clearly very upset, and I'd like to get an idea of what's going on.'

'Please answer my question.'

'No, you're not in an experiment. You can sit and tell me what's going on.'

'Not going to take notes?'

'This isn't a session.'

'So it's off the record?'

'What kind of record do you think I'm keeping?'

'I want to know if you will treat me as an equal, right here and now, as a fellow human being, and look into my eyes and answer my questions truthfully.'

'If I know the answers, I'll be truthful.'

'Do you know Ingrid Fox?'

He laughs softly. 'Oh no. *No*. How could I? If I knew Ingrid Fox, Jean, then certainly you'd have a reason to think... to believe you were being duped in some way. But I don't know Ingrid Fox, of course I don't. I do not know, personally, the woman you have spoken about over a period of six months and whose provenance we now know to be seizures.' He looks up at me, willing me to sit and talk to him. 'Or,' he says, shrugging, 'I could be making it all up. If you believe what you're thinking, you've probably already heard me say something like this in your mind. Am I right?'

'Yes.'

'So let's deal with that. You're right to be suspicious. If I were a bad man or a mad scientist, I would talk to you in a rational way, and reassure you. Take your concerns seriously. I could do a great job of it if I had to. How do you know I couldn't?'

'I don't.'

'Of course, a lot more people than me would have to be involved. It would be quite an operation. It's likely your husband would be involved.'

'I guess he'd have to be. So what do I do? How do I get out of this?'

'Well… I would take the proposition very seriously and subject it to the best test I could think of. I might, for instance, press to understand what the point of the experiment was. If I could come up with a plausible scenario in which a medical doctor would breach his legal obligations to you so completely, as well as enrol others to play certain roles, then I'd proceed to the next question.'

'Which is?'

'Why?'

Finally, I sit. 'Well. You'd have to be an imposter. Or it was part of the therapy.'

'Cure you of your autoscopy by putting on an elaborate performance of your symptoms out here in the real world? That would be ingenious if it worked. Is it working?'

'I don't know. I feel like I'm getting very close.'

'To what?'

'To something that'll be true. So. You don't know Ingrid Fox.'

'No. I don't.'

'What about Inger Wolfe? Do you know her?'

I see it immediately on his face. Or I'm imagining it. Or he's doing it on purpose. 'What would it mean if I knew a person named Inger Wolfe?'

'What about Rabbi Shoshana? Who's Clark Steele? Or

Cullen Gossage? Is Cullen your mole in the Clarke? Maybe those little children's Aspirins really are No-mind! How can I know?'

'Try to calm down, Jean. You're safe here. But I'm concerned now that you're not right, and you should maybe go back to the hospital.'

I laugh at him.

'What is no mind?' he asks me.

'You're trying to upload me. You and Cullen. He's *like* you,' I tell him. 'He knows what he's talking about.'

'Cullen is bipolar.'

'Sure.'

'Come on now.' He stands. The power dynamic in the room shifts. 'You know what this is. It'll be easier to fight once you recognize it. That's not half the battle – it's the entirety of it. Knowing when you're sick.'

'You want them to go back in and poke around my brain again? You know what you should do?'

'Jean?'

'You should get a lawyer.'

He doesn't really block my way, but he accompanies me to the door and gets there first. 'Where are you going?'

'Somewhere you can't find me.'

'If you're right and you're part of an experiment, what makes you think I can't find you anywhere? And how can you trust *anyone*? What if your husband *is* in on it?'

'I see through you. I'm going to Phoenix tonight. I'll be safer with my sister.'

He lifts his hand off the doorknob and steps away. 'All right then, go.' I pull the door open. 'You don't have a sister, though. Paula is not your sister.'

'Really? Who is she?'

'I don't know. I don't think she exists.' I remember him

writing in his little spypad when I first talked about her in his office. *Sister?* he must have written. *Delusional?*

'Why don't we ask her what she thinks of that?' I'm already at his front door with my phone out. I have one dot of reception, but it Skypes her.

'When *did* you last see your sister, Jean?'

'Hold on, she's answering.'

My screen moirés, and then there she is.

'Hey,' she says. I step out onto his front lawn. The snow's playing havoc with the signal; she breaks into lozenge-sized pixels. 'I'm so sorry.'

I hold my phone out to him. 'Okay? That's Paula! *Paula?* Hold on a second, I need more reception – ' He makes no further attempts on my liberty, but follows me and stands in his doorway. Little feet come galloping. Two faces appear on either side of him, two boys, identical twins. I hold the phone up above my head so they can all see Paula's face.

'– haven't been close,' she says. 'I don't know whose fault that is, but it doesn't matter now.'

'Tell him who you –'

She continues over me; she can't hear what I'm saying. 'Sorry to put this in a note, when it's too late. I thought...'

Her voice keeps changing. I have to bring her face to my eyes. There's no moving picture; the screen shows shards of her face. It forms for the briefest of moments, and there she is and she's crying. 'You were right about me,' she says. 'I never figured out how to get along in the world. Please don't feel guilty. I love you, Inger. I know you love me. I know one day you'll understand and you'll forgive me.'

The screen goes black. I look up and Morbier's front door is closed and there's not a single light shining in the windows of his house or in any of the houses on Denison Avenue.

IAN IS NOT HOME, BUT the kids are, asleep and alone in their beds. No doubt Morbier has already alerted him to my visit and he felt the urgency of the matter excused leaving his children unprotected. He won't have thought that I'd come straight home. I probably have ten minutes, fifteen at the most.

I start filling a backpack with necessaries. Underthings, T-shirts, an extra pair of jeans. Recharger cord, toiletries. I grab the $500 from the hollow book that's shelved among the old travel guides Ian still keeps from his vagabond days.

Nick is asleep with the covers pinched between his legs. I watch him from the doorway. I listen to him breathing, in and out, with that body I made him. I do the same in Reid's doorway, but he senses me standing there and turns over, murmuring. Their father loves them and I know they'll be okay until I get back.

I'm almost ready to leave when I see his car pull into the driveway. I put the knapsack in the closet. He calls from downstairs: 'Jean? Jean, are you here?'

I can't hide. 'I'm upstairs.'

He comes up to the bedroom looking flushed and worried. 'I got a call!'

'I know.'

'Do you? Do you know who called me?'

'You left the kids here, all alone.'

'You gave me no choice. They don't feel there's a choice now.'

'Excuse me, but who's *they*?'

A look of fear – fear of *me* – crosses his face. 'Jean, I have to take you in.'

'I don't even care now. I just want this to be over. Can I wash up first?'

'I need to take you now.'

'You can wait for me downstairs, *officer*. I'm not going to jump out the window, for chrissake.'

His eyes fill with tears. 'Jesus, Jeannie. You really don't know how sick you are. I wish I –'

'Get out.'

He leaves me. I stuff two more fistfuls of underwear into the knapsack. 'Come on, Jean,' he says from the hall.

'I'm almost ready.'

The bathroom window slides up silently – thank god we got the old shitty ones replaced. I shrug the knapsack on and step out onto the roof.

4

AFTER I BREAK JIMMY OUT of CAMH, I find someone to charter us to one of the airfields in Westmuir County, close to the town I used to call home. It costs four of the hundred-dollar bills.

Jimmy's never been on an airplane before, and he finds the changing topography fascinating. Roads give way to lakes and then forest and the north goes on and on. He says it looks like a huge animal clawed gashes in the earth and centuries of rain turned them into lakes.

Over Georgian Bay, the plane bucks and shears. Down the cabin, people brace their forearms against the sides of the plane, as if they can keep it from flying apart.

Jimmy looks ridiculously serene. 'You l-like this?' I ask him. 'The plane shaking all over the place?'

'It's not usually like this?'

'No. This isn't normal. This is heavy air tur... bulence. You're allowed to be scared.'

'I don't scare easy.' The plane hits a pocket and drops for a full second. A toupée flies up amidst the screams. Jimmy laughs. It's fantastic! This is life!

My own immediate fear is mitigated by the fact that I've been on medium sizzle, anxiety-wise, for weeks now. Having something to be afraid *of* is nice for a change. And if the plane breaks apart and our last, heavily adrenalized, slow-motion moments on planet Earth end with the waters of the bay rushing toward us, so what. We won't remember any of it. There will be nothing more to find out, to try to forget, to have to remember. Death is nothing compared to knowledge. Some days I'd rather die than find out one more

251

thing. The captain comes on and tells us he's going to look for some smoother air.

I don't think you get much of those trippy death ludes in a plane crash. Too sudden. What a huge rip-off, to live your whole life and not get the loot bag. What is the end like? A great swell of feeling? Will it be of love or regret? Maybe it will be a vivid dream to reassure me of my selfhood before it's led or lured away to permanent night.

Jimmy sleeps. Twenty minutes later, we're banking and descending. The wing slices a cloud.

The only stuff online for Ingrid Fox had been her books, reviews of her books, and snippy articles about her pseudonym. But when I put her real name into Google, it spat her life out. For the first time, she'd published a book under her own name. A fictionalized memoir or a novel based on real events, people weren't sure what to call it. She was touring the book and she was appearing at the Underwood Festival in Brigham. It's one of two writing festivals in the country that's held in the woods, and the only one in wintertime. 'The quintessential Canadian book festival!' the website boasted, over a time-lapse movie of people raising an enormous yurt within a stand of burr oak. Its roof is forty feet high and there's room in it for a restaurant and a number of venues.

Underwood is just a stop on her tour, but it's today and she's giving her first interview at the festival. Her book has been lavished with praise and her public is walking into a forest in their parkas to hear her speak.

Jimmy's the only person I can trust right now. It was easy to persuade him to come with me. Nothing strikes Jimmy as beyond the realm of possibility. His own mind partakes of the impossible often enough that he refuses to judge it, and the news that my doppelganger was doing a public interview under yet another name struck him as notably organic. I also offered to be his witness at any custody hearing he might have regarding his son, Tommy. His job was to keep watch for Ian, or Morbier, or anyone else who might take too much of an interest in me.

The station nurses barely blinked when I signed him out. We took the elevator down instead of up and he changed into Ian's things before we got to the ground floor. I told him I wanted him to be my eyes and ears. I had to clarify that my eyes and ears would still be involved. 'On your meds,' I told him, 'you're the clearest-thinking person I think I know.' He'd taken a half dose of his Seroquel for a few days and stockpiled the rest so he'd be covered for the trip. He seemed pretty steady to me, but I'd also seen him at his worst.

I booked an 11 a.m. flight, to keep a low profile. We rested on the benches in Terminal 3 outside the fast-food joints. Jimmy slept; I sat absolutely still with my eyes staved open while the clock on the opposite wall marked time in slower and slower increments. I spent every minute fearing we'd be discovered.

WE SIT SHIVERING TOGETHER IN the back seat of the cab from the airfield. It's fifteen degrees colder here than it was at home and Jimmy doesn't have an ounce of fat on him. I've reserved us a B&B in the town, but I don't plan to check in until after we go to the festival. We're travelling light. Jimmy has the clothes on his back and a twenty-dollar bill I gave him in case we get separated. I have my knapsack.

The festival's on provincial land and there are three trail-heads leaving from three different parking lots, depending on which direction you're coming from. There's a road in, but only for service vehicles. Part of the fun is walking in, so the website claimed, but I want to get there.

Four inches of snow blanket the fields north of the Westmuir Memorial Airfield. Snow-capped corn stubble sticks up. 'Why'd you bring those shoes?' I ask Jimmy, noting for the first time that he's wearing a pair of crummy Keds. 'You're going to freeze in those.'

'I've spent half my life in the cold,' he tells me. 'It keeps me focused.'

His jacket is better, although not by much. I grabbed a fleece from his room that he must have found in a charity pile because it hangs off him, but the combination should keep him warm if we walk fast enough. For his sake, I hope the path is already well stomped.

Our driver finds the packed and silent lot at the junction of Highways 91 and 121 and drops us after charging me $62.50 of my last eighty bucks. At least we're warm. When the sound of his motor vanishes, we're alone with about fifty cars, most of them with an accumulation of snow on their windshields. We're the stragglers. A colourful festival placard marks the trailhead to take. I put Jimmy on the path in front of me and follow him in.

We can't see beyond twenty metres, so thick are the trunks below treeshadow. This part of the forest is mainly pines, some of them towering. I keep my eye on Jimmy's back as he trudges forward, his head lowered to keep the cold air out of his face. Where the sun comes through in little spotlights, the snow has melted to a muddy slurry and his Keds shimmy on the slicker patches. A frozen mitten clings to a tree.

The trail thins and climbs a ledge over the forest floor. Wet leaf litter and slush make it difficult to keep my balance, but Jimmy's inner mountain goat is showing. While I'm stepping carefully with my arms out to my sides like a tightrope walker, his long legs keep a clockwork pace. 'Slow down,' I call to him.

'Keep up,' he says.

'Trail's only six kilometres, Jimmy. We don't have to rush.'

'I don't walk slow, don't know how. Six k in the cold is like ten in the heat. Don't fall behind.' That's the last thing he says to me. He even seems to step up his pace. Maybe he's making a run for it, a real escape. But why stage a break when you're about to be released? My intention is to get him back before nightfall, but the room in Brigham is there if we need it. I don't want his unauthorized furlough to get him into too much trouble.

A light snow falls. I check my phone for a signal and there's a sliver. I look for where I am on the phone's map: a blue bead beats in a featureless green landscape some distance away from Highway 41. The trails don't show on the map, nor in satellite view. Cold flakes blot the screen.

The snow is starting to fill the footprints of those who walked in before us. The sky is bright, and the low sun against empty branches strikes them in silhouette. From one angle, they join together in an endless black calligraphy.

Goethe's twin appeared on a forest path, dressed in grey and gold. He'd been on horseback, much more romantic than skidding through mud at the end of winter, abandoned by an undermedicated mental patient, on the way to meet one's doppelganger in the middle of a forest. I ask myself: Do I really want to go to the end of this path? Don't I know that when I get there, everything could change? Have I seen my family for the last time? Have I seen my home, the ever-protean multropolis of Toronto, for the last time? Goethe: *This strange illusion in some measure calmed me at the moment of parting.* He'd been going to see his beloved Frederica one last time. Did he see her, though? How did he know that his galloping doppelganger hadn't already replaced Frederica with her likeness, and that this likeness in turn would be replaced by another copy and another and another, in an ever-blooming cycle of selves, none of whom was the woman he loved?

The way forward is swallowed again and again in dark green, like a shadow galloping ahead of itself. How I'd miss this world.

Under my feet, new flakes are falling on a pristine layer of snow. Mine are the only footprints now. I hunt around looking for the path.

'Jimmy! Jimmy, can you hear me?' The tree trunks chop my voice into clatter. 'Jimmy, where are you? I've lost the trail...'

He's too far ahead. He'll come back. I have to stop and catch my breath. I clear a boulder of snow and get one of the six-dollar granola bars I bought at Pearson out of the knapsack. Greek-yogurt-dipped almond crunch. I flash on the throbbing blue dot on my phone, seeing it in my mind's eye, and make a decision to destroy it. I could be leaving electronic breadcrumbs. I put it down on the boulder and find a fist-sized rock to smash it with.

But I hesitate. What if I need to be found? I turn it off instead and put it away.

The underbrush crackles about a hundred metres from me. 'Jimmy? Is that you?'

Break's over! I jump up and start walking again, keeping the sun on my left. North.

Large, shadowy wings skid across the tree trunks.

THE SPICEBOX AIR IS HEAVY with oxygen. I can't find the path. I go toward an open area and the forest gives onto a small grassland with a patch of dead trees in the middle. Denuded pine, stripped to the trunks. It looks like a quiver of lightning bolts. I walk through the middle of the clutch, wondering how it came to be these pines grew here alone and then died. Forests are constantly digesting. I could lie down in this patch and let the grasses return me to the earth.

Fairy tales are suited to forests. If you go in far enough, you might come upon the ways things aren't. Trees older than Confederation growing out of decomposed stumps ten feet wide. The girl in the red shoes has to travel in deep to find the woodsman who can free her from her cursed dancing. Almost every Grimm hero suffers into the forest at some point. Do they ever learn, the Hansels, the Gretels?

Death feels like a fairy tale you never get to hear the ending of. It seems impossible that something of me will not survive it. What if I disappear *almost* completely, but *almost*? What might remain? Maybe a few flickerings of consciousness dimmed to their pilot lights but still viable, like sourdough starter, each bit irradiated with a tiny scrap of inner life. I recall Cullen's description of the transmission layer. There could be an ocean of raw consciousness waiting to get into the game. And while the saltings of what was once your semi-coherent self drift around inside this ocean, you have a long dream, and that's death. You see no faces but the seasons pass. There's no language except chemical reaction. No self, but mood, a universal roomtone, a vibration with intent milling itself from stellar debris. The

Horsehead Nebula is a tantrum. The 'Assassin' supernovae are regret.

High overhead, a bird tries to match its song to another's. *Chiddiup chee chiddi chiddi*, it says. Far away comes *chiddi chiddi chee*.

On the other side of the clearing is a river clogged with snow and ice. The water moves under it making water sounds, but muffled. After another five hundred metres, the river is pinched off altogether and vanishes beneath the forest floor. Sugar maples reclaim the space where the river had been, and in another clearing – a bare spot of dirt and snow surrounded by enormous trees – I come upon Jimmy. He sits above me on a boulder the size of a school bus, smoking a joint. 'Oh, thanks for waiting for me!' I say. 'I got totally lost!'

'The trail led you right here,' he says, and I look down and see I'm in other people's footprints again. 'Come up. I can see the lakes we saw from the airplane. Follow the break in the path to your left.'

The well-worn trail – people have been walking in this forest for thousands of years – brings me into the trees and onto the backside of the rock, which rises in long, broken chunks to where Jimmy sits. 'It looks like someone hacked the forest in half.'

'It's a fault line. Look down.'

His legs dangle over the edge and I lean out to see what he means. It's not a boulder but a stone wall. The cliff and the ground were once level. Near the cleft, the ground is warmer, and in the snowmelt there's an ecology of flowers and fronds and moving water. 'This is the high point above the bay. It has drawing power.' He puffs on the joint, but it's out. He tries to light it again with a little yellow Bic.

'I think I can help you there.' I pass him the matchbook from Steele's Tavern, the one with Ingrid's secret name written in Shoshana's hand. 'Keep it.'

He puffs a lungful of creamy smoke. 'You want some?'

'No. I need a clear head. Where are your meds?'

He shows me the joint. 'I fed them to the toads.' He directs my attention to the forest floor and I realize what I thought were little orange flowers are Jimmy's Seroquels. I don't see any toads.

'What the hell are you thinking?'

'I don't want them. I'm straighter on pot.'

'Whatever. You're an adult, I'm not going to fight with you. Just don't leave me behind again.'

'I thought you might have some deep thoughts if the trees closed in on you. You might figure out what you're here for.'

'Don't be my guru, eh? Just make sure I don't get eaten by bears, and watch my back at the festival. I know what I'm here for.'

'You gonna share?'

'I'm going to ask her how she knows August Morbier, and depending on the look on her face, I'm either going to kill her or we'll go home.'

'Which do you rather?'

'To go home. And know it's home.'

He looks skyward and his pupils almost vanish into his head. 'I'm glad one of us has a plan.'

'Go get your pills. Stay sharp.'

'Medication dulls my receptivity to intersticial wavelengths,' he says.

'I don't care what that means. Do you know how to get to the festival from here or not?'

He stands at the edge of rock and takes a survey. 'Yes,' he says. He takes us down the ridge, back to the forest floor, and finds the path. In places it's only wide enough for one and he goes in front again, but he allows me to keep up. When the clearing is well behind us, the trees crowd in. In some places, there's no sky.

It smells loamy – rotten-sweet with notes of wet cardboard. Being dwarfed by so many things this close together makes a person feel they're being watched. But what kind of mind is watching in the forest? If Jimmy's being directed by voices – and clearly he is – there are plenty in these winds to pick up on.

Then there's a sound in the distance – a flock of pigeons taking off? Or the wind bashing the branches back and forth? Surrender! I feel like running for cover.

But it's applause…

THE FIRST SIGHT OF THE festival is an autumnal wall of striped tent filling the distance, with holes in it for trees. That's where the applause is coming from. We're approaching it from the rear. Canvas sheets in orange, tan, and red rise into the canopy and wrap around to the left and right.

We continue our circumnavigation of the structure, and as we go, voices come through in one place, the sound of flatware and glasses in another. Finally we see where the people are, coming and going from the mouth of what is two-thirds of a giant yurt rigged in and around the oaks. The opening makes it look like a head with the face taken off. Inside is a honeycomb of spaces on different levels within the trees, most of them facing east, toward the entrance where we stand. They're performance spaces, a bar and a restaurant, with a swept forest floor temporarily spread with bar tables and chairs, like a piazza, but with mature trees in it. There must be three hundred people inside, drawn there like they were to Bellevue Square. It's hung with coloured lanterns. Even Jimmy says *wow*. The existence of this place and its scale makes it hard to know where to look. Once we've reached the middle, I can place the feeling. This is what it's like when you enter a great museum and stand in the foyer. You shrink and expand all at once. It's a pull focus.

Jimmy hands me a program. It's on recycled leaf paper. It crinkles like leaves in my hand. 'Your friend is being interviewed *right now*. Look.' He shows me her name in the program. 'Now where is the Algonquin Room?' He cranes his head over the crowd and points out a ground-level area where people are filling chairs. It's a large space with a raised stage at the front of it, complete with a black backdrop and a red velvet curtain, which is open and sleekly shining. 'You better go. They're going to start.'

'Stay here,' I tell him. 'I'll catch up with you afterwards, okay? Like in an hour? And Jimmy. Listen, don't talk to anyone about anything. Just keep to yourself.'

'I'm here to make sure *you* don't get into trouble.'

'I'm not going to get into trouble. You're the one off his meds. Just keep saying that to yourself – *I'm off my meds* – before you make any decisions.'

'You doubt me.'

'I do,' I say quietly. 'You doubt yourself all the time, though, so you should be used to it. I wouldn't have wanted anyone else for the job, okay? What if we land on that?'

'Do you doubt yourself?'

'Of course I do.'

'Because what if she's lured you out here?'

'Then she's lured you, too.'

It's on the dot of four now and the sun is deep in the sky behind the festival tent. The canvas has been taking on deeper hues; what were panels of drab autumnal colours have lit up warm and glowing behind the stages. Crosshatching the colourful stripes are the rectilinear shadows of the burr oaks.

I catch up with the back of the crowd looking for seats. It's much warmer here, among other bodies. The stage is set with two comfy-looking chairs, two microphone stands, and a small white table with two bottles of water on it. I need to install myself where she won't see me, and I find a good seat – in the corner, behind a man who is tall seated – when a young woman I've never seen before takes my elbow and steers me away.

'There you are,' she says. She's got a complicated badge holder dangling from her neck, a Bluetooth thing in her ear, and a bulging binder under her arm. 'I got her,' she says to no one.

'What are you doing? I want to listen.'

She gives me a hard but somehow comical stare. 'You can listen later. First you have to talk. Come on. They weren't even aware you were a lost lamb!'

Right, she thinks I'm *her*. A cop pokes his face into a curtained-off area, then swings our way. 'Okay, let's go,' I say.

I follow her inside a network of passageways clogged with people trying to get from one part of the immense backstage area to the other. I see waiters and people wearing headsets, everyone ID-badged but me. Up ahead, my rustler is saying hello to people or expressing herself into the wide open to the listener in her ear. 'I'm just about to point her to it.' She cups a hand over her microphone. 'Did you sign a waiver?'

'I –'

'Never mind. We put one in the welcome kit, but I always carry extras.'

She finds another waiver in her binder and folds it neatly in three before handing it over to me. 'Okay, this is it. Feel along the black cloth until you see the light from the stage. Someone will send you on when Linda is ready.'

'Okay!' I give her a big thumbs-up.

I duck into a break in the passage and emerge into a small area that, apart from a variety of tree trunks, is empty. There are some cracked and crushed plastic cups underfoot, some of which have red wine in them from, I presume, a backstage toast. What do they say to writers? Break a spine?

The audience I'd been about to join is amurmur some distance ahead, and I carry on through a door in a plywood barrier beyond the abandoned party space. It's suddenly much darker, although my eyes adjust and I make out some plywood set pieces – a rainbow leaning against a Doric column made of cardboard and plaster. Worktables are scattered where they fit and taped cables come down a couple of the trunks and terminate at a bank of generators. Rows of human faces are visible through a break in the black backdrop.

A woman stands in the wings, clasping a folder in her hands, and now I can make out the mixing guy at his bank of computers. I have to wonder if they're really waiting for me, but I know that my Ingrid – their Inger – is standing in the other wings, waiting for her cue before she walks onstage. Stage lights turn the gap in the curtain blinding white. The lady with the folder steps forward and there's applause.

I creep to the backdrop and stand behind it, my nose touching the noise-dampening cloth. I'm close enough that my peripheral vision is in darkness. I imagine I can see through the barrier and that I am looking directly at the two water bottles on the round white table.

The interviewer's voice is further mangled by a PA system that is louder than what is happening just a few feet from my nose. She's introducing her guest. She gives a history of the author's four novels, all of them grisly small-town mysteries, 'but that's not what we're here to talk about today, is it?'

'No,' says a woman with my voice, and there's nervous laughter both on the stage and in the audience.

'Were you worried when you wrote this book, that you'd alienate the people who were expecting another mystery novel from you?'

'Well, this is probably the best mystery I've ever written!' There's laughter, then more applause.

'Why did you use your writing pseudonym as a character in the book? A book you've called a novel in some places and a memoir in others. Which is it?'

'I think with the troubles I've had, it's better to treat the story as fictional. But a lot of it *happened* to me.' They laugh. She must have made air quotes. They like her. 'I used my pseudonym to put some distance between myself and the people I wanted to write about. Because there's me and there's *her* and then there's HER. And I don't think I could have written about any of it until I could get outside or above it, if you know what I mean.'

'You had to feel separate.'

'Yes. So I could imagine for myself again what it really felt like. And to give her her due.'

'Inger Ash Wolfe, when did you first start experiencing the symptoms you describe in *Denison Square?*'

'In the spring of 2014. I was walking around in downtown, and I happened to see myself, in the front window of a shop. But I didn't realize it was me at first. I just didn't. I thought there was a woman inside the store, and she was staring right at me. She looked like she was upset, but also trying to hide her feelings. That's what I saw in her face. I decided it was none of my business – maybe she was looking at someone inside the store who I couldn't see. But I glanced back once more, and she did too, of course at the exact moment.

'I kept walking, but I couldn't get the look on her face out of my mind. I felt I had to… confront her, ask her if she thought we knew each other or something. So I went back to the store and I went in. I couldn't find her anywhere. I asked the lady at the till if she'd seen a woman in a blue dress, wearing little hoop earrings, and she said, "Well, there's one standing in front of me right now."'

Good-natured laughter in the audience, a nice release. I touch my ears. I'm not wearing mine.

Linda says: 'I see you've got them on tonight.'

I walk down to the dark inside the wings. Her earrings, like the ones I own, are gold, half an inch in diameter, and thicker at the bottom. Ingrid... *Inger* is wearing jeans and cork heels. And lipstick. She looks good.

'It happened a couple more times,' she's saying. 'I'd see this woman deep in a store or a restaurant, and she'd look right at me. Sometimes I'd be in the car and turn my head, and there she'd be, sitting in the passenger seat of *her* car. I finally told my husband about it. He was the one who broke it to me!'

'That you'd been looking at *yourself*, all this time, in mirrors.'

'I couldn't believe it. How could it be I didn't know I was looking at myself? We read up on it, and the more we read, the more scared we got. I told my GP I couldn't recognize myself in mirrors – and they did the tests and then he asked me to come back to his office, like the next day. Something he didn't want to discuss with me on the phone.'

'You must have been terrified.'

'I don't remember the drive over. I could only think: this is it, I have cancer. The look on his face is going to tell me everything the second I walk in. But when we got to his office, his expression was, like, *you're not going to believe this*. He told us the MRI and the X-rays both showed a lesion between my parietal and temporal lobes –'

'For those in our audience today who might not be brain surgeons?'

'Uh, in the brain, there are lobes? And the temporal lobe is mostly about processing sound. The parietal has a lot of functions, like establishing where things are in space, a lot of your visual and language processing, sense of your own body.'

'Proprioception.'

'Yes. Imagine not knowing where your own body parts are. Like in space? Hey, why's this fork pointing at me?'

'Soon after your diagnosis, the symptoms got worse.'

'Yes,' Inger says quietly.

'You began to see yourself out in the world... walking around, in stores, in the street. But at a distance. And you and your twin's movements were not synchronized, which I understand is unusual even for people who experience autoscopy.'

'It is. It's called asymmetric autoscopy. There are only eight known cases.'

'In the book, you talk about how your family reacted to your diagnosis. Your daughter thought you were making it up.'

'Well, she didn't like me having a wilder inner life than she did. She was ten at the time, full of her own imaginary friends, and now Mummy has one? Then she got with it. She started telling me about my doppelganger, how she'd see it sometimes near her school and it looked sad because it wasn't really her mummy. It was sweet! She said it came into the house one day and made her a sandwich.'

For some reason, there's applause again. There must be a rip-roaring scene of me making that child her gorilla. Linda asks Inger if she was worried that when the book came out her condition would become public, and Inger recites what sounds like a prepared statement, about mental illness and stigma, and cashing in on her own problems, et cetera et cetera, and the audience responds like it's stroking her hair. But – Inger continues – she found the strength to publish. Praise be.

'Your husband was a great help,' Linda says. 'You dedicate the book to him.'

'For one thing,' Inger says, 'he was the one who found Dr Mourguet, and it was through applying some of Mourguet's techniques that I was able to... reassociate. Sometimes when you have a trauma, your mind can splinter. Not good for a writer. He taught me how to focus again. But yeah, Larry has been a rock. I'm lucky to have him.'

'I want to ask you about your sister. You talk about her a lot in this book.'

'When I got sick, I didn't know if I was going to tell her about it. Paula and I had been estranged for such a long time I didn't even know where she was living. I thought she was still in Phoenix, and I did write to her, to tell her that I was sick and to ask after her, but she didn't reply.'

'You found someone who knew her, a man who did custodial work in her building. She'd never left Phoenix.'

'No. Because she's buried there.' I mishear it at first. I hear Inger say Paula was spared. 'She killed herself,' she continues, and the word *killed* penetrates me like a bullet in the head. 'It hurts that she didn't reach out. We barely spoke, but I thought she'd ask for help if she needed it. I was wrong. I don't know if she ever tried to get help, but if she did, it didn't stop her.'

'She's gone, but during your illness, and since, you say you've felt much closer to her.'

'My memories of Paula are ancient. There were months in our childhood when she didn't live with us. She could be unpredictable and violent. They shuttled her back and forth between the group home and our house, but this was the seventies. They weren't sophisticated about her problem.'

'What was her problem?'

'Borderline personality? Psychosis? Maybe she had a vitamin deficiency. We'll never know.'

My entire body feels cold.

'Has it helped to write about her?' Linda asks.

'I feel like we suffered together while I was writing this book. We didn't do that when we were little and our house was full of drinking and fighting. And I miss her now.'

'Your doppelganger doesn't know that Paula's dead. Jean can see you, talk to you; she walks the same streets you do. We might say she knows you inside out, but for her, Paula is still alive.'

'Someone should have Paula. And Jean's got so much on her plate. She deserves some company, and Paula was beautiful company. Not for herself, I guess, but for me when I was a girl. She was like a protective layer in my life.'

'You could have used that in recent years.'

'I suppose in some ways, she's been here for me.'

There's a rustling on the PA and a squeak. Linda says, 'We can take some questions now if you like.'

'Sure.'

Someone asks, 'Do you still see it?'

'It?'

'Your doppelganger.'

'Oh yeah, gosh. All the time. Flare-ups. I can see her now, actually.'

Excited chattering. I back away from the light litter in the wings and stand nearer to the mixing guy.

'You can see her?' asks the audience member. 'Right now?

'Yep. She moved when I looked at her. She's like a floater in my eye.'

Linda leaps back in. 'But what does it mean when you see –?'

'She's like an aura before a migraine. That's kind of what

270

this is. But it's not a migraine, it's a, a seizure.'

'Are you okay? Do you need a glass of water?'

Inger laughs, and my guts churn. I tuck deeper against the canvas where it's cool and dark. 'I think I'm okay,' she says.

Linda's voice is excited, or worried, I can't tell. 'May I ask? Do you still see her?'

'No, but she's in the back, listening.'

'You're a fraud!' I shout. 'You're an imposter!'

'What's happening?'

'She's calling me an imposter.'

'Who is she, Inger? What does she think she is?'

'She's like everyone else. Me, you, everyone in this audience. She thinks her first-person experience is unique. She can't see that she's a variation on a theme.'

'And what's the theme?'

Quaking with rage, I creep along the plywood wall behind the technician's table, feeling with my hands.

Linda says 'Inger?' in a strange way, but then the sound from the stage warps. I open and close the door in the plywood barrier as silently as possible, and once through, I can't hear anything. I look at my watch: it's only been twenty minutes. Apart from a couple of patches of light, the backstage area is too dark to see in. My hands shake uncontrollably. I try to focus on the rainbow against the pillar, the only thing in the room clearly lit. Sitting there in the dirt, it seems to me an abject thing.

I'm startled by a voice nearby. 'Is it over –?'

I turn around; no one's there. The canvas ripples in the air currents. I hear the voice again – 'We should all get the hell out of here.' I look down and there's a toad the size of a teacup on the ground. 'Oh, she's going,' it says. 'Just now they attend her on the stage. Lissen.' There's a different sound emanating from the faraway speakers. Confusion, people crying out and calling to each other.

I crouch down. 'Are you talking to *me?*'

'Hello?' Jimmy steps through one of the backdrops. 'If you're going to kiss that thing, make it snappy. We have to get out of here.'

The toad's run out of things to say. 'I thought it was talking to me.'

'Maybe *you* should be on my meds.' There's a scent coming off him, the pot maybe, but no, it's smoke. Voices from the front rise in urgency. 'I figured out what I am in Ingrid's dream of you,' he says.

'Oh yeah?'

'I'm the alarm clock.' He has the matchbook I gave him. He tears a match off, snaps it alight, and tosses it onto a tabletop.

'Fuck, Jimmy!' I rush over to stamp it out, but he lights them one after another, tossing the eager little flames onto a table covered with crumpled napkins. I grab the matchbook out of his hand and pound out the redglowing napkins with my fist. My sightline to the tent's entrance reveals flames running up the canvas walls and people screaming and running for the single exit. I rush back to the interview stage to see the audience fleeing into the piazza. Inger is not among them. Where she'd been, the stage is littered with a semicircle of sterile wrappers and syringe covers.

'They must've took 'er already!' Jimmy says behind my left ear. 'I think she had an attack.'

I shove him away from me. 'What the fuck have you done?'

The smoke rushes in from left and right. People run past us, stumbling and crying out, and I hear sirens. Jimmy yanks me into the crush, and the mouth of the yurt is on fire like the entrance to the worst ride on Hell's midway. Beyond, the dead leaves from last fall shiver in the rising heat and begin to glow. More bodies converge on me and I'm pressed, pushed down from behind until I'm on the ground. Feet stampede past my head. The empty Steele's Tavern matchbook scatters from my palm and a black shoe steps on it. Someone wrenches my arm behind my back. 'Run outta matches, sweetheart?' A woman's voice. She pulls me to standing and starts pushing me through the entrance. 'You're under arrest,' she says.

All around us, people are coughing and struggling. The cop pushes me forward, her hand clamped to the back of my neck, driving me through the crowd panicking in the heat-shimmering air. Then her hand slips off and I feel her against my back. She knocks me to my knees. When I can scramble away and stand, I see Jimmy behind her holding a blood-smeared chunk of rock.

'Oh my god. Jimmy!'

'She was taking too much of an interest in you,' he says. Burnt skin hangs off his face and his brown irises float in red pools. He collapses to his knees. The officer, whose nametag reads WINDEMERE, lies on her back insensate but breathing. Blood trickles out of her scalp and into the snow. Jimmy takes her keys off her hip and tosses them to me. 'You should go,' he says.

People shriek and flee into the forest, and I look back and see a river of burning sparks flowing through the roof like an aqueduct of stars.

OUTSIDE THE TENT, THE GREY-BLACK pall has room to billow. It rises demonically. Behind, flames shoot up into the trees. Sirens come toward us along the service road, and a helicopter chops in from the west. Abandoned police cars stand empty beyond the smokewall, their lights going, a post-apocalyptic sight of bootless cries, and I run, crouching, to the nearest one. I get in and switch the flashers off. I know my way around a cruiser, until now a useless perq of being married to a policeman.

I try Windemere's keys in the ignition. No go. I slide over to the passenger door and get out to try the next cruiser. The door is locked and my key doesn't work. It won't open the third car along, either. But car 1266 opens and starts and its onboard computer immediately comes to life.

I navigate out of the small herd of cruisers and head down the service road to Route 41. A line of police cars and ambulances comes stampeding north, sirens and lights blaring armageddon, and I continue beneath their notice.

I pick up the handset and depress the button. 'Car twelve sixty-six, car twelve sixty-six, come in.'

'Westmuir twelve sixty-six,' comes a male voice. 'What's your location, Windemere?'

'South of the fire at the Underwood Festival. Need backup, as much as possible, and more air support –'

'We're sending everything we have and Mayfair is mobilized.'

'Is that the hospital they're taking people?'

'Julia? You don't sound like yourself –'

'It's the smoke.' I put the handset back on its hook. If

274

Inger got out alive, they took her to Mayfair. There's no closer hospital. I watch the powerlines slide past, black and silver portioning the night sky. Below them lies some of the same forest Jimmy and I walked through this afternoon, the same green mantle that was here when I belonged here with my little family. Maybe nothing has changed in my life and I'm actually still here raising two young children while my husband adjusts to his important desk job after years on the force. Maybe I'm still here, crying for no reason by the creek with Nick strapped to my chest. I see us reflected in the water, the steely sky behind us.

'Jean?' Ian's voice, coming from the radio. I look at the handset. 'Jean, pick up. Or turn on your phone! Where are you? Peter MacTier swears he just spoke to you, and you were in a cruiser? Pick up the handset, Jean. Talk to me.'

I bring it to my lips, push the button. 'Don't say anything if you want me to talk.' I leave a pause long enough to confirm compliance. 'I'm doing something that's important to me, Ian, even if you don't understand it. You have to trust me.' Will he jump in here and plead with me? Reason with me? No... he's actually listening. 'I can get her to admit what she did to Katerina if I just talk to her. Get her to admit what she's trying to do to *me*. Ian? Do you understand now?' He doesn't answer. I push the button a couple more times and it dead-clicks. He's gone. I switch my phone back on and dial him, but the last dot of reception goes blank and I'm driving in two layers of darkness, the road and the sky. I'm in a zone impermeable to signals.

Around another and then another jagged silhouette of pine stand and oak stand, I see in the distance a blue glow, the hopeful hospital H against the star-clad sky. I pull the cruiser in under the ER hood and park it between ambulances.

I go into emergency. Some of the victims from the fire are already here. I don't see Inger among them. It smells like burning hair, and black soot smudges the railings and the registration countertop.

I don't want to draw attention, which precludes standing in the line to ask a question. I huddle in among the people on the orange leatherette chairs in the waiting room and study the situation. There are a few cops around, but they're waiting near the exits. I scan the other half of the waiting room and make out at least two people who were probably brought in by them. Drunks with bleeding faces. I have to take note of the police a few times a minute to make sure one of them hasn't received instructions that pertain to me and/or my capture.

Past the registration area, painted footprints in red, yellow, and blue lead the way along the floor to various destinations: blue to the exam rooms, yellow to triage, red to the ICU. Choose your own ending. I get up and look like I know what I'm doing and then follow the yellow footprints. Doors hush shut as I go.

The triage lounge is quiet, but the ward is full of people waiting on beds behind half-closed curtains, most of them hooked up to something, looking grim in blue paper slippers. I continue down the infectious corridor and peer through the windows into the isolation rooms, but I don't see her. Somehow I find myself in radiology, where I pretend to look for someone named Joe. I make eye contact with no one. I walk under ominous signs and past the arrows to nowhere. Cardiac Ward Disease Management Pediatric Oncology. I go through the doors to a stairwell and take the stairs up a floor, retrace my steps along the hallway back over triage and descend the stairs on the opposite side. I join the red footprints and find my way to the doors of intensive care. Behind me, police and paramedics come crashing into the silence, pushing a gunshot wound alive and groaning on a soaked gurney and I tuck myself in behind and go through the doors into the ICU. I peel off behind a curtain and find myself face to face with a nurse. He's taking the blood pressure of an elderly man in a gown. 'Are you a relation?'

'I'm sorry, I'm lost. My sister's here. Last name Wolfe?'

'Mr Abrams, your arm is too small for the cuff. I'm gonna get a nurse with a wrist one.'

Mr Abrams says, 'Whist?'

'We're going to take your blood pressure at your wrist. Two curtains down,' he says to me. 'They have her on something to stop the seizures.'

'She's having seizures?'

'She's not my patient. Check with the duty nurse.'

I go through two more cubicles, pushing the hanging curtains one way and then the other, looking for the openings. In one bed a child sleeps with a tube up his nose. The fluffy white dog in his arms isn't a plush toy. It growls at me as I pass through. When I get to where Inger's supposed to be, even the bed is gone.

THE DUTY NURSE TELLS ME that Inger's in surgery. There's a recovery waiting room in the surgical wing on the ninth floor. She won't reveal what the surgery is. I wait for one of the four elevators with a family of three, a young girl with her parents. When we get in, the father presses nine and asks me my floor.

'Same,' I reply.

'Sorry to hear it. Our son Seamus is getting a new liver.'

'Oh. Well, they're really good with the transplants here,' I say, like I know something about it.

'The liver is still on its way from another hospital, but thank god we got one. They told us it's a good liver, a young person's.'

'Don't be so thankful, Dad,' the girl says. 'The only reason Shame's getting a liver is because some other family lost *their* son.'

'I swear to god, Emily.' The doors open on the fourth floor and we wait while no one enters. 'There's no comparison. It's not Seamus's fault that the boy died.'

'Shame is going to have a dead person inside him!'

'HEY –'

The mother stops the father from slapping the girl. She's only twelve or thirteen. Violence is near, I can feel it like heat on my back. It's a bright yellow rising tide.

We step out at nine, and the mother, scanning the signs hanging from the ceiling, announces the direction. I hang back. The girl slips her hand into her father's. 'Hey, the information people are over here,' he says, and they change direction, trading the lead like a flock of geese.

I continue down the hall alone. I can hear my breath coming too hard. I pass gurney after empty gurney, the beds with their sideguards lowered, as if waiting to catch something that strays too near. I'm still sufficiently overstimulated that I can't put the thoughts together that would help me find a hospital map or think of where they might be keeping her. Finally, I see: The Sam and Connie Litvak Recovery Waiting Room. A laminated sign by the door tells of Shelley Litvak, dead at fourteen. She's pictured on a bicycle. She's smiling. Once you're dead, you look dead in pictures, too.

THE WAITING ROOM IS A large space in two distinct sections. One is bright and the televisions on the walls are all on. The other part is dark and people slouch across the benches with their coats keeping them warm. That's where the family has gone. They took another route but ended up here as well. I sit in the light half and stare at the news crawl below footage of a fatal car crash. Maybe that's where Seamus's liver is coming from.

It's well past two in the morning when anyone official comes into the room, but she summons one of the hibernators, a man on his own. A fog of dread descends. Every thought and feeling that I have *had*, as in *I have possessed*, as in *I contain it in the little vessel of my body*, will be extinguished. I'm a being. I can no more give my beingness away than someone can take it from me. Inger thinks she can have it, but it's mine.

No one has come looking for me yet. Here I am in the wide open, like I was at the Dominion when I lost my mother, but I'm invisible. At four in the morning, Seamus's family is given news that causes the parents to sob and the girl to laugh. They are taken away, another story I can't know the beginning or the ending of. I pick up the phone and dial to the last digit of our home number before hanging up.

Jimmy must be dead.

SOMEBODY FROM A VOLUNTEER ORGANIZATION comes by just after sunrise to offer coffee and packages of low-sugar cookies. The news cycle renews. The stories that played until the middle of the night have been winnowed to the most sensational and spiced up with fresher horrors. The sun bangs around inside the elevator foyer.

More people have arrived in the meantime, families and next-of-kins, and they're discovering the magazines and choosing where to park themselves. Another doctor enters at last, but he doesn't call a name. Tall in white and capped in blue. I'd forgotten how much surgeons looked like chefs. He comes directly to me, silent, and I know I'm being summoned; I recognize when things have gone beyond words. I follow him through the warren of back rooms and hallways. The smell of disinfectant hangs in the air and we begin down another corridor of gurneys, but these ones are occupied with every kind of mortal shock. Luckily for these post-ops, they're unconscious. At the end of the corridor, we come to a frosted glass wall with muted light behind it.

'What's this?'

'This is our quiet room.'

'It's pretty quiet up here already.'

'It's for a special kind of quiet.'

My eyes want to bolt from my head. 'So she's gone?'

'No. But I don't want to paint too rosy a picture. It'll be good for her to hear your voice. It'll give her some strength and maybe she'll rally. She's in that room there.' He indicates it with his chin, as if her condition is so serious she might not survive a pointed finger. Then he returns the way we came, at one point reaching down to put the dangling arm of a gurney-bound patient back into place.

INGER LIES ANAESTHETIZED IN THE hospital bed, a tube coming from the inside of her elbow and another one going into her nose. A respirator hose disappears down her throat, and a glowing red clip pinches her finger. She wears a plush white turban of medical gauze.

She's breathing on her own, but her skin has a waxy cast. The wall behind her looks like the cockpit of a spaceship with flashing lights and buttons behind protective clear plastic boxes. I can read the blood pressure monitor. She's at 82 over 58, not enough pressure to water hanging plants.

I pull up a chair. An eyelid trembles but not enough for dreaming. There's no sign she knows I'm here. The half-dozen machines connected to her chatter and sigh like ladies at a book club. The heart line on the pulse monitor keeps moving in peaks and valleys like it does on television when there's still hope. 'One day people are going to understand what you've done,' I say to her.

Her gauze bonnet is very white. Because the lights are dimmed, it seems extra vivid, like a lighthouse emerging from fog. I want to unwind it and see what's under it. One piece of surgical tape keeps the wrap closed. It comes away easily. A second piece of surgical tape secures a deeper layer. In black marker, the words NO BONE are written across the tape. I peel it away and keep unwinding.

Her hair is really bad. She has bandage-head on the right side and she's bald on the left except for an open porthole of skull about the size of a nickel. Through it, red rivers flow over ivory dunes. Surgical plastic is stapled to her scalp. 'Is that where we are right now, Inger?' I toss the gauze onto the bed.

Morbier asks: What does it mean that she is profoundly asleep but you are awake?

Well, I answer him, maybe it means there's an afterlife.

Be serious, Jean. You have just looked into the woman's brain. What did you see?

Just meat. Red and yellow and white meat, like you'd see in a butcher's window.

We used a medical auger. It's like a drill. We put a three-quarter-inch hollow bit on it. The bone popped right out.

A strip of gauze drapes Inger's throat, limp against her clavicle. The respirator inflates and deflates her chest. I stroke her head, the half with hair on it. She's in no shape to answer any questions or confess. I have to go straight to sentencing.

I get on top of her in the bed and hold her between my knees. She opens her eyes and looks at me shining as I make two turns of her throat with the gauze. She watches me, but there's nothing behind her eyes. I pull the gauze closed over her windpipe but I can't draw it tight. She's a part of me.

I hear her voice in my head. It says, Do it, Jean. Be yourself for once.

I pull the respirator hose from her throat. Inger emits a wet gurgle as I press my thumbs into her neck and feel for her ribbed windpipe. I compress it. Her eyes go wide. I breathe in. One two three four. I breathe out.

One two three four.

Inger's pupils tighten and her focus travels beyond my shoulder, high above me. Her mouth opens in awe.

I look up, and there's one on the ceiling now, hanging down, clinging to it with her fingers splayed against the sound-proofing tiles. She's wearing her red crying coat and her short hair is dripping wet. She gazes down into our eyes and the machines start going crazy. I keep the pressure on Inger's throat until the nurses come running. One of them sticks her head in the door.

'Code blue!' she shouts.

The corridor springs to life. Nurses fly in, pushing diagnostic machines and carrying IV bags. The resident in his green gown dances through, holding the end of his stethoscope high in the air. I get off the bed and navigate the room through the flow of personnel. They're paging the specialists, and shadows rouse in the quiet room and stand at the door. It opens and her husband and their kid emerge, their faces drained of colour. They walk by me like I'm a ghost.

I see Ian is in the quiet room as well. Unlike the two men with him, he's not wearing his uniform. I can't help but laugh. How many men does it take to bring me to justice? He must think I've really lost it, running to him with tears pouring down my face. He takes me in his arms. He strokes my back. 'Oh my god, Jean. I thought you were dead!'

'I'm not!' I push away to see his face. 'But she is.'

The uniforms have emerged from the quiet room. They're getting impatient. 'These boys want to ask you a couple of questions, okay? Then I can take you home.'

'Of course! Just show me the way.'

I'll agree to anything now. Look how agreeable I am! I just want to go home. I love my life. I love my children! This was just a rift. In my perception, or someone else's. In my thinking, my beliefs. And I believe Cullen Gossage now. I believe in the transmission layer because it's everything everywhere all the time. It's the only thing I'm certain I'm *in*. I'm in the rift.

I follow one of the 'boys' into the quiet room. It's very

calming in here. I can't believe how light I feel.

I take a seat and wait as he gets the elastic band off his notebook and finds a new page to write on. He clicks his pen to life. 'Let's start with your full name,' he says.

# ACKNOWLEDGEMENTS

Thank you to Ellen Levine, my agent, champion, and friend.

Thank you to my editors Martha Kanya-Forstner and Kiara Kent, who lavished love and attention on this book and helped it become itself.

My gratitude to Ashley Dunn, for getting it into all the right hands and me to the right places, and to everyone at Doubleday Canada who saw the book through with such warmth and professionalism.

To Joanna Knooppathuis, Liz Phillips, Linda Redhill, Esta Spalding, Linda Spalding, and Kevin Temple: love and squalor for reading earlier drafts of this novel and for being brilliant and fearless in their feedback.

I am indebted to the Canada Council, the Ontario Arts Council, and the Toronto Arts Council for essential support at different times during the writing of this novel. I'm grateful to live in a country, a province, and a city that supports the arts.

In the spring of 2017, as the fictional timeline of this novel was expiring in the 'real' world, the city's Parks, Forests and Recreation division razed Bellevue Square to the ground. My regards to the City of Toronto for enthusiastically illustrating some of the themes in my work.

*Bellevue Square* is part one of a triptych of novels called *Modern Ghosts*.

# NO EXIT PRESS
## UNCOVERING THE BEST CRIME

'A very smart, independent publisher delivering the finest literary crime fiction' – *Big Issue*

MEET NO EXIT PRESS, the independent publisher bringing you the best in crime and noir fiction. From classic detective novels, to page-turning spy thrillers and singular writing that just grabs the attention. Our books are carefully crafted by some of the world's finest writers and delivered to you by a small, but mighty, team.

In our 30 years of business, we have published award-winning fiction and non-fiction including the work of a Pulitzer Prize winner, the British Crime Book of the Year, numerous CWA Dagger Awards, a British million copy bestselling author, the winner of the Canadian Governor General's Award for Fiction and the Scotiabank Giller Prize, to name but a few. We are the home of many crime and noir legends from the USA whose work includes iconic film adaptations and TV sensations. We pride ourselves in uncovering the most exciting new or undiscovered talents. New and not so new – you know who you are!!

We are a proactive team committed to delivering the very best, both for our authors and our readers.

Want to join the conversation and find out more about what we do?

**Catch us on social media or sign up to our newsletter for all the latest news from No Exit Press HQ.**

**f** fb.me/noexitpress **🐦** @noexitpress
**noexit.co.uk/newsletter**